foot^{steps}

footsteps

DiAnn Mills

BARBOUR
PUBLISHING

This book is dedicated to my dear husband, Dean,
who has always encouraged and believed in me.

Many thanks to Martina Schamp,
Darrell Sheffield, Jack Sheridan,
and the members of my critique group.

The sacrifices of God are a broken spirit;
a broken and contrite heart,
O God, you will not despise.
PSALM 51:17

chapter 1

"L isten, kids. Stay right here while I get the car." Standing under the shelter of the covered mall entrance, Debra fixed her gaze on one precious child then the other. All the while, a downpour hammered against the roof above them. "Chad, Lauren, don't move. You know the rules. I'll be right back." She slipped tiny Lauren's hand into Chad's. "We did have a good day, didn't we?"

Chad offered a thumbs-up, and Lauren smiled and nodded. Oh, how she treasured her children's innocence—their clean smell and the taste of her lips on their peachy-soft cheeks.

Debra grabbed the many packages, evidence of their school shopping, and dashed out into the rain. She winced at the liquid needles bruising her flesh and soaking her clothes. Moments later, she started the engine of her SUV and eased backward from her parking spot. Rain pelted the windshield, and although the wipers sliced through the cloudburst faster than she could blink, she still found it difficult to see. Pressing the air conditioner button, she anticipated the rush of cool air in the hot, humid temperatures of a Houston summer.

With her fingers gripping the steering wheel, Debra rounded the corner of a department store. She could only imagine what Michael would say when he discovered the cream-colored leather interior of his new SUV soaked from her wet clothing and, in a few moments, their rain-kissed children.

She detested the driving rain, no matter how badly the scorched August ground needed it. A flash of jagged light and a crack of thunder caused her to jump. "That was close," she said and realized she'd been holding her breath.

A few people darted about to retrieve their vehicles. Most of them had the sense to bring an umbrella today. But not Debra. She hadn't noted this morning's weather report in the hustle to get the kids to the mall.

She eased on the brake and stopped in front of the pavilion where she'd just left Chad and Lauren. They were nowhere in sight. Cursing under her breath, she yanked the keys from the ignition and leaped out into the rain. Once the door slammed, she pressed the lock button on her alarm and raced toward the mall entrance, determined those two would definitely receive a sound scolding for disobeying her.

The wind and rain drenched her. Frustrated, Debra considered all the things she planned to say to Chad and Lauren, and for certain, they would not rent any video games on the way home.

Agitation coursed through her veins. After all she'd done for those two imps today, why couldn't they have stayed where she left them? The metal bench was empty. Chad knew better. An eight-year-old entering third grade in two days should realize the importance of following a few simple directions. What an example for Lauren, who would be entering kindergarten.

She looked up to him as the all-knowing, perfect big brother. That little girl had better be holding his hand when she found them.

Debra caught sight of herself in the glass entrance door. Her shoulder-length hair hung in ringlets, and no doubt, her expensive makeup streaked down her cheeks. Embarrassment warmed her face, and irritation rose from the soles of her feet like smoke signals. Just wait till she found those two kids.

Stopping at the empty bench with water rolling down her arms and legs, Debra's gaze swept to a young black woman with a baby stroller standing nearby.

"Excuse me, but have you seen two children, a boy and a little girl? They were supposed to wait here for me while I got the car."

The woman shook her head. "No, ma'am."

A faint twinge of apprehension tugged at her heart, and the reply thickened in her throat. "Thank you. If you see them, would you ask them to stay put until I return?"

"No problem." The woman reached down to stroke the cheek of her ebony-skinned baby. "I hope you find them soon."

Glancing about, Debra stepped inside the mall. The closest store to the entrance happened to be Funville Video Arcade. She clenched her fists. *That's where they are. They both have money left over from Mother Patterson's last visit.* Earlier Chad had begged to check out the latest swords and demons games, but she wanted to get home—get dinner started for Michael.

Through the dim lighting with the sound of beeping, clanging, and sirens, she searched every game but couldn't find a trace of her children. Her fingernails pierced the skin of her palms. *Where could they be?*

Next to the video games stood a small earring and accessories boutique. Standing at the entrance, she took in every square inch. Two teenage girls giggled over earrings, but no children were there.

Across the way, a candle shop boasted of every size and scent known to tantalize the senses. Debra swallowed the lump in her throat and moved toward the storefront. Chad and Lauren had helped her select pumpkin spice and apple votives earlier in the day. *Those two are busy sniffing all those candles.*

Debra explored every corner and display but emerged from the busy shop without her children. Again, she scanned the area outside where she had left them. The empty bench seemed to mock her tortured emotions. More people mingled about as the rain poured unrelentingly. Concern had long replaced anger, and in its stead, a gnawing fear curdled her stomach.

Standing in the middle of the mall's walkway, she turned a complete circle. "Chad, Lauren. . .Chad, Lauren." Nothing.

Hysteria began a rapid ascent. She clasped her arms about her, freezing. Why did malls have to turn their air-conditioning so low?

"Ma'am," a woman said from a children's shoe store across from the candle shop. "Ma'am," the same woman called again.

Debra lifted her gaze in reply.

"Can I help you with something?" the woman asked.

She moistened her dry lips. "I left my children at the entrance while I ran to get my car. It's pouring out there." She avoided the woman's stare. "When I drove back around to pick them up, they weren't on the bench, and I can't find them anywhere."

Still not meeting the woman's scrutiny, Debra peered in every direction.

"And you've checked all these stores?" The woman waved her hand at the nearby shops.

"Some. I've looked through some," Debra said, and for the first time she met the woman's eyes. They were brown, a warm, soothing color. "This isn't like them. They're good children."

"I'll help you." The woman turned to another clerk. She quickly explained she would be gone for a few minutes. "What are their names?" she asked, joining Debra.

"Chad and Lauren Patterson. He's eight and she's five."

"And how are they dressed?"

Debra scrambled to remember. Where was her mind? "Chad is wearing a red and blue pullover shirt and jean shorts, and Lauren has a yellow, short overall outfit with a yellow and pink T-shirt. Both are wearing tennis shoes."

"Okay, I'll look on this side, and you take the other."

Debra nodded, briefly acknowledging her. She took a quick assessment of the woman—blond highlighted hair, medium height, and wearing a navy blue pantsuit. "Thank you," she whispered.

"And what is your name when I find them?" the woman asked.

"Debra—Debra Patterson." Her voice quivered, and she took a deep breath to control her staggering emotions.

"I'm Nelda." She smiled. "Don't worry, honey, we'll find your children."

She forced back down her throat the tears that threatened to well up in her eyes. For certain, those two would receive a good scolding for this one.

With each store—a cosmetic and perfume shop, cards and gifts, and an exclusive men's store—no one had seen two children who fit Chad and Lauren's description. She raced from one business to another while panic wrapped its icy fingers around her heart. She hated to stop and take a breath for fear she might miss them. Surely, they wouldn't think of this as a game.

Straight ahead, Nelda met her at the information booth empty-handed. "I think we should call security." Her voice was laced with compassion, and a furrow spread across her forehead.

"Yes, of course." Debra hurried toward the covered booth and quickly explained her problem to the lady perched behind the counter.

The customer-service representative, near the age of Debra's mother-in-law, stared at Debra as though she needed a lesson in motherhood. The older woman pressed her ruby-red lips firmly together and picked up the phone. "I'll call security."

"Why are you looking at me that way?" Debra leaned over the counter at the woman. "Didn't they train you to be more helpful? Can't you see my children are missing?"

There, she said it.

The older woman picked up a radio, without a trace of eye contact. "Customer Service to Public Safety. I have a woman at the desk who has lost two children." She gazed emotionless. "Ma'am, can you describe the children?"

Debra repeated the same information she'd just given to Nelda, adding Chad's cinnamon-brown hair and Lauren's blond curls secured in a ponytail. Ignoring her body's reaction to the trauma assaulting her, she looked beyond the booth to a candy store on the opposite side of the mall. *Lauren's favorite red gummy bears.*

Wet leather sandals beat a rhythm against the tiled floor. She brushed the shoulder of a long-haired male teen who told her to watch it, then she dashed in front of a woman with two little girls near the age of Lauren. The candy store had standing room only; its bright colors and enticing smells attracted all ages.

"Chad, Lauren, are you in here?" Several people stared, but she didn't care. "Chad, Lauren, you'd better not be hiding."

"Excuse me," a young woman sporting a short, purple, spiked haircut asked from behind the candy counter. "Can I help you?"

"My children." Debra searched over heads and around bodies and feet. "I thought they might be here."

She shrugged. "What do they look like?"

Debra described them while scrutinizing young and old. Nothing.

Walking outside the store, she glanced back at the customer service booth. A uniformed security man waited beside Nelda. Misery replaced the wetness from the rain.

Debra's breath came in short spurts. She made a conscious effort to gain control. Nothing worked. She clenched her fists but couldn't stop the quivering. Chad and Lauren would not be found any sooner by her losing control or hyperventilating. The mall had several trained security people who must have exact procedures to follow in circumstances like this. She must believe their expertise would find her children.

Quickening her steps, Debra wove her way back through the throng of people to the information booth. She needed to be strong. She needed someone to tell her everything would be all right. She needed to find Chad and Lauren.

"I can't find my children." She stared into the placid face of the dark-skinned security officer who hosted a mustache. His badge read JAMES THATCHER—SECURITY DIRECTOR.

"Yes, ma'am, I'm here to help you." His voice relayed confidence; his looks were professional, but he annoyed her instead of offering the hope she desperately craved. In the next instant, he produced a form and began firing questions, the same ones she'd already answered.

All the while Debra answered his questions, her gaze darted about, always looking. . .hoping to see her children. After she gave Mr. Thatcher their description, he radioed a general lookout to all the security officers.

"How many people do you have here?" Debra's voice shook.

"Twenty plus the mobile units outside."

"Does this happen often?" She forced herself to focus on his coffee-colored eyes. Perhaps this wasn't unusual, possibly a common occurrence.

"Sometimes." Mr. Thatcher smiled. "Don't worry, ma'am, we'll find your children. Most likely in the next fifteen to twenty minutes."

Twenty-five minutes later, Debra paced the front of the information booth. Nelda had excused herself and gone back to her store while the security director attempted conversation. A knot twisted in her stomach.

"Do you have a picture of your children?" Mr. Thatcher asked, too kind and understanding for Debra's liking. She didn't want sympathy; she wanted Chad and Lauren.

Her heart pounded furiously against her chest, the pain intensifying each time she took a breath. "Yes, in my purse." She glanced toward the mall entrance. "I left it in my car."

"Let's go get it." His competent tone wavered, or perhaps her trust had diminished.

He stepped beside her, and they made their way through the mall doors and out into the pouring rain.

A mobile unit had stopped beside her SUV. Mr. Thatcher waved the vehicle on.

Debra's trembling fingers couldn't find the button to release the alarm. "Stupid thing." She dug her perfectly manicured nail onto the car alarm and willed herself to, once more, find control. Rain bludgeoned her body as though attacking her as an unfit mother.

"Ma'am?" Mr. Thatcher asked.

She shook her head and tried the alarm release again. This time it clicked, and she reached across the driver's seat to retrieve her purse. The sight of her ultra-expensive leather bag with her cell phone sticking out of the top caused her to consider calling Michael. What would he say? She'd lost the children? Snatching up her purse, she slammed the door and locked it.

"I've posted security people at the mall exits with instructions to stop every person who has a boy or girl fitting your children's description, and I've called the police," Mr. Thatcher said once she reached him. "Also, your car will not be towed."

"What does this mean?" Suddenly the tears flowed as swiftly as the rain.

Mr. Thatcher studied her face. "It's policy, Mrs. Patterson. We are committed to finding your children."

"But you said you could find them in fifteen to twenty minutes." Her voice rose with the terror threatening to overtake her body.

"Please." He took her arm. "Let's go back inside and wait for the police. We can use your children's pictures to help the security guards. It might be a good idea to call your husband."

Debra sensed another wave of panic. Yes, she'd call Michael. He'd come to the mall and stay with her until the police found Chad and Lauren. She needed his arms around her. She hadn't done anything wrong. *The rain. Chad and Lauren would have been soaked. He'd have done the same thing.*

"Mrs. Patterson," the director said, "try to calm down."

Debra heard sobbing. Her own. This couldn't be happening.

"I understand how you feel."

Something inside her snapped. "You have no idea how I feel! Have you ever lost your children?"

"No, and you're right. I've never been in your position." He touched her elbow and escorted her toward the mall's business area. "We'll go to my office and meet the police there."

"But what if my children are looking for me? Shouldn't I stay here?" she asked.

"I think you'd be more comfortable away from the crowd. You'll appreciate the quiet and privacy when you phone your husband and find your children."

"Yes. . .I guess you're right."

They passed a sea of nebulous faces, reminding her of a horror movie she'd once seen. Did anyone care that a nightmare had invaded her perfect, secure world?

Mr. Thatcher ushered her to a small sterile area labeled SECURITY DIRECTOR and assisted her into a chair across from his desk. A photograph of a pretty, black woman with three young children rested on the corner. They looked happy. . .and safe.

"Do you know your husband's number?" Mr. Thatcher

handed her the receiver. "You can contact him while I post your children's pictures on the security monitors."

Fumbling through her wallet, she nodded and handed him the photos of Chad and Lauren.

Michael. She wanted to hear his voice, but she didn't know how she could tell him what had happened.

Swallowing hard, she took the phone Mr. Thatcher offered and punched in Michael's cell phone number. One ring. Two rings. Three rings. The waiting unnerved her. She caught the scent of the security director's uniform. It smelled of greasy burgers and fries.

"This is Michael Patterson. I can't take your call right now, but if you'll leave your name and number, I'll get back to you shortly. If your call is an emergency, please contact—"

"Michael, please call me immediately. We have an emergency." Replacing Mr. Thatcher's receiver, Debra pulled her cell phone from her purse and checked the battery. Fully charged. She punched Michael's pager number into the desk phone and left their 911 code.

She watched a long minute tick by on the desk clock. The second hand jerked as though possessed by a nerve disease. Maybe Michael had gone home for something. She snatched up Mr. Thatcher's phone again and raced through the number for home. One ring. Two rings. Three rings.

"You've reached the Pattersons. We're unavailable to take your call at the present time, but if you'll leave your name and number, we'll get back to you." Chad and Lauren had recorded the greeting weeks ago. Their sweet voices were filled with enthusiasm.

"Michael. Michael, please, if you're at home, please pick up the phone. Michael. I'm scared. I need you." The receiver fell from her hands, and she sobbed. Glancing up at Mr. Thatcher, she wanted to lash out at him—at someone for the guilt sweeping through her. *What kind of mother loses her children?*

A moment later, two police officers walked in. She could not utter a word. The nightmare only continued. Another thought entered her mind. She'd call Michael's office. Lynn would know how to find him.

She grabbed a tissue from Mr. Thatcher's desk and hastily swiped at her nose. Control, she needed control. Snatching up the phone, she punched in the law office number of Patterson and Doyle. Michael's secretary seemed to take forever to answer.

"Lynn, this is Debra. Is Michael there?"

"No, he's not. In fact, I've been looking for him. He hasn't been in today or returned any calls."

chapter 2

Debra dropped the phone. What did this mean?

"Mrs. Patterson." James Thatcher bent to her side. "I'm so sorry about all this. If you're able, these officers need to get more information."

She stared into his face and saw the compassion. For a brief moment, his kindness soothed her frenzied nerves. Debra silently agreed.

"I'll get you some water," Mr. Thatcher said.

"Thank you." She gripped his arm. "You'll be right here while I talk to them? You won't leave me alone?"

"Of course not."

Suddenly embarrassment seized her. How foolish to rely upon a stranger, but her world had crumbled before her eyes. Everything she held dear had disappeared.

"I'm okay now." She peered up at the officers. Mr. Thatcher patted her shoulder before he left the office.

She took a deep breath and turned to the policemen, one a light-haired man near her age and the other a black man. She wanted to trust them and believe they could find her family.

"My children are missing, and so is my husband."

One of the uniformed men pulled a chair next to hers. "I'm Officer Morton." He pointed to the black officer behind him. "And this is Officer Sanderson. I have to ask you some questions and verify everything you've already told the security director. But I want you to know that as of the moment the security guards were first alerted, every child leaving the mall has been carefully scrutinized by a trained professional."

"I understand. The security director explained the procedure to me." She clasped her hands together. Hysteria would only lengthen the process of finding her beloved children.

"Your cooperation is our best asset." He removed a notepad from his pocket and pulled off the cap of a pen with his teeth.

"I saw a news special about organized kidnappers," she said and remembered the suffering parents who were victimized; some never recovered from the loss of their children. Some couples divorced in an effort to ease the anguish. "I never thought I might face the same thing." She squeezed her eyes shut to keep from crying. *Be strong.*

"I'm sure this is a misunderstanding," Officer Morton said. To her, it sounded like rote, a guard against involvement. Anger moved her to want to scream at him. What did he know?

Mr. Thatcher returned with a paper cup filled with cold water. She grasped it with trembling fingers, as though it promised to bring answers to her aching heart. Once she finished, she turned to Officer Morton still seated across from her. Slowly and deliberately, Debra explained how she'd left the children under the mall pavilion while she rushed to get her SUV.

"And you're certain your husband intended to work today?"

"Yes, sir." A lock of hair tickled her cheek, and she tucked it behind her ear. "Is this a nightmare?" She glanced first at the light-haired policeman, then on to Officer Sanderson and to Mr. Thatcher.

"No, ma'am," Mr. Sanderson said. "I wish it were. Hopefully, we'll have this taken care of shortly."

"I don't understand why my family is missing. My husband had better not have taken them." She paused. "It's grounds for divorce. Or murder." Debra didn't mean for the words to echo like an empty tomb, but the moment they escaped her lips, she shuddered.

Officer Morton cleared his throat. "I'd like for you to think back to this morning, before you left home with your children. Try to recall everything." He hesitated. "Take a deep breath, Mrs. Patterson. We're here to help you." He whirled around to the other policeman. "Dispatch a specialized unit to the Patterson address."

"What's that for?" Debra closed her eyes. Were they going to take her to jail because she'd lost her children? What would it matter if they did? She had nothing without Chad, Lauren, and Michael. She deserved to be locked up.

"Mrs. Patterson, are you ready?" Officer Morton's tone sounded impassive and impersonal—canned questions waiting for polite answers. Her mother's weather-band radio produced the same voice.

"Don't you see or care how this affects me?" She massaged her shivering arms. A vortex of fear, guilt, and anger swirled around her heart. *I am stronger than this.*

"Yes, ma'am. We're only trying to do our job."

Shaking her head to dispel her vacillating emotions, she focused on her French-manicured nails, done yesterday. Perfectly shaped, natural, and no chips or hangnails. Her thoughts drifted back to last night then on to early this morning.

"Last night Michael brought me white roses and took me to dinner and a play. We had a wonderful time. It was perfect. We planned a vacation to Disney World with the kids and talked long into the night. I didn't see him this morning until breakfast.

"Chad and Lauren were already seated at the table eating when he joined us. He'd gotten up before me and was in the shower when I left our room to see about the kids."

Inhaling deeply, she continued to keep her eyes closed, remembering every word, every gesture. . . .

"Good morning, kids." Michael planted a kiss on Lauren's nose and hugged Chad's shoulders. The morning sunlight danced off the top of her husband's thick, light-brown hair.

He sat at his place at the head of the table and placed the napkin on his lap. She loved the look of him—the way his hair fell across his forehead and his curtain of dark lashes. Michael carried himself with assurance and wore only the most expensive European designer clothes. Today, he'd chosen black.

"Pancakes?" He flashed Debra a disapproving look through gray green eyes. "Really, dear, the children need a healthier breakfast than carbs and sugar."

"I'm sorry. They asked for a special treat since we're spending the day together." Her pulse quickened.

"We like 'em, Dad." Chad stuck his fork into a gooey morsel then dragged it through a puddle of syrup on the way to his mouth.

Michael ruffled his son's cinnamon-colored hair and smiled. "I know, but growing children need a nutritional start for the day." His gaze swung in her direction. "It's up to you to guide them properly. Sound nutritional habits will stay with them all of their lives."

"I'm sorry," Debra repeated and reached for her black coffee. What had happened since last night?

Her husband glanced at her empty plate. "At least you aren't eating them. I've noted a pound or two recently, and we can't let that happen, can we?"

"Of course." She smelled the tantalizing aroma of the pancakes. "I thought I'd have orange juice."

He shook his head and reached for a plain pancake. "Umm, not a good idea. I know for a fact you didn't run this morning, and orange juice has way too much sugar. I think you should refrain from eating and just have diet soda and water until those few pounds are gone."

Debra felt her reflux problem gaining the upper hand, but she refused to let it take over.

"After all, my beautiful wife wants to keep her youthful figure, right, kids?"

"Yes," the two children chorused.

He grasped Debra's arm, a little too tightly. "We love you and want the best for you."

"Daddy, we're going to have a special day." Lauren clumsily set her glass of milk on the table directly at the two o'clock position at the right side of her plate.

"And what are you going to do, princess?" Michael flashed his daughter a dazzling smile, orthodontically correct and chemically brightened.

Debra relaxed slightly and listened to Lauren explain the day's activities.

"We're going school-clothes shopping at the mall, eating at a nice place, and seeing a movie." She smiled, her cherub face reflecting all the love she professed for her father. She looked like him, whereas Chad had his mother's eyes, wide mouth, and thick reddish-brown hair. Sometimes she thought Michael resented the mother-son likeness.

Her husband lifted a questioning brow to Debra. "Where are you having lunch?"

She felt the all-too-familiar tug on her senses. "Not fast food. There's a nice restaurant in the mall."

He jutted his chin and whispered in her ear. "No wine, hon. You have the children."

His comment didn't warrant a reply. She'd had enough the night before, and he was right.

He turned to Chad. "And what movie are you going to see?"

"Hmm, it's the new one about talking animals," the little boy said, his gaze dancing.

Michael smiled approvingly then carefully folded his napkin on the table. He glanced at Debra. "Why aren't you using the book I purchased instructing you on how to fold napkins? I detest a meal without some sort of formality."

"I was in a hurry this morning, but I'll have more time at dinner." She felt her hands tremble. A drink would settle her nerves.

He stood and kissed her forehead. "I need to get to the office. Busy day in court." He studied her for a moment. "Why didn't you shower and put on makeup before breakfast?"

"I slept later than I intended," she said. "I'm sorry."

Concern etched his brow. In the next breath, he kissed her again, this time a brush across her lips. "Why don't you pick up something frilly today—just for me? Don't be concerned about the price. You are beautiful, Debra, and I'm sorry I criticized you." He turned to his children then back to her. "Everyone have a wonderful day, and I'll see you tonight with all your new clothes." He turned to her. "I put five hundred dollars into your debit account for today."

Debra smiled. She adored Michael, and she hated to displease him.

A few moments later, she heard his sleek, black Porsche leave the garage. Rising from the table, she watched him pull out of the driveway. Any other day, a little orange juice and vodka would help when she displeased Michael, but not when she planned to drive her children to the mall. . . .

Officer Morton's voice pulled her to the present. "Are you ready, Mrs. Patterson? Anything at all unusual about your husband this morning?"

Debra shook her head vigorously. "No, he acted fine this morning, even said he would be in court all day."

"A normal morning?"

"Oh, yes. Michael is a wonderful, adoring husband and father. He's genuinely concerned about all of us, insisting upon the best of everything."

"Why do you think he didn't report to work?" Officer Morton didn't lift his head from his notes.

Debra stared down at her hands, her knuckles white in an attempt to stop the shaking. "I don't know. Something must have detained him."

He cleared his throat. "Doesn't it seem odd to you that your husband *and* your children are missing?"

Dread wove a treacherous path around her heart. "Are you

saying my husband might have taken them? He simply had a busy day in court."

"Ma'am, it's a strong possibility."

"But. . .Michael? Why would he do such a thing?"

"We don't have an answer, Mrs. Patterson, and we don't really know if he has them. Are you two experiencing marital problems?"

Officer Morton's voice faded as she recalled what her friend Jill recently said to her. "You should leave him, Debra. Take the children and get out of the house. He's crazy, a real mental case. One minute he adores you, and the next he treats you like dirt. I'm afraid for you and the kids."

"Mrs. Patterson?"

She lifted her head to meet the officer's stare. "I don't know if we're having problems or not."

"Mrs. Patterson, I understand your feelings right now. This has to be a horrible ordeal, but we have to get all the facts in order to locate your family," Officer Morton said. "A specialized unit has been called to your home. They will search for any signs of criminal activity—suitcases gone, missing clothing, any notes left behind."

"Yes, of course." Her voice sounded hollow, empty. "What is this unit?"

"Officers trained in locating missing persons," he replied in the same mechanical voice.

"Could you phone a family member or friend to meet you at your home?" the black officer asked. "This is not a time to be alone."

"I don't have family in Houston." She refused to think about contacting Michael's mother who lived southeast of town in Clear Lake; they'd never gotten along. Debra's mother was in the middle of chemo and radiation treatments in Kansas City. "I–I can see if a friend is available." She picked up the telephone receiver and, luckily, Jill's number came to mind. One ring. Two rings. Three rings.

"Jill?"

"Hi, Debra. Back from the mall?"

"No, not exactly. Are you busy right now? I mean could you meet me at my house?"

"Sure. What's wrong? You sound awful."

"Jill, the kids are missing."

"What?"

Debra moistened her lips and felt her throat tighten. "The kids are missing, and Michael hasn't been at the office all day. I'm with the police, and they want to search the house."

"Honey, I'm sure there's been some kind of a mistake."

"I hope so. Right now, I need a familiar face."

"I'm on my way."

The phone clicked in her ear, and Debra gently replaced it. Determined not to give in to the panic, she gave her attention to the officers. "My friend will meet me, but I'm not so sure I should drive."

"One of us will take you," Officer Morton said. "If the circumstances at your home indicate a crime has been committed, this trained police force will take over the investigation."

"And someone will continue to look for Chad and Lauren here?" She squeezed her hands together until her fingers hurt.

"Yes, until closing tonight."

Debra rose from the chair. The room spun, and her stomach churned. Where were her legs? She grabbed the back of the chair, bracing herself before turning to the mall's security director. "Thank you, Mr. Thatcher." She glanced about her. "You've been very helpful."

He shook his head. "No problem at all. Just concentrate on assisting these officers."

"Yes, sir. I'll do whatever is needed." She stood on wobbly legs, reminding her of Chad and Lauren when they first learned to walk—both at ten months old. They were excited, pleased with their new mobility, not at all like the fear gripping her now. Snippets of different stages of her children's lives flashed before her eyes: first words, discoveries in their little world, birthday parties, and holiday excitement. Then Mr. Thatcher opened his office door. She heard the busy hum of shoppers, and the sounds jerked her back to reality.

chapter 3

Debra moved through the mall with the policemen. All the while, a strange sensation of floating enveloped her. Nameless faces passed in a haze, and she searched each one looking for her two beautiful children.

Voices. She heard Chad and Lauren laughing, calling. "Mom. Mom. I can't find you." Debra clutched her ears, unable to bear the haunting cries.

Outside, the rain continued—dark, menacing, and mocking. Once at her SUV, she handed Officer Morton the keys. He helped her onto the front seat of the passenger side, and somehow she managed directions to her gated community. As they rode in silence, her thoughts screamed like the sea gulls near Galveston, and her tongue fastened to the roof of her mouth.

She hoped the wet seat of the driver's side had dried. Michael would not be happy. The windshield wipers swished back and forth, beating out the words *Michael's mad. Michael's mad.*

"Turn left at the next light," she said, "then left at the first street past the stop sign."

He followed her instructions. A young mother walking

with her toddler beneath a wide umbrella recognized Debra and waved. Debra stared, unable to respond with even a smile. What would Michael say about her escort home from the mall and the police car following them?

"Turn right at the next street. My house is the second house on the right," she said.

The massive, two-story house looked menacing, a trait she'd never noticed before. It contained over five thousand square feet set on two oversized lots. Michael had done quite well with his law firm, and this home had been his dream. He planned every square foot, staying up late at night to labor over each detail.

She remembered when Michael hired the landscaping architect and the interior designer during the construction. Chad hadn't started school yet, and Lauren still nursed.

"I'll take care of the final touches," he'd said. "Why don't you take the children to visit your mother until the house is finished? You don't enjoy making decisions anyway. I promise it will be your dream home."

She did as he asked and returned three months later to a new home, where the exterior held no flowers, only non-blooming shrubbery. A home should have colorful growing things to depict the seasons. She loved gardening, the feel of earth and the satisfaction of planting growing, beautiful things. And a dog, a beautiful fun-loving pet to teach the children responsibility, but she dare not voice her sentiments to Michael. No reason to upset his generous spirit. After all, most women would have done anything to have her home—and her handsome husband.

As soon as Debra and Officer Morton pulled into the driveway, she noticed a strange car parked in front of the house filled with people. The specialized unit. She riveted her attention on the closed garage door. Michael and the children could be inside waiting for her to arrive. He'd be furious with the police officers. She shivered and wondered if she really wanted to enter her own home.

Ignoring the rain, Debra emerged from the passenger's side of her vehicle and peered toward the alcove framing her front door where Jill waited. Her friend held a red and white umbrella, but she didn't need it under the front door's protection. Their gazes met. Over six months ago, Jill had smashed her vodka bottle. The possibility of losing her only friend still tortured her.

Jill strode in Debra's direction. Her gait slow and easy, exactly like the quarter horses she raised. An ash-blond ponytail swung back and forth, and Debra knew her nails were chipped. Jill's husband didn't care if the napkins weren't folded like the book said. Most times, they used paper.

"Hey, lady," Jill said, giving her a hug. "What can I do?"

Debra glanced at the front door behind her friend. "I'm not sure. Just having you here helps. Are they. . .are they home?"

Jill shook her head. "I rang the doorbell several times and phoned, too."

"Mrs. Patterson, would you like for me to unlock the house?" Officer Morton asked against the backdrop of water gushing from the downspout.

She'd forgotten he held her keys. "Yes, please." Suddenly, she seemed surrounded by strangers. One woman wore a police uniform. For a moment, Debra couldn't breathe. Michael would be humiliated. What would the neighbors say?

The alarm sounded its ominous countdown the moment

the key turned the lock. Debra slipped past Officer Morton to disarm it, ever searching for an angelic face or a deep voice.

The traditional furnishings in dark, rich cherry mixed with antiques and lavish collectibles seemed to mock her: Michael Patterson's treasures. She swung her gaze back to Officer Morton, waiting for his lead.

"Mrs. Patterson, these people are the specialized unit I told you about." He turned to a silver-streaked, dark-haired woman. "This is Alicia Barnett, and she's in charge of the investigation."

Alicia stepped forward and extended her hand to Debra. She reached for it—in no mood for formalities or eye contact.

"I'm leaving you with her capable unit," Officer Morton said. "My work here is finished. I'll notify you immediately if your children are located at the mall."

Debra grappled for something appropriate to say but could only stare blankly at him.

"It's all right," he said, and for the first time she saw the lines fanning from his eyes. "These people are here to help you." He turned to the squad car parked in the driveway.

For a brief moment, she wanted to call out to him. Perhaps he could stay until her children were found.

Shaking her head to dispel the foolish thought, she gave Alicia full attention. "Go ahead and conduct your search." Debra hesitated. "No, I want to look, too."

Jill reached for her hand. "I'm right here with you."

With a deep breath, Debra glanced down at her friend's jeans, designer brand with a smudge of something white. No doubt flour; she loved to bake. Michael didn't approve of Jill, claimed she wasn't their kind. "Thank you. I'm so glad you're here." She held back her sobs and inhaled deeply. Later she'd release these pent-up emotions—later when she could touch her children.

Jill led the way down the hall to the master bedroom. Nothing appeared out of order, until Alicia opened Michael's closet and discovered his clothes were missing.

Debra gasped and swallowed the terror rising in her throat. No need to check for his toiletries. She knew they were gone. Rushing from the bedroom, she stumbled up the steps to the first room—Chad's. She stopped and stood in the doorway. Her heart hammered against her chest. With clenched fists, she moved toward his closet door. Anxiety gripped her senses. The door loomed before her. As if in slow motion, she reached for the knob. Before the automatic closet light switched on, she saw Chad's clothes were gone. Like a mad woman, she turned and tore through his dresser—empty. A quick glance around the room revealed missing toys. Even his Game Boy had disappeared from his nightstand.

A feral scream escaped from deep inside while she raced down the hall to Lauren's room. Her pink and white room with its canopy bed and white lace curtains looked sweet, inviting. Debra flung open the closet door: empty. Mr. Spot had vanished from atop her pink, custom-made bedspread, and her Victorian-dressed teddy bears no longer shared tea from a miniature round table.

Sinking further into a world of sheer madness, Debra managed to descend the stairs with Alicia and Jill's help.

"I want to look for a note," Debra said through a ragged breath.

They found nothing.

Debra released Jill's hand and collapsed on a kitchen chair, too afraid to grieve for fear she couldn't stop.

"Is there anything you haven't told us?" Alicia asked.

"I. . .don't think so."

For the first time, Debra noticed Alicia carried a slim briefcase. The investigator slid it onto the table and pulled out a pad of lined paper, a yellow legal pad like Michael used.

"Tell her." Jill placed her hand on Debra's shoulder. "Now is the time."

"Tell me what?" Alicia slid into a chair. "I know this is hard, but you have to tell me everything if I'm going to be able to help you."

Debra tried to speak, but the words hung in her throat. Dare she tell this stranger what it was really like to live with Michael Patterson? With her mind spinning like Lauren's baby top, she peered up at Jill. Surely, her dear friend would tell her what to do.

"Honey, this woman knows how to find missing children. That's her job. Now it's your job to give her all the information she needs."

She nodded and peered into the face of Alicia Barnett, a near double of her high school chemistry teacher. In contrast to the teacher who seldom passed any of her students, Alicia's face radiated with kindness. The little creases around her eyes and the streaks of silver combing through her hair spoke to Debra of trust and wisdom. And Debra desperately needed both.

Alicia gathered up her hand. "I have children and grand-children whom I love dearly. And although what you are expe-riencing has never happened to me, I've seen the fear and panic in other mothers' eyes. I can't begin to imagine how I would feel, but I know this has to be a nightmare. I want to help you, Mrs. Patterson. Let me, please."

Debra wanted to withdraw her hand from the comfort Alicia offered, but she had no energy left. Staring down at the spotless, white, Italian-tiled floor, she began, "Michael can be a little peculiar. He insists things be done a certain way and easily becomes upset when they're not." For a moment, she thought she heard the distant sound of crashing, reminding her of the times he'd broken things that were not stored in the cabinets and cupboards as he'd instructed. "Despite his some-times strange behavior, I have no doubt he loves his children. And there are times when he is loving, generous, and fun."

"Has he been abusive?" Alicia released her hand and began writing on the yellow legal pad.

Debra shook her head. "Not to me or the children. In fact, he's never spanked Chad or Lauren."

"Debra, that's not true," Jill said, her voice firm. "What about the bruises on your arm? He may not mistreat the chil-dren, but he treats you like a stray dog."

Debra leaned her head back and stretched the tense mus-cles in her neck. Her gaze swept to her upper arm where only a few days ago Michael had been angry because his steak was not rare enough. Since that outburst, he'd apologized several times.

"Is this true?" Alicia asked. "Does your husband beat you?"

"No. . . Once in a while he gets a little rough when he's annoyed with me." Debra hoped to sound as though Michael's behavior was normal—as if she had a clue to what that meant.

"Debra," Jill said, as though disciplining a child.

She brushed back a strand of hair that hung in her eyes

and drove her crazy. "He has squeezed my arm when he really needed my attention."

"I see." Alicia scribbled on the pad. "You mentioned he does peculiar things. Can you explain what you mean?"

She'd never told anyone. Oh, a word here and there to Jill, but not the fear she felt when Michael cast his piercing glare her way. "It's really nothing. I'm sure every husband wants his home and family looking nice. . .so he can be proud of them."

"I sense there's more," Alicia said. "You can tell me, Mrs. Patterson. I'm here to help you, remember?"

Debra pondered over the request. If revealing Michael's strangeness brought back the children, then the risk of facing his rage was worth it. "I guess, you'd say he's a perfectionist with the house, my appearance, his job, and the children. He has an ordered way of living. Without it, Michael cannot function."

"What kind of lawyer is he?"

"Corporate. He has a partner in the firm—Patterson and Doyle. They are in the Galleria area."

"Do you believe he took the children?"

She struggled for a reply. "He said I did a good job as a mother, and my other faults would disappear in time." *Why do I sound so weak? Is this what I've become?*

"What kind of faults?" Alicia's tone conveyed sympathy.

Debra stared at Jill, and her friend nodded.

"Managing household responsibilities, taking better care of my personal appearance, mastering social graces, and things like that. I tend to be shy, not extroverted as Michael would like."

"There's more," Jill said, lifting her chin.

Debra shot her a disapproving glance.

"What else, Debra?" Alicia asked.

The ugliness of Michael's demands made her feel vile. "Sometimes he wanted me to. . .take part in swinger's clubs."

"Wife swapping?" Alicia asked.

Debra nodded. "I refused. I simply couldn't do that."

"And how did he respond?" Alicia scribbled away. Would anyone else ever read those words?

"Angry. . .guess you'd say sexually. . ."

"Abusive?" When Debra whispered yes, Alicia paused. Her face spoke fathoms of the depths of her compassion. "No woman should be bullied into any acts of aggression." She hesitated then continued. "Back to my other question. Why do you think he took the children?" Alicia patted her hand and gently massaged the chill-bumps flaring on Debra's arm.

She paused, wondering which one of her weaknesses had led Michael to take the children from her. "Probably the many times I've failed him as a wife and proper mother. And, well, I do drink a glass of wine or vodka and orange juice when the pressures at home are overwhelming."

"Overwhelming in what way?"

She took a deep breath. "When Michael is at home." She spoke in hushed tones. He might be listening, hiding somewhere in the house. "I'm so nervous that sometimes I make mistakes."

Alicia caught Debra's gaze, silently urging her to voice those things weighing on her heart, except she'd confessed enough.

Debra swallowed hard. "When he's in one of his black moods, it's hard to please him."

"I understand. Mrs. Patterson, do you have a problem with alcohol?"

Debra studied her fingernails. "I don't think so. I've never craved it, except to ease my nerves when Michael needles me about things, just one glass now and then to calm me down."

"I can vouch for her about the drinking," Jill said. "I didn't agree with her using it as a crutch, but I never thought she had a problem."

"And what about an affair?" Alicia asked.

Debra's eyes widened. "I have never looked at another man."

"What about your husband? Is he faithful?"

She sighed, thinking back over the past several months and the mounting tension when Michael was around. "I wouldn't know. He often works late."

Alicia produced a form from her briefcase. "Okay, Mrs. Patterson, while the others are upstairs looking around and dusting for fingerprints, I need a few things to help us."

Debra turned to peer up at Jill who placed her hand on Debra's shoulder. "I'll do whatever you want."

In the same soothing tone, Alicia continued. "Have you ever had your children fingerprinted?"

Remembering the harsh disagreement she and Michael had a few months ago about the same topic, Debra shuddered. "No, he opposed it, said it invaded our privacy. Good parents don't. . .don't lose their children."

"That's not true, Mrs. Patterson. Unfortunately, loving parents like you do have their children abducted."

Debra fought the tears. Michael had told her last week if she loved the children, she wouldn't embarrass them by wearing jeans and a T-shirt to pick them up from their private school.

"I could use pictures of your children."

Debra pointed upstairs. "The game room is filled with them. You can take all you need, as long as I can have them back."

"Of course. We'll scan the photos and return them right away." Alicia smiled and stood. "Let's select a few now, and I would also like a good photo of your husband."

Debra rose from the chair, and the three women ascended the circular wooden staircase. Specialized unit members worked in each of the children's bedrooms, with another downstairs, and a fourth in the game room—down the hall from Chad and Lauren's rooms. She took one step into the game room, filled with all the modern electronics available for Michael and the children. She gasped. Her knees buckled beneath her, and if not for Jill and Alicia, she would have fallen.

"My babies' pictures," she said barely above a whisper. "He's taken their pictures."

chapter 4

Debra shook off the other two women's support and hurried to the far closet where all the photo albums were stored. The shelves stood empty.

She wanted to scream, but all she could muster was a flood of tears. "I have nothing," she said. "My children, their pictures, everything. . .gone." She turned to stare at the two women. "Why would Michael do this?"

Remembering Chad and Lauren's photos in her purse, Debra broke away from Jill and rushed to the staircase. Her sandals clapped against the back of her heel as she tore down the wooden steps. Snatching up her purse, she dumped it upside down on the kitchen table. Her fingers raked through her belongings searching frantically for the small blue book trimmed in gold letters.

"Oh no." She'd given away her only picture of the children to the police officers.

A shrill cry rose from the bottom of her heart. Gone. Every trace of her beloved children had vanished.

It took nearly thirty minutes for Debra to gain control of

her emotions, but with the control came a determination to find her children. If only she could hear their voices and not the mocking laughter rising from her nightmares. What she wouldn't give to pull them into her arms and feel the softness of their little bodies. She'd never let them go, no, never. Michael. She'd kill him with her bare hands when she found him. It suddenly occurred to her that he'd been watching her and the children all morning, waiting for the right moment. *What an animal.*

Seated on the stairway with Alicia and Jill on each side, she swallowed hard and gave them her attention.

"What are you going to do?" Debra shivered, wringing her hands like a dripping cloth.

"This type of case falls under the category of parental kidnapping. You and your husband share legitimate custody of the children. Either of you has the right to take them wherever you want to go. Once we are finished here, it is my responsibility to contact the custody unit of the juvenile department to see if the facts warrant a call to the district attorney."

"Then what?"

"The DA determines if the elements are criminal in nature and if charges should be filed against Mr. Patterson."

How had things gotten so complicated? Couldn't the specialized unit simply find Chad and Lauren?

"Mrs. Patterson, we can get the photo of your children back from the police officers, but is there someone who might have additional ones?" Alicia asked. "One of your husband is crucial."

Debra moistened her lips. Peering into Alicia's face, the woman she'd grown to trust in less than two hours, she knew she couldn't put off calling Mother Patterson any longer.

"I'm sure Michael's office has pictures. My mother-in-law has several. I suppose she needs to hear about this from me."

"Right." Alicia's gentle voice temporarily eased her racing thoughts. "Do you have a good relationship with her?"

"No." Debra twisted her wedding ring with its glitzy two-carat diamond. "Michael's mother doesn't care for me—believes her son married beneath him." She took a deep breath and brushed away a tear from her dampened cheeks. "What if she's in on this? What if Michael and the children are with her right now?"

"Oh, honey." Jill's eyes brimmed with tears. "With all of their clothes and toys? And Michael's things, too?"

Debra felt her lips quiver, and she bit down hard to stop the display of weakness. He'd succeeded. He'd destroyed her only hope and joy.

"I'll make the call," Debra said. She accepted the cordless phone Jill offered, dreading the confrontation sure to follow with Mother Patterson. "I will find my children, and those who have done this will pay."

When Michael's mother answered, Debra's heart drummed in her ears. She willingly rested her hand in Jill's grasp. "Mother Patterson," she said through a weak voice. "I have some unfortunate news."

"What's wrong? Has something happened to one of the children? Michael?"

"They are all missing—and their belongings, too."

"What do you mean missing?"

"It looks like Michael has taken them." At the admittance, Debra felt the anger tear through her body.

"Are you crazy? My son would do no such thing—unless you provoked him. Goodness knows, you're a lousy excuse for a wife and mother. He could certainly do a much better job of raising those kids on his own."

The words sparked a smoldering fire, and accompanying it came a resolve not to let her mother-in-law triumph. "It doesn't matter what you think of me. I'm here with a specialized unit from the police department to help find my children. All of Chad and Lauren's pictures and the photo albums have been taken. The police need yours to scan for the investigation."

"I don't think so." Mother Patterson laughed. "You lost your children; you find them. You'll get no help from me."

Click.

❦   ❦   ❦

Dr. Cale Thurston dropped his briefcase at the door, shut it with his foot, and deposited his keys on a small marble-topped table in the foyer. Snapping on a light, he trudged down the hallway of his high-rise condo en route to the kitchen. Stale, musty air met his nostrils, and the deafening quiet pealed in his ears. Sometimes he thought a dog might keep him company in those few hours he spent at home, but good sense told him an animal deserved better treatment than being shut up for twelve to fourteen hours at a time. On occasion, he even had to spend the night at the hospital.

Maybe this computer age would provide the technology to produce robots with the capabilities to speak and carry on conversation. He smiled. From what some of his doctor friends said, a robot might be the ideal wife—low maintenance.

He wouldn't know. Cale didn't have time to seek female companionship on a permanent basis. He was married to a surgeon's scalpel.

Tired—too tired to breathe, Cale glanced about at the emptiness threatening to envelop him. His condo looked more sterile than the hospital. That's what he got for hiring a decorator who preferred sleek contemporary fashion. So now he lived with black, white, chrome, artificial plants costing more than the real ones, uncomfortable chairs, and original paintings that resembled his gloved hands during surgery.

With a heavy sigh, he rubbed the back of his neck. No chance of ever getting rid of the knots plaguing his shoulders. He'd done nothing but work since joining the staff at Houston's St. Luke's Hospital. He'd thought life might get a little easier when he left his position at Henry Ford Hospital in Detroit, but Cale had traded one headache for another. At least the headaches here were work related.

His hazy mind swept back over the day, which began at seven o'clock this morning: first a boring staff meeting, then hospital rounds, overbooked patient appointments, and the accident. A huge pileup on I-45 tonight in the middle of the pouring rain had sent three people into emergency surgery. A child died.

Sometimes he hated being a doctor.

Ambling over to the refrigerator, he reached for the milk, the only item there except for a partial loaf of stale bread.

Cale sniffed the milk before pouring a tall glass. More times than he cared to remember, he had tasted the sour variety. Reaching into a cabinet, he grabbed a half-full package of Oreos—the new kind with peanut butter in the middle.

"Sensible eating." He chuckled. "Nutritious, well-balanced, low fat, high protein." He popped a milk-soaked cookie into his mouth. "Definitely an energy booster."

Habitually, he picked up the remote and aimed it at the small TV scooted up next to the coffeemaker. Time for the ten o'clock news. Time to hear what manner of chaos had rocked Houston and the world today. A local news reporter recapped the tragic accident during rush hour, causing him to flash back to the frenzy of events in the emergency room.

He didn't even taste the second cookie as his mind shifted to the accident report blaring over the TV. Three others died in the fire resulting from the collision. Kids. A carload of fun-loving teenagers had run a stoplight and hit a family with a small child, the one he'd tried to save. Closing his eyes, he muted the TV's sound until the segment ended.

A moment later, a vivacious newscaster offered the viewers a dazzling smile and artistically applied makeup, no doubt touched up seconds before the camera lights hit her. He upped the volume.

"And now a sad story. Mothers and fathers everywhere can identify with this woman here in Houston. Today, during a downpour at a local mall, Debra Patterson left her two young children on a bench beneath a pavilion while she rushed to get her vehicle. When she returned moments later, they were gone. Authorities believe the father, Michael Patterson, a local attorney, abducted them. Investigators are combing the city for the father and children."

Cale set his milk and half a cookie on the counter. Picking up the remote, he powered off the TV. No sports or weather tonight. The Astros had lost the last three games in a row, and the weather had hit record highs for August. He'd heard about as much good news as he could handle for one day.

Dunking another Oreo, he poked it into his mouth and downed the rest of the milk laden with chocolate crumbs. He wrapped the tab over the cookie bag and jammed it into the cabinet.

A familiar series of beeps notified him of a page on his cell phone. Cringing, he pulled it from his pant's pocket: St. Luke's Hospital. A quick call alerted him to an emergency heart surgery.

"Doctors need their sleep, too." He headed back down the hall to the front door. "I'm not God, neither do I want to be, but I sure could use His help."

Halfway to his extended cab pickup, Cale remembered the carton of milk still sitting on the kitchen counter.

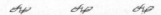

In the wee hours of the following morning, Debra grabbed a blanket and curled up on a love seat in her bedroom. The rain had stopped, but puddles stood as reminders to the earlier downfall. In the streetlights, the little pools of water fairly glistened, like tiny sparkling diamonds. Like her children.

She'd tried to rest, but her body refused, and she couldn't bring herself to crawl into bed. A rattlesnake once lay beneath those sheets with her, and his memory made her feel dirty. She'd been so naïve, so stupid. His varied mood swings flashed across her mind in vivid detail. His highs used to excite her, but the lows were frightening. This bed was where her children were conceived and where her husband had thrived on duplicity.

She'd roamed from one area of the house to another, lingering in Chad and Lauren's rooms and hoping to find their little bodies tucked in their beds. Eleven hours had gone by. Where were her children? Were they all right? Even now, she had difficulty believing Michael had taken them. Lauren would cry for Mama.

"Where is Mom?" Chad would ask. "She's gonna be worried about us."

She could almost hear Michael's agitation, see him tighten his jaw, narrow his eyes.

Fortunately, Chad hadn't seen the times when his father used his strength to reinforce his words. Perhaps that's why Michael took them—before they grew too attached to her and told someone about life at home—a bruised mother who drank too much and a demanding father.

In the darkness, Debra longed to hear her mother's sweet voice. Her words of comfort and wisdom always soothed the agony of whatever bludgeoned Debra's heart.

Mother suffered from the debilitating side effects of chemotherapy and radiation. The treatments to shrink her liver cancer devoured the very life the doctors aspired to prolong.

"Can't we bring Mom to Houston where she can receive the best possible care at the medical center?" she'd asked Michael.

"I don't want the interruption in my home. You'd have to take her back and forth to doctor appointments and most likely neglect the children."

"But since Daddy died, she has no one in Kansas City but her brother. I want to take care of her. Michael, we can afford to make her suffering a little easier, and the doctors might even have a cure."

One seething glare silenced her. "The answer is no. Don't bother me with it again."

Yesterday afternoon, Debra made excuses for Michael, thinking he may have been forced to pack the children's things and leave, but now she knew better. She knew her role as mother and wife left room for improvement, yet it did not warrant his insidious behavior. If she ever got her hands on him again, she'd scratch his eyes out. Murder seemed too kind.

Sighing, she considered her commitments for later this morning. Jill had volunteered to drive her downtown to the police station where she'd face more questioning from Alicia.

"Bring a list of everyone—friends, family, and business associates who might have information about your family's whereabouts," Alicia had said. "In the morning I'll serve your mother-in-law with a court order for the release of family photos. Officers are already on their way to see if your husband and children are there."

"What about the media?" Debra asked. "Can they help?"

Alicia jotted down something on her note pad. "They'll be contacted for a city-wide search. Possibly the DA will have made a decision by then."

A bit of hope rose in her. People were looking for her family. She wasn't in this alone. No doubt once Mother Patterson saw the evening news or read a newspaper, she'd shudder in horror. What a pity if she lost her position at the country club or her presidency of the Junior League.

After the appointment downtown, Debra planned to visit the bank. Suspicion gnawed at her. She needed to know the status of their accounts. If Michael had conceived a plan to snatch away the children, what other treachery could he have devised?

Although silence draped an eerie cloak around her, she knew Jill slept close by in the guest room. Her presence comforted Debra with something she could not reach out and touch. Jill's devotion most likely stemmed from her church involvement, but whatever the reason, Debra needed her strength.

Dear, sweet Jill hadn't budged from Debra's side all afternoon and evening, and her husband didn't mind at all.

"I don't like those people." Michael had repeatedly complained about her dear friends. "They aren't on our social level. In fact, keep the children away from them. I'll hold you responsible if Chad or Lauren talk about religion or church."

Debra had gone against his wishes anyway and hoped Michael wouldn't find out.

She tossed aside the blanket and made her way to the window facing the street. Brushing back the heavy custom drapes that seemed to hold her prisoner, she searched the shadowed area for signs of the children. A stray cat stole across the yard, and a car wound its way down the street. The carefully placed landscaping could have hid a dozen children, but none of them hers. A lump rose in her throat. Only yesterday, she believed her two children were the only possessions no one could take from her. What a cruel, ugly joke.

On and on her mind raced, memories dipping in and out like stars on a clear night. She remembered sitting on her grandma's knee and listening to her say, "I wish I may, I wish I might, have the wish I wish tonight." Grandma's voice still whispered across Debra's thoughts. She desperately needed to believe in something.

Tonight the tears no longer flowed, but nothing stopped the

pain. If she believed in any god, she'd pray. The words of her mother from a recent phone conversation echoed around her.

"Debra, honey, I know you're not happy. Whatever is troubling you, Jesus can take care of it."

"I don't believe in God." Debra hoped her response sounded gentle and not condemning. "I'm glad you have your faith, but the God-Jesus thing is not for me."

Mom's smile shone through her words. "I understand. Someday you will see."

Poor Mom. She'd given in to a crutch.

chapter 5

When dawn lifted the darkness in chalky shades of pink and orange, Debra ceased her wanderings and endless deliberations and trudged into the mammoth bathroom for a shower. She allowed the steady stream of water to gently massage her back and shoulders, bringing a moment's relief until her thoughts ushered in reality. Tears mixed with the cleansing spray, fell to the tiled floor, and swirled into the drain, gone but not forgotten.

Suddenly she remembered her daily jog. "Fat chance, Michael," she said. "When I find Chad and Lauren, you will never intimidate me again. In fact, I'm smacking you in the face with divorce papers."

Dressed in the jeans Michael hated and her hair nearly dry but no makeup, Debra emerged from the bedroom to the alluring aroma of fresh coffee. The smell brought back all the mornings Michael complained it tasted too strong or too weak. Chad thought it smelled good.

"Good morning," Jill said from the kitchen. "I have breakfast ready." Her swollen eyes indicated she hadn't slept well either.

"Just coffee, please. I'm going after the paper. I want to see what they've printed."

"I can get it." Jill brushed back a stray strand of hair loosely tied in a ponytail.

"No, I will." Debra headed into the foyer and out the door. The *Houston Chronicle* lay on the driveway in the familiar blue plastic bag. On the way to retrieve it, she heard a woman's voice.

"Mrs. Patterson?"

She glanced in the direction of the sound just in time to see two men and a woman emerge from a TV van. As they hurried across the manicured lawn, the woman carried a mike while one of the men focused a camera on Debra.

"This is Jen Wiler live with Channel 6 News. We are at the home of Michael and Debra Patterson where only yesterday authorities believe Michael abducted their two children from Cranbrook Mall." She thrust the microphone in Debra's face. "Tell us, Mrs. Patterson, any news about your husband and children? Have they been found?"

Debra took a step back, disgusted at the scene before her. Suddenly the whole idea of the media parked outside her home infuriated her. "I have nothing to say to you," she tossed over her shoulder as she walked up the driveway. "Leave me alone."

Trembling from the reporter's insensitivity, she rushed inside the house and locked the door. Leaning her back against the structure, Debra sunk to the floor. They knew nothing of the madness sweeping through her. They thrived on sensationalism and promoting their careers, not about people.

"Debra?" Jill called from the kitchen. The sound of her bare feet slapped against the wood floors of the foyer. "What happened?" Her friend placed her arms around Debra's shoulders.

"A TV van is parked outside." She buried her face in her hands. "They started asking questions, and I couldn't stand one minute more."

"This is ludicrous," Jill said. "They deserve a piece of my mind."

She scooted Debra away from the door, unlocked it, and stomped outside. A moment later, she heard her friend's voice. "Get out of here. Mrs. Patterson has nothing to say to you."

"All we want are a few words—"

"Forget it, lady. It isn't happening."

A moment later, Jill entered the house. She glanced at Debra and gave her a broad smile. "I feel better. God has a special place for people like them."

"God?" Debra shook her head. "There is no God, Jill. We're just here as a part of some sick joke to make the best of things until we die."

Her friend ignored the comment and helped Debra to her feet and into the kitchen. "Let's have that cup of coffee and some breakfast before we drive downtown."

An hour later, Jill backed Debra's SUV from the garage and past the Channel 6 van. At first it looked as if the vehicle intended to follow them, but Jill wound her way through the subdivision and sped onto the expressway.

At the police station, Debra gave Alicia the computer-generated list of all Michael's friends, relatives, and associates compiled during her all-night vigil. Jill's husband, Drake, had helped her with it, since Debra had no computer skills.

"I'll get someone on this right away." Alicia opened her office door and called for an officer to follow up on the names. Once the door closed, she took a moment to inquire about

Debra's night. "Until this is all over, you might need to see your physician for a prescription to help you sleep. I'd also like to suggest a counselor or a pastor—a professional who can help you through this trying time. Right now, maintaining good health is critical." She gazed into Debra's face, as if to say more but stopped. "By the way, your mother-in-law relinquished her photos without a court order."

"Good." Debra studied Alicia's round face while the woman took a phone call at her desk. She appeared to be more of a grandmother than an investigator, which left a few doubts about her capabilities.

I'm simply exhausted. She took a deep breath and noted the ache in her back and shoulder muscles. *I have to believe Alicia can help me. She must be top-notch, or she wouldn't hold this position.*

The woman replaced the phone and eased back in her chair. "I have additional information," she said. "Your husband's car has been found near Huntsville on a back road."

Debra stiffened and toyed with her wedding ring.

"Police found no evidence of foul play or clues to your family's whereabouts." Alicia hesitated. "The DA has decided to pursue criminal charges."

She didn't know whether to rejoice or grieve. "Will this speed up the investigation? I mean with the pictures and the charges against Michael?"

Alicia offered a faint smile. "We'd like to think so. Let me give you a status report on what has been done since your children disappeared."

Debra felt Jill take her cold, trembling hand and squeeze it lightly.

"From the very beginning, we broadcasted a bulletin to local and statewide law enforcement agencies alerting them to the children's abduction. They entered Chad, Lauren, and Michael's names in the National Crime Information Center registry of missing persons. Contrary to what most people think, there is no waiting period for adults."

Alicia shuffled through a stack of papers. "I'm not sure if you were aware of everything that went on yesterday afternoon while the specialized unit worked at your home, but let me explain why they took your children's bedding."

Debra glanced down at Jill's hand clinging to hers. "You're right. It made no sense to me."

"Those items were placed in secure plastic bags so the tracking dogs could use them to search your home and the surrounding area."

She remembered the dogs combing the house and yard last evening. At the time, she had trouble focusing on all the events.

"Also, we are looking for traces of valuable DNA through the same personal items. We would have preferred toothbrushes and combs or brushes, but obviously those are not available."

"But I do have extra toothbrushes that the kids pack when they spend the night with their grandmother," Debra said. "At least I did have them. I'll check as soon as I get home." She released her hand from Jill's grasp and picked up her purse. "I do have a brush in here that I use on the kids." She pulled it out and handed it to the woman. At least Debra could do something.

"Excellent. Just lay it on my desk." Alicia waited for Debra to ease into her chair again. "Late yesterday afternoon, the children's pictures were faxed throughout the country to various law enforcement agencies. Also, the FBI was alerted to investigate the abduction. They don't step into every parental kidnapping incident, but instead their decision is based on a case-by-case basis. When we are finished here, Special Agent Steven Howell will want to speak with you about FBI procedures. We will be working together on this. In fact, let me see if he's available now."

Alicia stepped from the room and immediately returned with a short, balding man who reeked of cigarette smoke. After introductions, he explained to Debra about possible extortion attempts, although that aspect most likely did not apply in Chad and Lauren's case.

"We have alerted the National Center for Missing and Exploited Children and faxed photos of your children and your husband to them," Agent Howell said. "The police and FBI will continue to work closely together until your family is found."

Debra nodded, trying to maintain control.

Agent Howell continued. "Every form of transportation in Houston has received posters of the children and has been notified about the role their father may have played in their abduction. This includes taxis, buses, rental car agencies, airport grounds, and the airlines."

He crammed his hands inside his pant pockets. "Investigators are examining the daily logs of traffic violations for signs leading to the children's whereabouts. Even known sex offenders are being questioned."

The turmoil inside Debra whirled in a mass of helplessness. She didn't know what to say. What could she do but wait? The investigators had considered more angles and measures than she might ever conceive.

"Another point was brought to our attention earlier this

morning when two police investigators discovered all of your husband's business records are missing. He didn't leave an electronic or paper trail behind."

Debra stiffened. "He'd planned this for some time," she said barely above a whisper. "How could he do such a horrible thing?"

Agent Howell pressed his lips together in an effort to form a compassionate smile. "We were hoping you might have additional information about your husband's business dealings."

"I can't help you there. He was a very private man. What does Mr. Doyle say about all of this?"

"Your husband bought out Mr. Doyle about five months ago."

A mixture of shock and disbelief wrapped its cloak around her. "I feel so stupid, so naïve."

"Why don't you go on home, Mrs. Patterson?" Agent Howell said in a tone indicating he had nothing more to convey. "Alicia and I will keep in touch."

"I'm taking her to the bank to check on her financial affairs," Jill said. "Then we'll be back at the house."

"I have my cell phone," Debra said. "Until the children are found, I'll sleep with it."

Numb and in dire need of sleep, she half-listened to the two women discuss the remainder of the day. Her ears perked when Agent Howell mentioned a lie-detector test. She'd agree to anything if it helped return her children.

✐   ✐   ✐

"Mrs. Patterson, I'm sorry, but your husband closed all of his accounts with us weeks ago," said Adam Crenshall, the vice president of Community National Bank.

Debra's breath came in short, quick gasps. "But he just left yesterday." The continuing realization that Michael had planned for weeks to abduct the children and clear out their finances sent a sick, twisting sensation to the pit of her stomach. She knew he had various investments but had no knowledge what kind or where.

"I'm sorry, Mrs. Patterson." He folded his hands on the exquisite mahogany desktop. "I know all of this is devastating, especially in light of your missing family."

"No, Mr. Crenshall, you don't understand at all. My children have been snatched away by their father. I have no idea where they are or what has become of them." She glanced about the richly decorated office—green and plush. Every bit of it oozed with money and power—the things Michael valued. Jill reached over to touch her arm, but Debra couldn't look at her.

"Has the home mortgage been paid this month?" Debra asked.

"Yes." His bushy brows knit together while he searched the computer screen. "In fact, he paid two months in cash." No signs of emotion touched his corpulent face. Obviously the vice president seldom passed on a meal.

She shuddered. *Paid in cash?* Michael said checks and credit cards were the only way to keep good records. A clock on Mr. Crenshall's desk registered noon. Would Michael remember Lauren's food allergies?

"Did you say this month and the next have been paid?"

He licked his full lips. "Yes, Mrs. Patterson."

Take my children and pay the mortgage? Is that supposed to ease my grief? "I see." Debra rose from the plush chair. "Thank you, Mr. Crenshall. I appreciate your time with me."

Jill stood, silently supporting Debra as they made their way out of the bank office and into the engulfing humidity.

"I'm not surprised at this." Debra descended the steps leading to the parking lot. "It hasn't been twenty-four hours, and everything I knew and trusted has been yanked out from under my feet. I don't care about the finances. I want my children."

"We'll figure out what to do," Jill said, as they made their way toward the SUV.

Debra bit her lip to keep from crying. Did anyone fully comprehend how she felt, the devastating horror of losing her children? News reporters from the *Chronicle*, TV, and radio had assaulted her with phone calls this morning. Thankfully Jill took care of the calloused media.

"Why don't we get some lunch before I take you home?" Jill asked. "You didn't eat any breakfast."

"I'm really not hungry."

Jill unlocked the SUV, and they slid inside. Immediately the suffocating heat caused perspiration to trickle down Debra's face.

"When did you last eat?" Jill toyed with the key before sticking it into the ignition.

"Hmm. Yesterday at noon, I think." She stared out the side window.

"It's nearly two thirty, and you need your strength. Don't you remember what Alicia said about taking care of yourself?"

"Really, I don't think I can eat anything. Maybe later." She closed her eyes and fought the pain searing across the top of her head. "I haven't thanked you for all you've done. Drake must think I'm pathetic."

"No, he doesn't. We're just glad we can help. Look, honey, you need to take care of yourself. . . ."

Debra's thoughts moved in another direction. Once again, she heard Chad and Lauren calling for her, giggling as if at play. Their voices grew louder and louder, deafening sounds that pierced her ears. She opened the door and nearly tripped in her rush to find the source of the laughter.

"I can hear them." She scrambled to keep her balance. I know their voices. "Chad, Lauren, Mommy's right here."

Debra hurried to the middle of the parking lot. She peered in every direction, even under the cars. A man looked at her oddly, but she didn't care.

"Chad? Lauren?" Silence shed a grim reminder. She plummeted to her knees, the hot pavement burning through her jeans. Hiding her face in her hands, Debra felt all sense of control vanish in a puddle of tears.

chapter 6

Cale exited his office and took a right in the hallway leading from St. Luke's to Texas Children's Hospital. At the gift shop, he turned left and entered another hallway displaying a children's gallery of framed, original art. He passed a McDonald's restaurant, where the combined smells of French fries and hamburgers teased his senses, then on through glass doors and a covered walking area leading to the West Tower of the Pediatric House.

He had a good hour to himself and needed a break. Some days the only thing that eased his weary mind was a kid-fix, and today was one of them. He'd had an early morning surgery then back-to-back patients until four o'clock. Right now, he craved one of those million-dollar smiles from a pint-sized person.

Kids held a special spot in Cale's heart—always had. He remembered the dilemma when forced to make a career choice between pediatrics and cardiology. Back then, he feared becoming too involved with the kids and making poor decisions as a result. But God had given him clear direction into his current field, and he'd never regretted it.

Yesterday he paid a visit to Texas Children's and saw a little blond-haired girl who reminded him of one of the Patterson children. Ever since he'd seen the TV report about the abduction and viewed the two children's pictures in the paper, he'd been compelled to pray for them. The more he learned about the case, the more he felt compassion for everyone involved.

Cale remembered the sorrow depicted on the mother's face. *How tragic for that woman.* He hoped her grief was real. Maybe the media and law enforcement officials hadn't uncovered all of the truth. Maybe the woman had a history of neglecting her kids and ran around on her husband. Could be she frequented the drug scene or stayed drunk. From the looks of things, money probably ran in a smooth flow. No matter what the reason, those children were the ones to suffer. They were too young to be without both parents. And if Michael Patterson had plotted a clever scheme in light of his wife's innocence, then God have mercy on him.

Cale's thoughts turned to his initial impression about Houston when he first came to live there nearly six months ago. At first the city held little interest, except in the tremendous work done in the area of cardiovascular surgery and the opportunity to work with the renowned heart surgeon, Dr. Kenton. Cale came from snow country, and here the temps soared beyond sweltering. The sight of gun racks in the rear windows of good-old-boys' pickups and cows grazing beside the freeways shocked him. Subdivisions sprang up everywhere with more shopping facilities than he could ever imagine, and the ambiance of multicultural people and activities never ceased to amaze him. He'd traded his snow boots for cowboy boots and tossed his winter gloves in exchange for suntan lotion.

footsteps

Here in Houston, he could almost forget the past. Uneasiness settled upon him worse than the heat rising from the concrete on a mid-August day. An old haunting sensation crept into his mind and tightened its grip around his heart. Even with the Lord, he could not forget.

The entrance to Texas Children's loomed ahead, and once again, his thoughts turned to the little patients there. Some of them didn't receive visitors, and those were the ones he singled out, coaxing smiles and whispering in their ears that Jesus loved them.

This afternoon he knew exactly the kid he wanted to see—a young boy by the name of Wesley who recently lost his right leg to cancer. Grabbing a wheelchair from the nurses' station, Cale picked up his pace toward the boy's room.

Peeking inside the private room, Cale observed Wesley watching cartoons, one about superhero teens battling giant robots to save the world. *Whatever happened to Donald Duck?*

"I need a listening ear." Cale pushed the wheelchair next to the bed. "Got time to give an old man advice?"

Wesley grinned. "Yep, I got about an hour before my dad gets here. And you're not old." He threw back his sheet and powered off the TV.

Cale noticed the light reflect off the boy's bald head, a symbol of the side effects accompanying chemotherapy. Life-threatening diseases for children always wrenched his heart. He pasted a smile on his face. "Do you need the bathroom?"

"Nope, I'm good to go," Wesley said.

Cale scooped him off the bed and settled him into the chair. "Okay, hot rod, I've got the IV pole. Let's put some miles behind us."

Once they were in the corridor, Wesley turned to Cale, his pale face serious. "So what's botherin' you?"

Cale purposely drew out his breath. "My computer at home. I can't figure out whether to buy more memory or invest in a new one."

"How long you had it?"

"Nearly three years."

Wesley shook his head. "Get yourself a new computer. You can afford it. Heart doctors make big bucks. Besides, think about the speed."

Cale laughed. He liked this kid. "To tell you the truth, it's hard for me to find the time to research what's out there."

Wesley sighed. "Now I know where this is leading. You want me to figure out the best PC for your money, right?"

"Well, yeah," Cale said. "Do you mind?"

"Nope. Gives me something to do. You write down what you need, and I'll find the best buy. I'm sure cost is no big deal."

"Well, I don't want to get ripped off."

Wesley laughed. "Are you cheap, Doc?"

"No, just frugal." When the boy gave him a questioning look, Cale continued. "That means I want the best PC for my money."

"Gotcha. And what do I get in return?" Wesley twisted around to peer up into Cale's face.

"Name your price. I'm desperate." He doubted if he could keep one step ahead of his young friend.

"Probably software for my computer, but I'll let you know. Too bad you weren't the one to take my leg, or I'd ask for a reduction in your bill."

"And I'd have given it. You think about your price and let me know."

"Deal. Say, can we go back down the hall? I think it would be cool to see my dad when he walks off the elevator."

"Sure thing." Cale turned the wheelchair around. "Is your mom coming, too?"

Wesley didn't respond, and Cale wondered if his parents were separated. He should have checked Wesley's charts.

"My mom died of cancer when I was a baby," the boy finally said. "This is real tough on Dad, but I told him not to worry."

What a burden for his father. "Good, you're a fighter."

"More than that, I'm a Christian like you."

Cale's reputation spread through the kids at Texas Children's faster than among the staff at St. Luke's. "Is your dad a believer?"

"Yeah, but he says it's easier for kids to have faith than adults, especially when things get bad," Wesley said. "Guess we don't have grown-up stuff to worry about."

"I think you have your share." Compassion swelled in Cale's chest for the tragic situation.

"Naw." Wesley grinned. "I'm too busy looking for a computer for this doctor friend of mine."

A smile tugged at Cale's mouth. More folks needed Wesley's hopefulness, or rather his faith. For the next few minutes, he listened to Wesley talk about all the things he planned to do once he was released from the hospital. Wesley liked school, but he had mixed feelings about the challenges of an amputee.

"A couple of guys made fun of my bald head." Wesley's face took on the deep lines of one much older. He picked up the empty leg of his pajamas and twirled the fabric in a circle. "This will really make 'em laugh."

"But you're alive." Cale didn't doubt for an instant the cruelty of Wesley's peers. "And you'll get fitted with a prosthesis."

Wesley nodded. "Yeah, and that's why I have to go back to school, just in case one of them gets cancer and I can help 'em through it."

"Wise decision, hot rod," Cale said.

Wesley nodded. "Doctor Thurston, do you have kids?"

"No, I'm not married."

"You should have some," the boy said. "You'd be a good dad."

Cale smiled, but before he could reply a man stepped off the elevator and captured Wesley's attention.

"Are you waiting for me?" The man sported sandy blond hair and the same blue eyes as Wesley.

"I wanted to surprise you. Me and the doctor have been talking and stuff."

Cale shook the man's hand and introduced himself. "You two have a great visit. I need to head back to St. Luke's."

"Thank you," Wesley's dad replied, but a single tear escaped his eye. Cale excused himself, knowing his sentimentality would soon follow. He stepped toward the elevator a little faster than necessary.

Life could be so unfair.

"Why don't you try to get some rest once we're home," Jill said. The two sat at a red light in Debra's SUV. "You don't want to collapse again like you did in the bank parking lot and not be able to take care of the children."

"You're right, but I can't sleep. My mind keeps racing with

everything." Debra moved her head from side to side in an effort to stretch her neck and shoulder muscles. "I have to be doing something." The meeting she'd just had with the vice president of the bank replayed in her mind. "How very thoughtful of Michael to make the mortgage payment. He actually provided for a roof over my head until October while planning to kidnap our children."

"Humph." Jill said. "What a nice guy. I'll be sure to nominate him for the husband-of-the-year award."

"If I find him, he won't live that long." Debra crossed her arms over her chest.

"Honey, you don't want him dead, just Chad and Lauren found."

Debra clenched her jaw and dug her fingers into her palms. "At the moment, I could murder him and gladly fry for it."

chapter 7

Four gruesome days had gone by since the children and Michael disappeared. To Debra, the time seemed like years, a maddening ellipsis of time where she possessed no control. Neither the police nor the FBI had found a single clue, and deep down inside she felt like she was being punished for failing Michael and the children. One of the biggest problems in the search came from Agent Howell's declaration that Michael had vanished without a paper or electronic trail. The pain of knowing his plans were in motion the night before when he'd taken her to dinner and later made love to her cut Debra worse than any knife.

What a jerk.

Anger and panic boiled together like a volcano threatening to release its fury. Her family was gone, and no one could help her.

Saturday afternoon she sat at the kitchen table with Jill and toyed with a white coffee mug. A blank piece of paper lay before her along with a sleek silver pen, which belonged to Michael.

"Why don't you list all the people and agencies involved in finding the children?" Jill asked. "That way you can see how everyone is helping you."

"Surely Chad and Lauren will be found soon." Debra picked up the pen and viewed Michael's name inscribed across the barrel. She wanted to break it. Jill's optimism scraped at her nerves. "Four days ago, the kids and I were enjoying a wonderful day together. I had a husband whom I thought loved me, and now this. Seems like years. . .another lifetime."

"I've been praying." Jill's voice rang soft and gentle against the turmoil raging in Debra's mind. "And I've placed the children on our church's prayer list."

Debra gripped the pen until her fingers ached. "If I thought a religion would help, I'd join a sect or two."

Jill stood from the kitchen table and poured them both another cup of coffee. Her friend's shoulders drooped, and her normally upturned lips quivered. Debra couldn't bear to see Jill's despair. Selfish as it sounded, she needed her friend's support and encouragement.

Debra glanced about the solid-white kitchen. The only inkling of color came from an arrangement of blue and yellow silk flowers, artfully placed by a decorator during a recent visit—Michael's idea of upgrading. But at the moment, the flowers reminded her of Jill. Some color in a blur of bleakness.

"I'm sorry. I know you believe in this God thing, but I don't." Debra carefully chose her words. "I must have something tangible. I need to wrap my arms around something I can see and feel. Your God is like a fairy-godfather. What I'm going through is reality."

"I wish you didn't feel that way, because to me, God is life.

He's the reason I live and breathe."

"My children are the reason I live and breathe."

She gazed into Jill's warm gray eyes and thanked her for the coffee. Never had she drank so much of the stuff; Michael claimed it discolored her teeth and tainted her breath, but the hot black liquid kept her going.

Jill moistened her lips. "I don't know what to say." She scooted into a chair next to Debra. "The Lord is my hope and my joy; He gave Himself for me. I'm not into religion, but a personal relationship with Jesus. My faith sustains me through whatever adversity is thrown my way."

"You sound like a TV evangelist." Debra believed her lack of sleep had increased her irritation. "I don't want to be the one who disappoints you, but there is no God or heaven. Except I will agree to a hell; I'm living it."

"The Lord can give you peace," Jill said without a flinch. "If you trust in Him, He will—"

"Please." Debra interrupted her for the second time. "I don't want to hear this. If your God gives this peace you're always talking about, then why hasn't He returned my children?" She sighed. "Look, Jill, I love you dearly. You are the only friend I have. You've stayed right by my side since this whole thing started and thought of only the children's welfare and my state of mind. But your religion is for you, not me. Let's not argue. Please."

Her friend pressed her lips together and slowly nodded. Her eyes spoke a thousand silent words—all compassion. "All right, but it won't stop me from praying for you."

Debra took a swallow of coffee and burned her tongue. In her own misery, she'd forgotten Jill and Drake had no children of their own and adored Chad and Lauren. The couple remembered them on special occasions and took time to listen to their chatter. They had repeatedly tried to involve Michael in conversations and activities, but his condescending manner kept them at a distance. Yet, Jill and Drake loved his children.

"I hate the waiting," Debra said after several long moments. "Waiting for Alicia, waiting for Agent Howell, waiting for the phone to ring or not to ring." She wrung her hands, freezing in the midst of bleak reality. "I know I'm feeling sorry for myself, but I'm eaten up with worry. And you don't deserve me lashing out at you about your beliefs either."

"It's all right, honey." Jill curled up one leg beneath her. "Why don't you let me handle the phone calls and you get some rest?"

Debra smiled sadly and shook her head. "You already took care of the media—more than once—as well as all the other nasty tasks that keep cropping up."

The cordless phone rang and Jill grabbed it from the tiled counter. "Patterson residence." Her peaches-and-cream features remained placid as she listened. Quietly Jill expelled a breath before pressing the MUTE button. "It's your mother-in-law."

Debra shook her head, petrified at the thought of conversing with the woman. "I don't want to talk to her."

"Would you like me to tell her you're unavailable?"

She closed her eyes, dreading the confrontation. "No, wait. She might have news from Michael. Better let me talk to her."

Jill handed her the phone while Debra's heart thumped like a trapped animal. She released the MUTE button.

"This is Debra." The days of calling the woman Mother Patterson ended Tuesday afternoon.

"Have you heard from Michael?" the woman asked without a hint of emotion.

"No. Have you?"

"Really, Debra, would I have bothered to phone you if I had?" She cleared her throat. "I can't believe you have involved the FBI in this petty domestic rift. Think about how this looks to the public. Michael has an excellent reputation to maintain."

"The FBI's intervention is on request by the police department. I had nothing to do with it, but I'm glad the nationwide search is being conducted."

"Michael will be furious with you. I hope you understand your poor job of wife and mother is what drove him to this. A reputable woman would not have allowed such a scandal."

Debra nearly choked on her coffee. "Oh, please. I don't have time for your insults. I have things to do."

"I imagine you're lounging around and neglecting the house."

Debra bit back the fire that smoldered beneath her frenzied emotions. "I'm trying to locate my family."

Silence met her ears.

"Despite our differences, would you contact me when you hear from them?" Mrs. Patterson's voice sounded strained.

Debra's gaze flew to Jill's face. "Will you contact me if you hear from them?"

Silence met her ears.

"Don't expect me to jump through hoops for you if you can't oblige." Debra disconnected the call.

For the fifth night in a row, Jill slept in the guest room. Debra knew her friend should be at home with her devoted husband and not baby-sitting a grown woman. Tonight he'd brought Chinese food for their dinner, but the dear man had omitted the fortune cookies. He somehow knew Debra did not need the trite optimism. How perfect could a man be?

As on other nights, she wandered through the house, fingering her children's precious few belongings and shedding an endless pool of tears. This night she rummaged through boxes in her closet until she found Chad and Lauren's baby clothes. Sitting on the hardwood floor of her bedroom, Debra gingerly unwrapped each soft, delicate article from white tissue paper. Tears trickled down her cheeks at the sight of the tiny pink and blue shoes tied with matching ribbons; caps and lace bonnets; hand-crocheted blankets from her mother, stitched in pastel shades of yellow, green, pink, blue, and white; and congratulation cards from friends and family. She touched the pieces to her cheek, relishing the faint scent of baby powder. Sweet memories wafted through the room, each one embedded forever in her heart.

Her trembling fingers crept over a tiny red and gold sweater with the words "Little Slugger" embroidered across the front. Debra sobbed and drew the sweater to her chest. Farther down in the box, she found Chad's matching ball cap and a little pair of red tennis shoes. Michael had taken a zillion pictures the first time Chad wore it. Back then, she and Michael possessed a passionate, fervent love—long since lost. It ended with the merger of Patterson and Doyle Law Firm. Michael gradually shifted his affections from her to dollar signs and a table at the country club. His mother praised his every effort to climb the social and corporate ladder to success. Never mind he chose to distance himself from his wife, but not his children. That was why she felt certain Chad and Lauren were all right, wherever they slept this night.

Twice tonight, she'd stepped into the kitchen with an urgency to pour a drink. She needed sleep, and a glass of orange juice and vodka guaranteed to relax her body. She'd tried the over-the-counter sleeping aids as Alicia and Jill suggested, but still her mind zipped in and out of memories.

A chill sped up her spine and tickled at her nape. What if Jill discovered her drinking? Would she leave her alone in Michael's big empty house to face this living nightmare? Surely, she'd understand how desperately Debra needed a good night's rest.

In the darkness, she stole across the kitchen and opened the cabinet for a tall glass. She turned and stood in front of the refrigerator and stared at Chad and Lauren's artwork. She'd memorized every color and stroke of their drawings. Michael didn't like the pictures hung where others might see. He claimed the drawings made the kitchen look tacky. But who could possibly object? His mother? So every morning after he left for work, Debra taped them back on the fridge until evening when the Porsche pulled into the driveway.

Finally she opened the refrigerator door. The cool air captured her already cold fingers and held them suspended, taunting her. She took a ragged breath and set the glass on the counter. The orange juice rested on the top shelf behind a gallon of milk and a plastic carton of apple juice. After one minute more of deliberation, she reached for each container and set them on the counter. With the refrigerator door open, she splashed orange juice into the glass, filling it one quarter full. In the same painstaking manner, she returned the items and closed the door.

She'd hidden the vodka beneath the cabinets in a stainless

steel container marked "cookie cutters" jammed far into a corner with an angel food pan on one side and a Bundt pan on the other. In front of those, round cake pans were stacked according to size. Since Michael issued a no-sweets edict for her and the children, they were seldom used.

On her hands and knees, dressed in a pair of pure silk, azure pajamas, Debra quietly slid out the stainless steel container. While still on the floor, she wrapped her fingers around the orange juice glass and brought it down beside her. Her fingers itched to open the liquor bottle. Slowly, she turned the lid. A soft gurgling sound, in spurts and shoots, filled the glass and toasted the air. No ice, of course.

The glass felt smooth, like the first swallow promised. . . and the next. Her pulse raced, and her belly craved the warm glow of abandonment and the expectation of forgetfulness. She'd been contemplating this moment since Tuesday evening; now it existed in mere seconds. All she needed bordered on this one drink to settle her sleep-deprived body. Tomorrow they'd find Chad and Lauren; then she'd quit drinking and raise her children properly.

Holding the glass with both hands and closing her eyes, she leaned her head back as though paying homage to a carved image. Reverently she lifted the glass to her mouth—an iced-tea Waterford purchased by Michael's mother from an exclusive bridal store in the heart of the Galleria. Ten years ago, they were new, and Debra treasured them along with her Ivy League, personable husband. Now those glasses held the spirits of regret.

First a sip, she thought. *Then I'll put everything back in perfect order.* As soon as the glass touched her lips, she knew it ushered in everything she anticipated. Her stomach rippled, and she smiled in the shadows. With the air of a master, she screwed on the vodka lid, slipped the bottle back inside the cookie cutter container, and slid it in the corner of the cabinet. She eased into place the other baking items that covered her hiding spot.

With the contents of her glass nearly gone, Debra rose to her feet and noticed how her silk pajamas caused her to glide across the room. Amidst this pleasure, she could wait until the police and FBI found Chad and Lauren tomorrow. What strength she found in an iced-tea glass filled with orange juice and vodka. Liquid courage, she'd heard it called. It didn't make the pain go away, just easier to bear.

Debra remembered the boxes of baby clothes on her bedroom floor. She decided to sort through them again. Each one, four of them to be exact, marked a different age. This time, she promised herself not to cry so much and instead notice every detail of Chad and Lauren's tiny baby things, especially the items her mother had made. Maybe she would cry a little, maybe a lot. Her babies were missing, abducted into a terrifying world without their mommy.

The kitchen light flicked on, blinding Debra's vision.

"Debra, what are you doing?" Jill's eyes were wide and angry.

chapter 8

Debra dropped her glass, shattering the near-empty Waterford around her bare feet. A sliver anchored on the top of her foot and sent a flow of blood trickling alongside her big toe. She stared at the floor and the small crimson pool blending in with the orange juice and vodka. Suddenly she didn't feel so optimistic about her circumstances.

"What are you doing?" Jill repeated, not moving from her stance in the doorway. She folded her arms across her chest. "It's three in the morning, and you're dancing across the kitchen?"

"I couldn't sleep." Debra groped for a reasonable explanation to what Jill had found. Weeks before, she'd promised Jill not to use the problems of life as an excuse to drink, but back then, the problems hadn't escalated to this.

"And you thought liquor might help?" Jill's voice rose higher.

"What—what makes you think I'm drinking?"

"I'm not a fool, Debra. Look at you. Rather pathetic if you ask me."

"Who asked you?" Debra shouted, stamping her foot and

wincing with the pain of yet another piece of glass in her foot. "I have the right to forget my grief for a little while. I have the right to indulge in one drink or the whole bottle for that matter. This is a nightmare, Jill. I have the right to escape!"

Jill rubbed the palms of her hands together. "That's right, you do," she said. "But not with me. I'm here to help you, not enable you to continue down a drunken path of self-destruction and self-pity."

"Self-pity? Is that what you think? My children are out there somewhere with a man who is an insensitive, unfeeling. . ." A string of expletives followed.

"Cursing won't bring Chad and Lauren home any faster."

"Well, it sure makes me feel better." Debra's words echoed around her. Why was she lashing out at her best friend?

"Fine, then you can drink, curse, and do whatever you want by yourself. I'm going home."

Jill's ease and control unnerved Debra. Whereas a moment ago anger heated her veins, she now sensed a growing panic. Her lips quivered. "Oh, please, don't leave me, Jill. I couldn't bear to be left alone."

Her friend swallowed hard and peered into her face. "You were doing quite well before I interrupted you."

Debra's gaze flitted about the room. "I made the mistake of going through baby clothes," she said, wishing desperately her head were clear. She despised herself. "All of their tiny little things smelled so fresh, and it brought back memories of them and good times with Michael." She lifted a tear-glazed face. "It wasn't always this way with Michael, not in the beginning years. We loved each other then." She knew she rambled, but the words spilled out. "I know you don't want me to drink, but

I can't help it. I'm weak, Jill. He betrayed me. He made love to me the night before when all the while he plotted to take my children."

Jill took a step forward then shook her head. "If Michael walked in here right now, could he prove you are an unfit mother?"

"One drink doesn't make me a bad mother." Debra lifted her chin.

Jill pointed to the floor. "No, it doesn't, but you're standing there in the middle of broken glass and a pool of blood."

Debra glanced at her feet. She dare not move for the sharp pieces resting precariously about her. Orange juice permeated the air. It smelled rancid. "I. . .I didn't realize."

"I know, honey," Jill said, her eyes sleep laden. "Don't move, and I'll sweep this up. At least I'm wearing slippers." She padded to the utility room broom closet.

"And you're not leaving me?" Debra asked. Her friend could easily open the back door and walk down the driveway to her own home.

Jill stood still, as if contemplating Debra's question. "I plan to go to church this morning with my husband, and I'd like for you to come along. But in any event, I'll let you know afterwards. One thing is certain; you have to decide to be strong and no longer resort to temporary escapes or handle this mess on your own. I refuse to be anything but a good friend, one who won't stand by while you destroy yourself. Your crutch has to go or I do."

Debra stared, numb to anything but Jill's ultimatum. Her friend didn't mince words. She uttered the truth. Other women might hold her and tell her she had the right to drink. Some would speak kind words, but they'd all be gone as soon as they plastered a Band-Aid across her heart.

"I'll do better," she said, trying not to slur each word. "I won't drink, and I'll be stronger." She sighed. The confrontation had suddenly sobered her. "Please forgive me, but church is not what I want to do. You go on ahead with Drake, and I'll be waiting when you get back."

"What about your liquor?"

"I'll discard it, I promise. Jill, I realize you and Drake cannot move in with me until the children are found, and someday I have to face the world by myself."

Her friend's face softened. "If you only understood how much God loves you. He wants to be your rock and your peace."

"Right," Debra said. "If your God loves me, He has a poor sense of humor."

Later in her bedroom, Debra saw the clock read four and hoped she might still rest before dawn. She'd pulled the glass out of her foot, dabbed hydrogen peroxide on the cuts, and applied a gauze bandage without Jill's aid, simply to prove she could manage a small corner of her life. Together, they shoved the boxes of baby clothes back onto the farthermost shelves of Debra's closet.

"I won't bring them down again," Debra said, once they finished. "Hurts too much."

"Wise decision," her friend said. "Now, why don't you crawl into bed instead of trying to sleep on the sofa?" She glanced about the room. "When I'm having a bad night, I turn on the ceiling fan and listen to classical music. The combination lulls me to sleep."

"If it works for you, then it might work for me."

Exhausted, Debra crawled beneath the white down duvet, and for the first time since last Monday night, she drifted into a world where she dreamed of her precious children, safe beside her.

On Sunday morning, the sound of the phone ringing woke Debra from a deep sleep. At first she ignored it; her mind floated in the haziness between slumber and reality. On the third ring, she lifted the receiver only to drop it then pick it up again. The caller might be Alicia or Agent Howell.

"Debra Patterson?" a woman asked.

She bolted upright from the bed. Although she didn't recognize the voice, she might have news about Chad and Lauren. "Yes, this is she."

"This is hospice in Kansas City calling in regards to Cynthia Wilson."

"That's my mother. What's wrong?" Fear paralyzed her senses. Hospice meant the beginning of the end, when no hope remained for a patient.

"On Friday afternoon when meals-on-wheels attempted to make their stop, the delivery man couldn't get Mrs. Wilson to answer the door. He contacted a neighbor who had a key to your mother's home. They found her unconscious and made arrangements for an ambulance."

"Is she alive?" Debra's voice quivered.

"Yes, Mrs. Patterson. Her doctor plans to release her to-morrow into our care. He gave us your number."

"So the prognosis is not good," Debra said. A slow ache enveloped her body and tightened around her heart.

"No, I'm sorry. She doesn't have much time left, and I'm sure you will want to spend it with her."

Debra took a deep breath. "Can she come here to Houston where I can take care of her myself? Possibly MD Anderson could help her."

"She isn't strong enough to be moved. Is there a problem with you traveling to Kansas City?"

"A problem?" Debra felt hysteria mounting in her voice. "My husband has abducted my children, closed all of our bank accounts, and now you tell me my mother is dying? I don't have a penny to my name, to say nothing for purchasing an airline ticket."

"I had no idea." Compassion caressed the woman's words.

Debra broke into sobs. Her chest heaved, and her throat burned. She wanted to tell the woman she'd try to make arrangements to fly there, but where would she get the funds? What if the children were brought home, and she was gone when they arrived? "I don't know what to say or do." She fought the urge to scream.

Someone please help me. She must gain control. She told Jill she'd be stronger, find the courage to face each new day without a drink.

"I need a little time to figure out what's best," Debra finally said. "Can you hold on a minute while I get pen and paper to write down your number?" She laid the phone on the bed and rummaged through the nightstand. If only her body would cease trembling. A notepad inscribed with "Patterson and Doyle" lay inside the drawer. How ironic and cruel.

I hate you, Michael. I wish you were dead.

She snatched up the pad and fumbled for a pen. Her knees weakened, and she grabbed the corner of the nightstand for support. Willing her mind to focus attention on the problem in Kansas City, she wrote down the woman's name and hospice's number. "Thank you, I'll call you no later than in the morning."

"Mrs. Patterson, I'm so sorry."

"I appreciate your understanding." *But your sympathy won't bring back my children or heal my mother.*

Debra climbed back into bed and pulled the sheet up around her neck. What had happened to her world? If this was life, then she wanted no part of it. Without her children and her mother, she possessed nothing. Chad and Lauren had given her purpose; Mom had given her support.

She craved the depth of character so evident in Jill, but how could Debra attain the same stalwart demeanor? Perhaps Jill had inherited some kind of special genes enabling her to resist tragedies.

For certain, God had nothing to do with it. Her mother trusted God, and she lay dying. Maybe fate had simply dealt Debra a bad hand—preyed on her vulnerability until she slipped onto the edge of madness.

"Mom, your God has failed you," Debra had said to her about a month ago. "Your cancer count is not going down."

"He will heal me," Mom said. "If not in this life then in the next. Sweetheart, I'm not afraid of dying. My life has been rich; my blessings too many to count."

"How can you say that? Daddy died, leaving you with a pitifully small pension. Up until you got sick, you were forced to work or starve." Debra shook with anger.

"I am not the least bit bitter, and you shouldn't be either. Heaven is my home, and Jesus will escort me there."

Mom's words were laced with a passion that Debra didn't

understand; neither did she want to. "What will you do when you find out you're wrong?"

"I'm not, Debra. This is faith—knowing what I hope for is true, even though I can't see or touch it now."

"You talk in riddles, Mom. The cancer is eating your mind, and your church is poisoning what is left."

"My dear daughter, I pray one day you find the Truth, but for now let's talk of something else."

Mom's words neither condemned Debra's disbelief nor lessened the love she held for her daughter. Debra was confused as much then as now.

How could she go on without her mother? Although she knew nothing of what Michael had done, Debra still felt an element of security in knowing she was there. More than ever, Debra needed her mother's loving arms around her.

Loneliness crept over her like a damp chill. She studied the clock and calculated the hours until Jill returned, if she did at all. Who could blame her? Why should she baby-sit a drunk who was stupid enough to lose her children and her husband? At least her mother would be spared knowing how Debra had ultimately lost everything.

"I don't want to live without Chad, Lauren, or my mother," she whispered. "I can't go on."

chapter 9

arly Sunday afternoon, Debra heard Jill enter the back
door and call her name.

"I'm in the bedroom," Debra said. She'd slipped
into jeans and a T-shirt and forced a banana into her empty
stomach. But she hadn't disposed of the alcohol, and Jill
deserved to know she hadn't kept her word.

"Drake's with me," her friend said en route to Debra's
room.

"Good, I've done some thinking while you were gone, and
I need a sounding board." Debra hoped her tone reflected a
little confidence, certainly more than she felt. She was glad
Drake had come with Jill. He had a soothing effect upon
Debra, a certain confidence. Perhaps his exceptional height
had something to do with his ease, or possibly his dark hair
and piercing crystal blue eyes that attracted young and old to
give him a second look. Chad said Mr. Drake reminded him
of an eagle.

Jill and Drake appeared in the doorway, both wearing their
church clothes. Drake carried a white to-go bag. From the smell,

they must have enjoyed Italian food for lunch.

"We'll be glad to listen," he said with a smile and held up the bag. "I brought you something to eat. Just let me set it in the kitchen." He disappeared leaving Debra to fill an awkward silence with Jill.

Despite her queasy stomach, which seemed to have taken root inside her, Debra offered Jill her best smile, a quivering semblance of a greeting. She rose from the love seat to open the drapes. Perhaps the sunshine would lift her depression.

"How was church?" Debra asked.

"Exceptional," Jill said, her countenance glowing. "We wish you could have been there." Her ash blond hair hung loosely about her shoulders. She looked vibrant and definitely calm.

How does she do it? "Sometimes I think if it would help, I'd tag along."

Drake leaned against the doorway. "When you're ready, we're here to take you. But in the meantime, we'll be praying for that very thing."

Debra's smile turned to uneasiness. She brushed back her own tresses and remembered she hadn't combed them. "Thank you for all that you've done. I'm not so sure I could be as good a friend." Another uncomfortable silence passed. "Would you like some coffee? I need to discuss a few things with both of you."

"I'm ready for the talk, but count me out of the coffee," Drake said. "I drank a full pot early this morning before Jill got up."

"I'll have a cup," Jill said. "Would you like me to make it?"

"Go ahead, and I'll pour out the vodka before we begin. I

meant to dispose of it earlier, but a phone call left me rather worthless for a while."

"Alicia? Agent Howell?" Jill asked with a tilt of her head.

"No. I'll tell you about it when we sit down."

While Jill measured coffee and water, Debra pulled out the seldom-used baking pans and the stainless steel container holding her vodka. She thought she'd consumed only one drink, but the bottle measured half full, and she'd recently purchased it. The realization shocked her. She poured the liquor down the garbage disposal and tossed the bottle into the trash. She had no money to buy another one anyway.

Neither Drake nor Jill said a word, but their stares drilled a hole through her back. Yet she needed them to see her earnest attempt at cleaning up her miserable life.

Once seated at the table, Debra wrapped her fingers around her mug and stared into the black, steamy coffee. "I'm not sure where to begin." She hoped she could manage her composure. "This nightmare is getting worse, and I don't know when it will end." She glanced at her friends, but her gaze quickly reverted to the hot, strong brew. "Let me start by saying how much I love and value your friendship and what you've done for me since the children's disappearance. You two are the most sincere and unselfish people I've ever known. You've always given more to my children and me than we deserved. I remember the many times you tried to befriend Michael—even when he was obnoxious."

Jill reached across the table and touched her arm. Debra felt the warmth and comfort flow through to her bones.

"I've been rude and depended way too much on you," she said to Jill, "not once taking into consideration that I had pulled you from your husband and your life." Debra swallowed hard and stared into Jill's face. "I'm sorry." Turning to Drake she added, "I'm sorry for taking advantage of your kindness."

"We are here to help in any way we can," he said. "Neighbors are supposed to be like family."

Debra nodded. "I know, but I've become a leech. After some careful thought, I've decided to list the house with a Realtor as soon as possible and pursue a job. When we bought the house, Michael put the title in my name for liability reasons, so I'm free to sell it if I choose. Even if he did come back, our marriage is over."

"Even with counseling?" Drake asked.

"No amount of counseling could ever restore the trust."

"I see, and I understand," Drake said. "I'm glad you're thinking about the future. It's a good beginning."

"Well, this all brings me to a matter of importance." She turned to Jill. "I want you to go home and resume a normal life. Your presence causes me to behave like an emotional cripple. The longer you nursemaid me, the longer it will take me to find the courage to go on. Surely the investigators will find Chad and Lauren soon. They assure me they are doing everything possible to speed up the search. Once the children are home, I'll need to confront Michael and begin divorce proceedings. None of those things you can do for me."

Jill's gray eyes offered hope. "I understand, and I'm pleased with your plans to pull yourself together. The changes you want to make will take time. You shouldn't have to face all of this alone when there are people who love you. Is your mother well enough to travel to Houston?"

Debra blinked back the stinging tears. "Mother is not

well at all, which brings me to my other topic of concern. I received a call this morning from a hospice worker who has been assigned to my mom's care."

Drake groaned and leaned back in his chair. "Is this totally unexpected?"

"Not altogether." Debra willed her lips to cease trembling. "She has been undergoing chemo and radiation treatments for liver cancer, but it looks like nothing has helped. The deliveryman from meals-on-wheels suspected a problem when she didn't answer the door Friday. He alerted a neighbor who had a key. They found Mom unconscious and called an ambulance. Her doctor plans to release her from the hospital tomorrow under hospice's care. In short, he is sending her home to die."

"Oh, Debra." Jill's sympathy rang through her words. "How much more can you handle?"

"Precious little." Debra inhaled deeply. "I have no children, no husband, no money, and soon no mother. I'm frightened and don't know which way to turn." Immediately, her gaze met Drake's. "God is not the answer, Drake. At least not for me."

He said nothing, and she appreciated his silence. "What can we do?" he asked.

"Simply be my friends," Debra said. "Make me accountable when I conduct myself—well, like I did early this morning." She took a sip of coffee, and it hit the bottom of her stomach hard. "I've acted like an immature adolescent, and I want to escape any way I can." She sighed. "I need to call hospice back no later than in the morning. Naturally, they feel I should be there, but they also understand this nightmare with the children."

"But how are you going to purchase a plane ticket?" Jill asked. "Honey, let us help you."

"No." Debra sat straighter in the chair. "I've already phoned Mom's brother in Kansas City and explained the circumstances. He will take care of the ticket." Again, she swallowed hard to maintain her composure. "I also talked to Alicia and Agent Howell. Both assured me they could contact me as easily in Kansas City as here. I believe my children will be found today, but in case they aren't, my cell phone works anywhere. Until it's disconnected for nonpayment, I have its use."

"So when do you expect to leave?" Drake asked.

"There's a flight in the morning, and that is where I need your help. Could one of you drive me to the airport?"

Drake glanced at Jill. "I have a crucial meeting with a vendor in the morning, but I'm willing to cancel it."

"I can take Debra," Jill said. "In fact, I want to."

"Thanks. I don't know how long I'll be gone, and I didn't want to leave the SUV there in the parking lot. I'm hoping Mom improves to the point I can bring her here. Surely, with all of the technology available at MD Anderson, the doctors can help her."

"Possibly." Drake offered a reassuring smile.

"Look," Debra said, "I'm not a fool, and I understand hospice is the last resort, but I need to feel some sort of hope."

"Yes, you do." He combed his fingers through his hair. "I'm pleased with your courageous stand."

Jill and Drake spent the rest of the afternoon with Debra, despite her protests. She sincerely wanted to be the person her friends desired to see, but she did realize her weaknesses.

She packed clothes for the trip, not sure of how much or

what to take. The idea of visiting her mother for the last time tugged at her emotions. When Debra could not bring herself to pull a black dress from her closet, Jill chose one and slipped it into the suitcase.

The idea of witnessing her mother die an excruciating death added horror to Debra's ongoing nightmare. No matter what heartache she felt, her mother would not learn about the children's abduction. Debra tried calling her at the hospital, but the nurse said Mom was unconscious.

Debra's hope dwindled.

The following morning, during eight o'clock traffic, Jill drove Debra to George W. Bush Intercontinental Airport for a nine thirty flight to Kansas City. Groggy from another sleepless night, Debra's thoughts tumbled from Chad and Lauren to her mother—such turmoil, such confusion. Jill stopped for gas, and while she pumped it, Debra stared at the station's window where a sign read 3 TAMALES FOR $1.00.

Three tamales for a dollar. Debra sighed.

Three tamales for a dollar.

Three tomorrows for a dollar. What would it cost to buy my mother a few more tomorrows?

"Do me a favor?" Jill asked, as they pulled away and waited at a traffic light.

"I guess," Debra said, arousing from the depths of despair.

"When you get back, would you see a counselor?"

Debra nibbled on her lower lip. "I'd be glad to, but I have no money."

"One of our pastors is a licensed psychologist."

"Oh, Jill, will you ever give up?" Debra stared out the window and felt a tear slip down her cheek.

"No, I can't. You mean too much to me." Her friend paused. "Just think about it, okay?"

"All right." Debra would agree to anything to avoid the topic of God. "I really didn't mean to cut you off."

"I know," her friend said. "Don't concern yourself with it."

They rode the rest of the way in silence. Debra hated the barrier between them with the religion thing, but stress had pushed her beyond listening to such nonsense. Odd, the two women she loved the most—her mother and Jill—clung to this idiocy about God. Finally Debra forced small talk, avoiding any discussion about the children, her mother, or God. "I'll miss you," she said, which was truer than she wanted to admit.

"Call me collect," Jill said, "as often as you need. I don't care what time day or night."

"I'll be fine, and I'll keep in touch." The PASSENGER DROP-OFF sign came into view, and moments later, Jill slid the car next to the curb. Debra turned to give her friend a hug. "I love you, Jill, and thanks for everything." She stepped back and waved good-bye.

"See you soon." Jill opened her mouth to speak again but closed it abruptly.

Once inside the airport, Debra checked her luggage, received her boarding pass, and then waited nearly an hour in security. She glanced at her watch and tapped her foot. Why was she in such a hurry to step from one black pit to another?

At last the attendant called her seat assignment. The Jetway loomed before her, and Debra hesitated. For a brief moment, she remembered the time a dog chased her up a fence. Perched on the top, she'd screamed for help, but the only person who came to her rescue was a bully who threatened to push her into the dog's path. With nowhere to turn and no one to help, she'd burst into tears and lost her balance, tumbling to the ground beside the boy. Terror had caused her to become violently ill, and he'd laughed. Now she felt the same impending gloom. No matter where she turned, something horrible happened.

As though in slow motion, she forced one foot in front of the other. She stepped into the plane and found her seat and eased down next to a window. Perhaps she could rest for a few hours during the flight.

The cell phone rang. She considered not answering it, but the caller could be Alicia or Agent Howell.

"Mrs. Patterson, this is hospice in Kansas City." Debra recognized the woman's voice from yesterday.

"Yes, I'm onboard the plane now, and I'll be there in a few hours. Please tell Mother I'm on my way."

"I'm sorry, but I have bad news."

Debra's heart pounded, and she sat erect. "What's wrong?"

"I hate telling you this over the phone, but Cynthia Wilson, your mother, just passed away."

chapter 10

Usually Mondays hit Cale like an avalanche. The weekends always brought accidents and heart-related conditions through the emergency room. Of course all of the patients wanted to see a specialist on Monday. Many times, prayer and the Lord guiding his hands were all he could do.

Cale prided himself in getting to know those who en trusted their health to his care, not simply their names and if they had health-care insurance, but a glimpse into their lives. He prayed for all of them and many times with them.

Today brought a whirlwind of secret sorrows—the anniversary date of his sister and nephew's tragic death. From the moment he woke this morning, a black cloud had settled on his heart and mind no matter how hard he prayed. After all, he'd leased the plane.

"Are you okay?" Cale's receptionist asked after he'd seen his last patient.

He glanced into the brown face of this godly woman. "Well, Joan, I've been better."

"Anything I can do?"

"Not really. My sister and nephew were killed on this date a few years ago."

"I'm sorry, and I'll pray for you."

"Thanks, Joan."

He gathered up a few files that he intended to study this evening, but the memories played back like bad tapes. Eight years ago, his only sister Julie married Kevin Baxter, an anesthesiologist on staff at Henry Ford. On the surface, the marriage looked picture perfect, but Kevin had an abusive side to him. He took out his frustrations from the stressful pace at the hospital on his wife and their four-year-old son, Daniel. Julie kept it hidden when the physical abuse was aimed only at her, but when he leveled his anger at Daniel, she begged Cale to help her get away. Cale wanted to tear his brother-in-law apart with his bare hands, hurt him as he had hurt Julie and Daniel. "That makes you no better than Kevin. If you really want to stop him—see him punished—find me a good attorney," Julie had said.

Cale arranged for a private plane to take his sister and nephew to a hideaway in Vermont. They never arrived. The plane crashed into the White Mountains.

After examining the files he'd brought home, Cale gave into his rumbling stomach and heated a frozen chicken dinner. The food grew cold. . . .

Memories haunted him still. In Detroit, Cale avoided Kevin, but those times when he did see him, all the old animosity boiled near the surface. Repeatedly he took the matter to God, knowing He ultimately judged Kevin. Forgiveness was vital, yet Cale couldn't bring himself to let go. At times he believed his anger toward Kevin vented toward himself.

When Cale moved to Houston, he believed a change of scenery was not only good for his career but also vital to his relationship with God. Something had to change soon—and he knew the ball was in his court.

✐   ✐   ✐

On Thursday, a week after her mother's funeral, Debra ventured into a mall in Kansas City. She'd taken her mother's twelve-year-old Ford and felt guilty, as though she needed to ask someone's permission.

The moment she pulled into the parking lot, an invisible hand wrapped icy fingers around her throat. Every detail of the last day with Chad and Lauren rolled across her mind in vivid detail. She remembered the children's conversations, the humorous bickering, what they ate for lunch, and the clothes they chose for the new school year. Alone with her precious children, she'd shut out all the ugliness of her life and treasured their presence.

Why was she doing this to herself? Logic told her it made no sense. In the depths of her being, Debra felt she deserved the torture searing her soul. Her neglect had caused Michael to take advantage of the moment. She had to walk through this mall; it hailed as her executioner.

Debra closed her eyes and fought the whirl of emotions. Returning to her mother's empty home invited more pain. She'd done everything possible to avoid going through Mom's personal belongings, but they had to be sorted and disposed of by tomorrow night. Every time she opened a closet or cabinet door, her courage gave way. Yesterday she found all of her mother's shoes lined up in perfect order. The sight brought Debra to the floor in a pool of tears.

On Saturday morning, she had a plane ticket to fly home to another empty abode.

As she walked through the mall, a wave of dizziness caused her to bump into a young man and fall to the floor.

"Are you all right?" He bent down to peer into Debra's face. "Do I need to contact security?"

"No." Debra's tone was much too harsh for the young man's kindness, but her last encounter with security people still played across her mind. They couldn't help her then, and they couldn't help her now. "I'll be okay, just a bit light-headed."

"Are you sure? I mean, you're really pale."

Debra swallowed and blinked several times, willing the spinning in her head to cease. She should eat more like Jill and Alicia urged, but her appetite vanished with her children. The young man guided her to her feet and led her to a nearby metal bench.

"Thank you so much," she replied, uneasy with the young man's attention. "I'll rest here a few minutes before heading to my car."

"Would you like for me to stay with you?"

She glanced up into his face, marked with the telltale scars of acne. "It's not necessary. I'm feeling much better."

He gazed out across the storefronts. "I see a coffee shop. How about if I get you a cup?"

Nodding, Debra reached for her purse. She'd found fifty dollars in Mother's jewelry box.

"No, let me get it," the young man said. "Do you take cream or sugar?"

"Just black, and thank you for your generosity."

"My pleasure." He disappeared and returned a few moments later.

She gathered up the cup with both hands. Steam swirled from the small hole atop the cap, and the nutty aroma captured her senses. "Oh, thank you. This smells wonderful."

"You're welcome. I guess if you don't need anything else, I'll be going." He smiled, and she returned the gesture.

How nice to know some decent people still existed.

"Please, continue with whatever you were doing, and again thank you." Debra felt her face redden under the young man's scrutiny.

"I don't know you, ma'am, but God does, and He loves you." He walked away, leaving Debra confused and bewildered. He sounded like Jill. Were there any nice people who didn't spout the God thing?

Sitting on the mall bench, she contemplated the friends now dearest to her. Jill and Drake rated at the top, and they lived and breathed God and the church. Alicia came in next; she and Debra talked every day, sometimes more. The head of HPD's special investigative team in charge of finding Chad and Lauren always spoke calmly and offered encouragement. No mention of God, though, and for that Debra felt grateful.

Sergeant Howell appeared nice enough, but rather cold and formal. He stuck to facts and little else. She valued his expertise and knowledge. If he followed any religion, he certainly never made mention of it.

Of course, her mother believed in church involvement, and she had urged Debra to seek the Lord out for years. A lingering death had been her mother's reward for those years of prayer and devotion. At least she'd been sedated and pain free during those last hours. Debra remembered something the woman from hospice had said. *Your mother died with the most peaceful look on her face—rather serene.*

Debra took a sip of coffee and let it dribble down her throat. A wave of heaviness settled about her shoulders. She ached all over, had done so for days. The downward spiral of her life knew no bottom. Each new day dragged her further into a pit of despair.

When would the authorities find Chad and Lauren? The children were missing school and their little friends. Who read them a story before they went to bed? Who tucked the covers beneath their chins and turned on the night-lights? Did Michael relish in the silky softness of Lauren's hair? And did he allow Chad to play his GameBoy beneath the sheets? Did their father kiss them good night? The questions never ended, and, as always, she searched the crowds for signs of an eight-year-old boy and his gray-green-eyed little sister.

Sighing, she finished the coffee and stood on wobbly feet. She stared down at her baggy jeans held together with the first notch of her belt. Odd, the weight Michael complained about left with him.

Hours of work awaited her at Mom's. A charitable organization would be picking up the discarded items tomorrow afternoon. She should have sorted them earlier in the week but hated the thought of ever beginning.

She needed a drink.

Driving away from the mall to her mother's apartment, she saw a cocktail lounge advertising lunch. It looked like a nice place for a sandwich. One drink before she returned would make the afternoon go by more easily. She had enough money.

        ঔ   *ঔ*   *ঔ*

Debra opened her eyes and turned over on her back. Darkness and the effects of alcohol bundled confusion around her mind. She tried to think about what happened earlier in the evening, but the haziness shut out any memories of those lost hours. Obviously, she'd had too much to drink, and after she'd told Jill and Drake those days were over. Guilt attacked her spinning senses. She was an unfit mother; this afternoon proved it.

Odd, the room didn't smell like her mother's apartment— a mixture of sweet perfume and the scent of funeral flowers. The stench of alcohol hung about her and disgust wafted through the chilly air. She'd broken her word to Jill and Drake. The hum of an air-conditioning unit and snoring stirred her attention.

In alarm, her gaze flew to the figure beside her. Her heart hammered against her chest until it hurt. What had she done? What had happened since she stepped into the cocktail lounge?

Swallowing the acid rising in her throat, Debra picked her way through the cobwebs of her mind for an explanation. When nothing emerged, she ceased to wonder and stole from the bed. Light-headedness enveloped her, and she instantly sat back down until it disappeared.

Adjusting her eyes to the darkness, she saw her clothes piled in a heap on the floor. She dared not contemplate what she'd done while drinking. The evidence looked too horrible. How could she have sunk to such base means, especially when she didn't remember anything about the man sleeping beside her? Maybe shutting out the sordid memories had its advantages.

She glanced at the clock radio; the red letters flashed three thirty. Hot tears rolled over her cheeks, and she whisked them away. Debra gathered up her clothes and crept into the bathroom.

I've got to get out of here. Oh, please, don't let him wake up. Debra sensed the alcohol still had its treacherous hold on her. She slipped into her shoes and realized they were on the wrong feet. Another rush of tears spilled from her eyes. Fear and remorse suddenly shoved her into lucidity.

Her purse, she had to find her purse and her keys. What would she do if she couldn't find her mother's car? A cab, she could call a cab if she had any money left.

She detested the thought of what Jill and Drake might think. Courage, she had forgotten. Hope, she had abandoned. But she knew her life had ended unless she resolved to make some definite changes—not merely words but real life-altering improvements. If Chad and Lauren were returned to her today, she'd still need to deal with Michael and the difficulties of single parenthood. She'd find more and more excuses to drink.

God, if You're real, if You love me, like I've heard from Mother and Jill and Drake, why is my life so awful? I want my children back. I want Michael punished. Times, like now, I want to die. I need help. I need someone to love me.

Debra felt her way through the shadowy room and discovered her purse on the dresser. She patted around the laminated top. The man stirred. Stiffening for a moment, she wet her lips and willed her body to gain control. Satisfied the man slept, she felt around for the grainy leather case that held her keys. A moment later, she curled her fingers around them. The man uttered something, but this time she did not stop as she tiptoed to the door.

Her hand grasped the knob and turned it, her passageway to freedom. Debra ran along the carpeted hallway, following the arrow pointing to the elevator. She glanced behind her, as though the faceless man might pursue her. What if she had caught a disease during her drunken stupor? Perhaps she deserved it.

Finally, the elevator slid open and she stepped inside, stumbling in her haste. Luckily, no one stood about to stare at her disheveled hair and clothes. The numbers descended far too slowly. She smelled the liquor, its stench radiating from her body like cheap perfume. Downstairs in the hotel lobby, she searched for the ladies' room. Inside she scrubbed her face, as though rubbing it raw would make her feel clean.

Within moments, she'd combed her hair, straightened herself, and applied lipstick. A perusal inside her purse revealed she had but twenty dollars left, and she might need that at the airport on Saturday. Now, to find coffee and her car.

Adjacent to the front desk, a beverage counter hosted fresh coffee. It smelled as though it had sat there for twenty-four hours, but Debra filled a paper cup and swallowed the tepid, bitter liquid. With a deep breath and a determination for steady nerves, she refilled the cup and marched through the front double doors to the parking lot.

Beneath the streetlights, Debra searched the parking lot. When she could not locate her mother's sedan, she bit back the tears and tried again. This time she found the vehicle nestled between two minivans. She hadn't locked the car, another stupid move. Easing her tired, aching body onto the seat, she took a moment more to clear her mind. She couldn't find her way back to the apartment until she learned the address of the hotel.

She shouldn't be behind the wheel. She could get picked up for drunken driving and lose her children. How ironic. She finished the coffee in her hand and noticed writing on the side of the cup. Switching on the overhead light, she read the hotel's address—less than ten minutes from her mother's apartment. She could do this.

A few more deep breaths, and Debra stuck the key in the ignition. The car hesitated, creaked, and moaned, like an old woman trying to drag herself out of bed. Debra held her breath and tried again; this time the engine responded. Pulling away from the hotel and onto the street, she spied a police car behind her.

"Please, no," she said. "Just let me get to the apartment without an incident."

Somehow, Debra maneuvered the car to the residential area. Expelling relief, she locked the vehicle and hurried into the apartment building.

Sleep, she thought. *After a few hours' sleep, I'm putting some sense into this miserable life of mine. No more drinking—ever, and I vow to act responsibly.* Most important of all, she intended to find some sort of meaning to her wretched existence. Maybe she needed God after all. Anything had to be an improvement.

At eleven o'clock on Friday morning, Debra awoke. Shame haunted her with vivid memories of the night before. She showered, repeatedly washing her body. Never had she felt so sordid. She'd become what she used to whisper about to her girlfriends in high school and college. Trash.

But Debra meant her commitment made in the wee hours of the morning. Those days were behind her; she needed to deal with today. First of all, she needed to start eating properly. She trekked into the tiny kitchen and opened the cupboards. The contents were typical of an elderly woman: chicken noodle soup, saltine crackers, applesauce, and four cans of liquid nutrition. Inside the refrigerator sat a jar of pimento cheese. She forced herself to eat, although the pain in her head threatened damage to her stomach.

The second step came in a careful inspection of Mom's belongings. She knew she didn't have time to sort through every closet and drawer, so she chose to select only those things she wanted to keep: a few pieces of inexpensive jewelry that Daddy had given her, her wedding ring, a journal of her great-grandmother's, an embroidered handkerchief trimmed in faded yellow lace, old photographs, and a Bible. She fingered the black leather binding of her mother's prized possession but did not open it. If Mom deemed it so important, then she needed to give it proper consideration when she didn't feel pressed for time, perhaps tomorrow on the plane.

The other items could be organized and disposed of by Uncle Rick, Mom's brother. Debra simply couldn't manage the task and admitting her incompetence didn't make her feel any better. With shaky hands, she phoned her uncle.

"Uncle Rick, is it possible someone else could go through Mom's things? I simply can't bring myself to do it."

"Sure, Debra. I understand how you feel. How about if I give you the church's number and let you make arrangements with them?"

The woman who answered the phone at the church gladly

obliged, relieving Debra of the arduous task.

Late afternoon, she eased onto the threadbare sofa with the resolve to call Jill. Twenty minutes later, she mustered the strength to dial the familiar number.

"Jill, this is Debra," she said when her friend answered. "I really miss you."

"Are you ready to come home?"

"Yes, I am." Debra meant those words. She must go forward. "Can you still pick me up at the airport?"

"Of course. Five in the evening, right?"

"Right. You know, this time alone has forced me to face a few ugly things about myself."

"Do you want to talk about it?"

"Not over the phone." Debra curled a strand of hair around her finger. "But I believe I'm ready to talk to the counselor from your church."

Silence reigned on the other end of the phone.

"Jill?"

"Yes." Her friend's voice sounded strained.

"Are you okay?"

Jill sniffed. "I'm just so very happy you've decided to seek counseling."

"Well, it doesn't mean I have religion, but I must find some meaning and purpose to my life soon. This depression scares me. I have no hope."

"Pastor McDaniel has helped a lot of people."

"It would be nice to think I could be included with them."

"Have you heard any word about the children?"

Debra hesitated, swallowing an onslaught of tears. "No, not yet. Alicia and Agent Howell are optimistic, but the fact remains they have no clues or leads."

"You and the children are always in my prayers."

Debra didn't know quite how to respond. "Thank you for your loyalty to my children and me. I've always noted something in you and Drake that intrigued me, something I wanted but didn't know how to obtain. In the past, I credited my envy to your relationship with each other, but now I wonder if what I see and feel is your relationship with God."

"You have a start," Jill said and cried softly.

"But if I become a Christian, will God bring back my children?"

"None of us know His mind."

chapter 11

"Mrs. Patterson, I know a little about your situation from the newspapers and Jill, and I understand your children haven't been located." Pastor Rod McDaniel said. He took a quick glimpse at her completed forms and laid them on his lap. "I am truly sorry about this tragedy. Our church staff has been praying for you and your children."

"Chad and Lauren," Debra said, feeling a knot tighten in her stomach. "Their names are Chad and Lauren."

He skimmed over the forms and circled the information on her papers.

Debra nodded and wet her lips—anything to keep from crying. Liquid emotion didn't solve a thing. She liked the fact Pastor McDaniel sat in a chair facing her rather than behind a desk. It felt less intimidating. Plus, his silver hair gave the impression of a kindly man.

"I appreciate your prayers." She folded her clammy hands and felt a jagged thumbnail. Maybe this counseling thing wasn't such a good idea. Maybe she could dig herself out of this pit by herself, but the truth about her past futile attempts said otherwise.

Her gaze darted about the shadowy office, actually rather homey with the plush furniture and plants. She noted a few fly-fishing paintings. The pastor sat in a navy blue leather chair while she tried to relax on the matching sofa. The furnishings suited him.

"Would you mind telling me the story?" Pastor McDaniel stood and picked up a yellow legal pad and pen from his desk before resuming his position.

Debra stiffened. "Can you take notes on something other than that?"

"Certainly." He retrieved another pad of paper from his desk.

"Michael is a lawyer, and he used those things." She tightened the grip on her folded hands. Glancing down at them, she realized the protruding veins were the same as her mother's. "We have tons of them. I hate the reminders, although the lawyers today keep track of their cases on laptops."

The pastor smiled. "No problem. I don't have to take notes, if you like."

"No, sir, I understand you need to have a record of what we discuss." Perspiration dripped from her temples.

He leaned toward her, his attention fixed on her. "Mrs. Patterson, try to relax. I want to help you."

"I know. Guess I feel the whole thing is my fault. I never quite lived up to Michael's expectations of a wife and mother."

"Why don't you start at the beginning?"

She hesitated. Hashing over her marriage and the living nightmare since Michael began pursuing his career was like pouring salt into an open wound.

"I know it will be difficult, but in order to help you I must hear your story."

She managed a faint nod. "It may take awhile."

"We're not confined to time. I don't care if we're still here tomorrow morning."

Debra wanted to reveal the truth of her tragic marriage, the bits and pieces that chipped away from the love she once felt for Michael. She studied the pastor before her. His voice reminded her of waves breaking against the shore. Yes, that should be his name: Pastor Peaceful.

"My father died when I was ten years old. Mother never remarried, neither did I have living grandfathers as examples of how a man should treat a woman. I didn't have a measuring stick." She took a ragged breath. "I met Michael in college during my senior year. I majored in history and wanted to teach, and he was completing his law degree. After a few dates, Michael insisted we were destined to be together. Flattered at his lavish attention, his devilish good looks, and his desire to one day own his own law firm, I gave in to, well, whatever he wanted. I adored him. He became my lover, my friend, my daddy, and anything else I ever thought a man should be. Shortly afterwards, his father passed away unexpectedly. Michael's mother said the father and son were close, but Michael never spoke of him again. We were married a year later, and for the first few years, we had a storybook marriage."

When the tears seeped from her eyes, Pastor McDaniel handed her a box of tissues. "Would you like a soda or some coffee?" he asked.

"A little water would be nice."

He left the office, giving her time to compose herself. She

hadn't been able to dwell on those early years with Michael without tears of regret. She'd been so stupid back then, allowing him to manipulate her every move. Love had made her blind, and things between them grew worse over the years.

The pastor returned, and she gratefully accepted the water.

"How did things change in your marriage?" He closed the French doors behind him.

"When he began to climb the corporate ladder and later establish his law firm, his priorities moved from me to his career, although he adored the children. He said my backward ways were an embarrassment, and he began to mold me into the wife he needed. The sad part is I allowed it. I said nothing when he told me I didn't need to know about our finances. He purchased my clothes and eventually convinced me of my ineptness. He said my dream of teaching school didn't enter his plan for our lives. I didn't even know he bought out his partner, Mr. Doyle, until the investigation revealed it."

"And the children? How did he feel about them?"

Debra reached for another tissue and dabbed at her nose. "Until just a few days ago, I believed he loved them as I do. Michael could not do enough for Chad and Lauren, and he spared no money for private school, sports, dancing lessons, and whatever else they wanted. Now, I think he thought of them as possessions, something else he owned like ornaments on a Christmas tree. Naturally, when we were in public, he doted on us all, but in private, he demanded a lot. Of the two children, Lauren seemed to be his favorite."

"Why do you believe that?"

"Chad had started to take up for me. He spoke out against

Michael's bullying, which caused a wedge between father and son."

"Did he ever physically hurt you or the children?"

Debra shifted on the sofa. "It depends on how you define physical abuse—not the children. He never laid a hand on them, but he did grab me when he was angry about things."

"Grab you?"

"Well, sometimes he bruised me." Her heart pounded furiously. She'd admitted this to Alicia, but deep down she felt she deserved Michael's wrath.

Pastor McDaniel leaned closer. "That is abuse, Mrs. Patterson. Did he hurt you physically in any other way?"

She felt herself redden and could no longer look at him. Bitter memories of limping to the refrigerator for an ice pack brought a surge of anger. "At times," she said. "He hurt me when. . ."

"During intimacy?" The pastor leaned in closer.

Debra nodded, and the tears flowed faster.

"Do you want to continue?" he asked.

"I should, but this is so difficult." She inhaled deeply and took another sip of water. "Yes, I want to while I can." With another deep breath, Debra told him every detail about the day the children disappeared.

"And you've heard nothing from him since then?"

"No, sir, and the authorities haven't been able to locate any of them." This time she held her breath until the urge to weep had swept past her. Why couldn't she be strong and in control?

"But it couldn't all be Michael's fault," she said after several moments. "I'm not a good person. I'm incredibly weak."

"In what way?"

"I'll do anything to avoid a confrontation, and I tend to drink when I'm overwhelmed."

"And what do you drink?"

"Vodka and orange juice usually." She waited for the condemnation to set in. She knew Jill and Drake didn't indulge in any kind of alcohol and doubted if any members of their church did either.

"Did Michael know about this?"

"Yes. Actually, it merely confirmed his accusations that I was unfit as a wife and mother."

"Are you an alcoholic?"

The pastor's words rolled around in her head, reverberating until she pressed her hands against her ears. "I don't know," she said. "How do I find out?"

"Do you drink every day?"

"No. I don't crave it, either. Just when things are too difficult to bear, and I need to escape."

"When was the last time you had a drink?"

Debra laid her hands back into her lap and folded them again. She sat straighter. "Thursday night."

"Do you want help for your drinking?"

"I need help period. I want to be strong and find out what are the right things for me to do until my children are returned."

Pastor McDaniel nodded. He removed his wire-rimmed glasses and ceased to write. "Would you like to attend an AA meeting?"

"No—unless I realize I do have a dependence on alcohol. And if that is the case, then I will be at the next meeting."

"Who are you putting your faith and trust in right now?"

Confused, Debra searched for a proper answer. "I don't know," she admitted. "The police? FBI?"

"Has there ever been a time when you accepted Jesus Christ as your personal Savior?"

She shook her head and managed to look into his eyes. They seemed to glow with warmth. "I don't even know what you mean. I know my mother believed in Jesus and so do Jill and Drake."

"God loves you, and He wants to be your strength through this. He accepts us as we are and helps us turn from living life our way to living life His way."

"I'm not ready to make that kind of a commitment." She glanced down at her hands. "Not yet, anyway, but I want to learn more."

The pastor smiled.

"I believe God helped me through the week I spent in Kansas City after my mother died. I did bring back her Bible, and I've begun to read the book of John. Don't know why I started there. I guess that's what caught my attention."

"That's an excellent start."

She leaned back on the sofa. Her shoulders ached from the stress and pressure of talking about her problems. Guilt pointed its finger at her, the incredible guilt. "Pastor, I'm so tired, in every way imaginable. Can we stop for the day?"

"Yes, of course. When would you like to meet again? Wednesday?"

Debra stiffened. "So soon?"

He smiled again and stood from his chair. "I feel it's necessary to see you as often as possible to help you through this crisis."

She studied the carpet, where a coffee spill stained the cream color. "All right. What time do you want to see me?"

Pastor McDaniel picked up his planner. "How does Wednesday at ten sound?"

She nodded and swallowed hard. "I'll be here."

He jotted down the appointment.

"Pastor McDaniel?"

He peered into her face.

"If I become a Christian, will God give me back my children?"

He studied her through a kindly gaze. "I can't speak for God, neither can I tell Him what to do. But I will tell you this. He loves Chad and Lauren more than you could ever dream possible, and He knows exactly where they are. He wants your faith and trust so He can show you how much He loves you."

"You can't assure me He will return my children?" Her eyes pooled, and he handed her another tissue. "I asked Jill the same question, and she couldn't promise me either."

"No, but I know the power of prayer and His never-ending love."

"So you're telling me I'd be taking a chance by doing the Christian thing?"

"You never take a chance with God and His precious gift of life. You only win all He so desperately wants to give."

"It's difficult for me to understand that." She paused, hoping she could remember everything he said later. "I'll read some more of John, although most of it is difficult for me to grasp."

"Are you reading a King James Version?"

She thought for a minute. "I'm not certain. I just know

my mother received this Bible from her parents when she and Daddy married."

"There are other, easier-to-understand versions. Why don't you bring the Bible on our next visit, and we can discuss the passages that are giving you problems?" He opened the French doors, and she stepped into his outer office. He pulled a business card from his shirt pocket and handed it to her. "Call me night or day if you need me. My pager and home phone are there, too."

"Thank you." She exited the church, her burdens weighing heavier than before.

I thought I'd feel better after talking to the pastor. But I don't really, and he can't guarantee God will return Chad and Lauren. Why should I go through the motions of the Jesus thing if my life might not get better?

chapter 12

For Debra, Monday evening after her first counseling appointment dragged on. Her mind spun with the afternoon session and fueled her increasing anxiety. Snippets of her conversation with Pastor McDaniel held meaning, while others rolled across her mind in confusion. She found nothing to grasp and hold on to. She had to believe he could help. Without him, her life looked bleak. When ghostlike darkness enveloped the house, she curled up in her bed and waited as always for word that Chad and Lauren had been found.

Unbidden whispers besieged her resolve to stop drinking and act responsibly. She considered phoning Jill for support, but Debra loathed the weakness raging through her heart and mind. Her friend needed to spend the evening with Drake, not holding a drunk's hand. *I refuse to be an alcoholic.*

The phone rang, but she had learned to allow the answering machine in the kitchen to screen her calls. She climbed from her bed and hurried to check it, in case Alicia or Agent Howell needed her. The machine held no message, only the click of a hang up. With a weary sigh, she ambled toward her bedroom, the silence ringing in her ears.

Television offered no escape. The sitcoms aired either dim-witted comedy or family dramas that reminded her of how she'd failed as a wife and mother. Even the commercials depressed her.

Remembering Jill's suggestion to listen to classical music, she tuned in the radio, but it didn't soothe her restless spirit either. The clamoring orchestras merely pounded in her ears and increased her unrest.

She switched off the radio and stared at her mother's Bible on the nightstand. A marker indicated where she'd stopped reading in John the day before. Although she felt strangely drawn to the book, she couldn't recall any of the information. Again she tried to concentrate on those first few verses, but the words jumbled together, awkward and meaningless.

In the beginning was the Word, and the Word was with God, and the Word was God.

What word? Maybe if she'd grown up involved with Sunday school and church, she'd understand the material. But Mom didn't get religious until Debra started college.

Fully clothed, she crawled beneath the sheets, not sure if she wanted to tackle reading any more of the Bible or not. But in memory of her mother and her promise to Jill, Debra tried yet one more time.

As before, she read and reread the first few verses of chapter one.

Nothing made any sense; this John wrote in riddles. Did she need a secret code? Frustrated, she closed the book.

If only she knew God really existed, that He loved her

despite all the horrible things she'd done in her life. If only she could believe what Jill, Drake, her mother, and Pastor McDaniel said about a real heaven. If only she knew for certain God sent His only Son to die for her sins. *If. If. If.*

Debra's thoughts trailed back to the young man at the mall in Kansas City. She'd nearly forgotten his kindness. He'd gone out of his way to befriend her and then said God loved her. Nothing else about him proved unusual, except his deep acne scars. Michael would have been repulsed by the young man's appearance and shunned him with one condescending glance. Looks meant so much to her husband.

Glancing at the worn cover of the Bible in her lap, Debra wondered if she dare believe in God. Truth be known, she wanted to believe. The theory of everything in the world happening by chance pulled her further into a well of hopelessness. This life had to mean more.

"God," she said and shocked herself by speaking aloud. "I need to know if You are there and if You love me. Please talk to me. I don't understand the Bible, and I desperately need help. Are my children okay?"

Silence. Her fears shouted a mocking, *I told you so. No one loves you.* Disheartened, she sobbed herself into a fitful sleep.

The next morning, she awoke to her normal routine of a long, lingering shower and the ritual of calls to Alicia, Agent Howell, and Jill. She forced down a banana with black coffee while watching a TV minivan stop in front of her house. Would they never give up? Vultures, all of them, preying on the emotions of hurting people—picking at the bones of despair.

A notion struck her. A long walk might calm her ragged thoughts. She phoned Jill, and when her friend asked if Debra wanted company, she declined. As much as she craved Jill's calming presence, her friend couldn't play nursemaid forever.

"I need time to think. I've tried reading Mom's Bible, and everything is so confusing." Debra raked her fingers through her hair. "I need answers, Jill. I hate my life and what has happened with Chad and Lauren."

"Have you considered writing down your questions, and then I could help you find the answers?"

"The answers I need are whether God is really there and if He loves me."

"Okay, I understand."

Any other time, Debra would have bit back a nasty retort, but lately she wondered if what Jill and her mother believed really would give her purpose, meaning, and above all, love. And maybe, just maybe, belief in God might help her find her children.

Debra snatched up the cell phone with her purse and stepped toward the garage.

She drove to the nearest Starbucks drive-through and slipped into line. The TV van soon gave up and sped away. Debra pulled the SUV from the line and headed to where she could walk uninterrupted. Fifteen minutes from her home, near the soccer fields where Chad used to play, sprawled a two-mile walking and jogging trail. This early in the morning, it wouldn't be engulfed in sweltering heat, a perfect opportunity to deliberate those things that plagued her.

A slight breeze whipped around the oaks bordering the trail. A few people walked or ran by her, but for the most part, she strolled alone. She avoided scenes of mothers and their children; that hurt too much, so she simply looked away.

A colorful ball rolled across her path, and out of habit, she picked it up. A towheaded little girl stood just beyond the tree-laden path with her thumb sticking in her mouth.

Compassion flowed through Debra's veins. She bent and pushed the ball in the child's direction.

"Here you are, sweetheart." She smiled into the angelic face.

Debra lingered a moment while the little girl gathered up the ball and toddled away toward a woman. Her precious babies, where were they?

"She's a beautiful child," Debra said, the pangs of loss ripping at her heart.

"Thank you," the woman said. "Isn't it wonderful how God blesses us with children?"

"Yes, it is."

"Do you have children?"

"Yes. I have a boy and a little girl."

The mother patted her rounded stomach. "Guess I will have a little boy in three months."

"Congratulations." Envy laced every syllable. Debra resumed her walk, no longer able to bear the sight of the mother and child.

"God loves you," the woman called.

The magnitude of the words caused Debra to swing her attention back to the woman, but she'd turned and walked away. *God loves you* repeated in her mind like credits from a movie. Oh, how she wanted to believe those words.

After the walk, she dug through her purse for her cell phone and checked on messages at home. Agent Howell questioned whether she had remembered any of Michael's friends.

"Call me, Debra," Steven Howell said. "We've discovered something about Michael."

Curious, she punched in Steven's cell number. Had the FBI found a clue? A missing link?

"Hi, Steven. This is Debra."

"We've found out a few things about Michael."

She didn't know whether to be hopeful or not. So many times her expectations were destroyed. "What have you learned?"

"He was skimming off the top of the law firm and had been for some time."

She nearly dropped the phone. "I thought all of his records were missing."

He chuckled. "Michael just made it a little more difficult for us. We also found out he'd been depositing the funds into a bank on the Channel Islands—off the coast of France."

"France?" Debra's mind raced. "He always talked about the French—how he envied their way of life."

"Now you know why."

"Steven, by now I shouldn't be surprised at anything."

He sighed, and she imagined him in a tight-lipped smile. "Greed has a way of changing people, and not for the best."

How well Steven nailed Michael, and the agent didn't even know him. "Does this information mean you can find him and the children?"

"Maybe. Looks like he's changed his identity—could be anywhere. We'll have to dig deeper."

"I see," she said. "Are you saying my children could be living outside the U.S.?"

"Possibly. Right now, we don't know. That's all I have right now."

Debra's head began to pound. She squeezed her eyes shut in an effort to ease the pain. "Thank you, Steven. I–I appreciate the call. Can I call you on Saturday?"

"I might not have my phone with me. I'm taking my son on a canoe trip. You know, guy stuff."

"Oh, I see."

"He's not the best kid, but then I'm not the best father."

"But you're trying. Have a good time with your son." She replaced her cell phone and leaned back against the headrest. Michael involved with embezzlement? Michael, who guarded every word and action? How little she'd known her husband, but she never thought he'd abduct their children either.

Shaking off the rising depression, Debra started the car and tuned the radio to a classical station. Once she got home, she'd take something for her headache and lie down for a while. Steven's news meant the FBI was working on the case. Realistically, she should be pleased—grateful of the progress. Instead, she wanted to sink into despair.

While driving by Chad and Lauren's school, she remembered Alicia's report stated Michael had withdrawn the children's school records the same day he abducted them. He'd thought of everything, and again she wondered how long he'd been planning to snatch away her babies.

A thought leaped across her mind. Although school had started and teaching positions had been filled, districts always needed substitutes, and she did hold a teaching certificate. The school district might require her to update her skills, but that could be done while she taught. Substitute teaching would be a way to get back into her field until a full-time position became available.

Debra turned into the parking lot of the elementary school and found a visitor's spot. Taking a deep breath, she rummaged through her purse for a nasal spray to combat the migraine seemingly pulling her hair out by the roots. Despite the pain, she could make an inquiry about where to complete a teaching application.

Stepping from her vehicle, Debra felt she'd made another positive step in making her life whole—first the counseling and now seeking employment.

Inside, the secretary immediately recognized Debra. "Good morning, Debra. How can I help you?" A muscle twitched in the tall woman's face.

"Hi, Linda. I have a question." A sharp throb cut across Debra's eyes, and she knew they must be red. "Excuse me, I have a bit of a headache." She inhaled deeply and attempted to will away the pain. "Can you tell me where I can apply for a substitute-teaching position?"

Linda stared at her strangely. "Do you think that's such a good idea?"

Debra stiffened. "Why do you ask?"

"I mean working with children might be a bit of a challenge. Oh, Debra, think of how agonizing it would be seeing children every day and not having Chad and Lauren."

"I have a teaching certificate, which makes me qualified." Debra felt her temper rising. The term "unfit" danced across her mind.

Linda nibbled at her lip. "I don't doubt your capabilities, but wouldn't teaching be agonizing in light of your missing children?"

"I'd rather be working with someone else's children than

have no contact at all. In fact, I think it might help." Debra ordered herself to calm down. Not everyone judged her mothering skills.

Tears pooled in Linda's eyes. "I'm so sorry. I've been meaning to call, but I really didn't know what to say, at least not without crying."

Immediately Debra regretted her near loss of temper. "We could have cried together."

"I hope—I hope you realize I didn't know what your husband was doing the day he requested the children's records. I said the same to the police and the FBI. I never dreamed—"

"No one knew his plans, and I have never once blamed you for any of this. Put those thoughts out of your mind, okay?"

Linda nodded and sniffed. "Thanks. Like I told the police, your husband said you were moving. Then when you came in just now, I naturally assumed you were going to let me have it."

Tears filled Debra's eyes. "And I thought you were questioning me as an irresponsible mother who had no right wanting to teach children."

"Oh, no. You are one of finest mothers I've ever seen. We could always depend on you to lead volunteer committees and help out at school functions. I told the authorities the same thing." She reached across the counter and patted Debra's hand. "They will find Chad and Lauren."

"Thank you."

Linda picked up a business card. "Here's the school district's office. Their hours are eight to four."

Debra took the card. She couldn't say more for the lump in her throat. The pounding in her head had grown worse; she wished this nightmare would end.

"Keep in touch," Linda said as Debra left the office. "And good luck."

I don't need luck; I need my children.

Outside, the shouts of children on the playground wrenched at her heart. *Oh, God, if You are really there. . .please help me.*

chapter 13

B y the time Debra had taken medication for her migraine and rested until the pain dissipated, the hour had passed for her to apply for a teaching position at the administrative office. Tomorrow morning, she'd take care of it.

She woke Wednesday morning with a sense of anticipation. For the first time in nearly a month, she had plans that gave her a reason for crawling out of bed and forcing herself into the shower.

After making her normal calls to Alicia, Jill, and Steven, she drove to her children's school district office. As soon as she had completed the necessary paperwork, she'd head toward Pastor McDaniel's office for her counseling appointment.

". . .and you don't feel spending the day with children would push you into depression?" asked Mr. Tanner, the superintendent of instruction and curriculum.

"No, sir," Debra replied. "It will have the opposite effect. I want to teach children, and I can do an excellent job."

"All right, Mrs. Patterson. I had to be sure. Currently all of our full-time positions are taken. Are you willing to substitute?" The middle-aged man shuffled through his papers as though anxious for Debra to be gone.

"Yes, by all means." *Why are you uncomfortable? I'm the one who lost my kids.*

"We'll be in contact as soon as your application is processed." He smiled and folded his hands on the desk. "Most of our subs are kept busy working two to three days a week—providing their references are good."

Debra felt her cheeks warm. The words to tell him what she thought of his insinuations nipped at her tongue, but she didn't want to upset the man who had the authority to approve her application. She thanked him and a few moments later, stepped into the humid air, about as heavy as what she left inside. Taking a deep breath, she climbed into the SUV and noticed the gas gauge rested on empty. *This gas-guzzler will have to go.* She couldn't afford the payments or the upkeep. Much like her house.

Suddenly she felt overwhelmed by the staggering circumstances in her life.

Breathe in and out, Debra. She refused to allow a panic attack to control her mind and body, or give into tears that lasted for hours. *Breathe in and out.*

She must handle one thing at a time, minute by minute if necessary. The investigators hadn't stopped their search for Chad and Lauren. Every hour brought them closer to finding them, and she would be strong and ready to resume her role as mother.

Gas, she needed gas. At the first station, she pulled in. Fortunately, she'd found five twenties in her lingerie drawer, money she'd put aside to buy Michael a nice birthday present.

It would sustain her for a little while. Michael a special gift? Right now, she wished him dead by his next birthday.

All the while she pumped gas, her thoughts dwelled on what she could do to speed up the process of finding the children. With so many free hours until the district called for a sub job, she could volunteer to file reports, make phone calls, or even brew coffee for the investigators. What else could she do with her time? Sit at home and cry while fighting the urge to drink?

"Hey, lady," a biker called from the pump adjacent to hers. Tattoos bulged from his sleeveless shirt and several earrings dangled from one ear. "Aren't you the Patterson woman, the one whose husband stole her kids?"

Debra refused to look up and give the crude man reason to taunt her.

"Oh, you are." His tone softened. "I'm sorry. Life must be tough enough right now without the likes of me asking stupid questions."

She peered up at him. The sympathetic look in the biker's eyes contrasted his hardened features. "Yes, I'm Debra Patterson."

He jammed the handle back into the pump and leaned against the side of his Harley. "Lady, God loves you. Believe that. He'll never let you down." With those words, he threw a leg over his motorcycle and sped away, leaving Debra with her mouth agape and the smell of gasoline in her nostrils.

She slipped back into the SUV and drove toward Spring Creek Church. Bewilderment with the biker's words moved her thoughts back to God. What good did it do for the woman yesterday to say God loved her or the biker today? She needed to hear God say it.

"How are you doing since we met on Monday?" Pastor McDaniel asked. He reached for a pad of white-lined paper.

Debra shrugged. "The same." She hesitated and took a sip of cold water. "In some ways better."

"How's that?" For the first time she noted his tanned face indicating he enjoyed the outdoors.

"The better part?"

"Yes."

"I'm fighting harder. I haven't given in to a drink, and this morning I completed an application to substitute teach."

"Looks to me like you're winning," he said. "Why do you think this is happening?"

Taken by surprise, she needed to ponder his question. *Am I winning the war against myself? Is that why I'm exhausted?*

"What are you doing differently? Bible reading? Prayer?" Pastor McDaniel's gentle probing caused her to dig deeper into her tangled thoughts.

"I'm still trying to understand the Bible, but I'm easily frustrated."

"Did you bring yours?"

"No, I forgot, but I did see it's a King James Version."

He reached for a Bible on his desk and presented it to her. "This one is written in more contemporary language. I've jotted down a few passages and slipped them inside the cover. Many of the verses speak of God's love."

She glanced up.

"What is it, Debra?"

Shaking her head, she didn't know whether she could voice her deep longing or not. *God's love?* She felt like a child asking if her daddy loved her. "Nothing." Forcing a smile, she wrapped her fingers around the Bible's binding. "Uh, thank you for the Bible, Pastor."

"You're welcome. You know, sometimes the hardest thing to accept about God is that He loves all of us equally and more than we could ever imagine."

Debra swallowed hard. Had the pastor read her mind? "How nice." His words sounded too good to be true, a fairy tale.

"Any news on the investigation?"

While Debra explained what little she knew, a nagging thought persisted. What was wrong with her? All of her thoughts needed to be focused on Chad and Lauren. How selfish of her to be considering a notion as self-centered as whether a god loved her.

"Pastor?" she said. "How does God speak to people?"

Pastor McDaniel raised a brow. "Through the Bible, prayer, other people, and circumstances. In the Bible, He sometimes spoke His messages through angels."

"How do you know it's Him?"

The pastor studied her for a moment. "If you believe God may be talking to you, then listen to what He is saying."

"Jill tells me to pray." She hesitated. "But I don't know if I'm doing it right. Is there a technique?"

"Not at all. Speak to the Father from your heart, like you would your best friend."

She managed a smile. "I will."

Once their session was completed and Debra arranged to meet him again on Monday, she returned to her SUV. Pastor McDaniel gave her so much to think about. He wanted her to accept Jesus Christ as her Savior, but he said it must be her choice. No one else could do it for her. Still, she hesitated. Possibly pride stood in the way, or did she really expect this love relationship that other Christians talked about?

A gnawing in her stomach reminded her she hadn't eaten today. Her watch read nearly noon, and she knew the refrigerator and pantry at home held nothing. A stop at the grocery for a few healthy items wouldn't take long.

On her way out, she glanced at the familiar liquor store that loomed beside the grocery. It captured her attention, just as it had in the past. She did have cash.

I will not, she told herself. *Liquor doesn't solve any of my problems. In fact, drinking adds to them.*

She forced her attention in the direction of her vehicle, determined not to give in to the urge of purchasing a bottle. Momentary escapes from pain would not rule her life anymore, no matter how tempting.

A teenage boy wearing the grocery store's emblem on his shirt hurried across the parking lot, no doubt late for work. His gaze met hers, and he grinned. She saw the little boy in him, the impish look that most likely won over his mother.

"God loves you," he said and stepped lively past her and into the opened doors of the grocery store.

As though someone had laid a fist into her stomach, Debra nearly doubled over with the realization. Three times in the past two days, she'd heard the words "God loves you" from three unlikely people. Had she not asked God to speak to her—to let her know if He truly loved her?

And He had. She felt certain of it. The three incidents went far beyond coincidence. In fact, who would ever believe the strange quirk of events?

Debra stumbled to her vehicle and dropped her keys twice in an attempt to disarm the security system. She shoved her purchases onto the passenger seat and switched on the engine. Moments later, cool air bathed her face, but even a reprieve from the heat didn't stop the strange sensation at the back of her neck. Coupled with a peculiar sensation in the pit of her stomach, it made her wonder if she would faint. Instead, a spurt of growing urgency to talk to God swung like a mighty pendulum.

She leaned over the steering wheel and closed her eyes. *Oh, Lord, I believe You love me, just as I believe You arranged for those people to cross my path. And if I believe this, then all the other things I've heard about You must be true. You sent Your Son Jesus to die for my sins, and You raised Him from the dead. A real heaven must be out there, a place to live someday with You. My life is such a mess, and I know I've done horrible things to lose my children. If You can't bring them back to me, let me know they're okay. I miss them so much. Help me, God, I beg of You.*

~ ~ ~

"This is the best news I've heard in ages," Jill said, once Debra told her about surrendering her life to the Lord. "Drake and I have prayed for this miracle."

"Tell him I said thanks, and I'm glad you two never gave up on me." Debra stood in the middle of her kitchen, sensing her tears would begin again, but now her weeping stemmed from recognizing the sea of forgiveness in the Lord.

"I'll admit the biker had me questioning my sanity," she said. "Oh, Jill, why have I been so stubborn? God gave me the first real sense of peace that I can ever remember. And with all of the dreadful things going on in my life, I feel. . .well, like everything will somehow be all right." Debra attempted a faint smile, although her tears clouded her vision of Jill's face. They fell into each other's arms, crying and hugging at the same time.

"God will make sense of this mess one day." Jill pulled away from Debra's embrace. "We simply have to trust Him."

"I have no choice but to believe you. If He loves me enough to tell me through three people in a few days, then I can only respond in the faith you have always told me about. Chad and Lauren will come back to me. I know it, and I feel it. Maybe this very hour. Maybe tomorrow or six months from now, but eventually it will happen."

Her friend nodded and blinked away her tears through a smile. "I will never stop praying for your precious children. His angels are watching over them."

Debra reached for Jill's hand. "Another comforting thought is I know Michael would never hurt them. He has done a ton of wrong things, but he does love his children in the best way he can. Michael believes I'm not a good mother and thinks he can do a better job raising them. Now, I must find Chad and Lauren and prove him wrong."

For the first time, Debra trusted in God to see her through whatever lay in the future. She had so much to learn from His words of knowledge and wisdom. Most importantly, she felt a shower of God's love beyond anything she'd ever imagined.

Tough days lay ahead—many of them. But she no longer had to face life alone; she had a Friend and a Father. At last, she had Someone to love her.

chapter 14

O n Sunday Debra trembled all the way to church with Jill and Drake. "I'm so nervous," she finally said from the backseat of their car. "I know it sounds stupid, but it's the truth."

Drake glanced at her through the rearview mirror. "You've made the decision to accept Christ in your life. This is the part where you obediently involve yourself in His church."

"Will this increase my chances of getting back my children?"

Drake exchanged glances with Jill. "We're not supposed to bargain with God."

Confusion crusted Debra's thoughts. "I thought it might make a difference. If I trust Him with my life, shouldn't that speed up the process?"

"It makes a difference in your heart and where you'll spend eternity."

"Having my children with me means everything to me," Debra said, wishing the choking sensation in her throat would vanish.

"God has to have priority in your life," Drake said.

"Above Chad and Lauren?"

He nodded. "A lot of things here in the beginning are going to sound strange. As you grow in your Bible study and surround yourself with godly people, the principles you now find difficult to accept will begin to make sense."

Debra gazed at the road ahead. "I know God loves me. He proved that in the miraculous way He assured me this week. Until I learn more, I will have to trust Him like a child trusts a parent—like Chad and Lauren must surely believe all Michael has told them about my absence."

Jill turned around to face her. "Oh, honey, we all have to be trusting children when it comes to God's will for our lives. You hold on to that and don't ever let go."

Sunday school surprised Debra. She didn't expect the warmth and offers of friendship. The members were genuine people, with not only humorous things going on in their lives but also real issues. She could get used to this.

Listening to Pastor McDaniel speak seemed more like an extension of his counseling sessions. She likened the way he presented his sermon to having coffee with an old friend. God's love was real in Pastor McDaniel, just as she had seen in Jill, Drake, and her mother. An urgency, like a flame, welled in her. She could think of no better place to be on Sundays than in God's house.

The following Monday, nearly four weeks after the abduction, Debra entered Pastor McDaniel's office for her counseling session.

He took one look at her and grinned. "Debra, let me guess what has happened to you. I know I saw you in church yesterday."

She returned his smile. "Does it show?"

"From here to eternity. I suspected your change of heart yesterday, but I needed to hear it from you."

"Have you talked to Jill or Drake?" She no longer felt uncomfortable around the pastor. He'd become her friend.

He ushered her to the leather sofa. "No. I've just been praying for God to make His love for you abundantly clear."

During the next few minutes, she told him everything that had happened the day she realized God's love.

"When we meet again on Wednesday, and in the sessions to come, I want to talk about all the good and bad times in your marriage. I believe it's important for your mental health to chart the circumstances that led to Chad and Lauren's abduction."

Curiosity nibbled at her thoughts.

He stuck his pen behind his ear. A few wisps of silver hair covered it. "People don't wake up one morning and decide to abduct their children and destroy their reputation. It's a grad ual process, and I think discussing it will help you deal with the trauma of Michael's abuse."

Debra wasn't so sure she could plod ahead with Pastor McDaniel's suggestion, but she'd trusted him this far. "All right. If you think it will help."

This time when Debra left Spring Creek Church, she felt at peace but exhausted from digging into the past. Now she understood the pain brought healing.

September trickled into October while Debra swept from one phase of her life to another. The school district hired her immediately as a long-term substitute when one of their teachers took a maternity leave. Four weeks later, after the teacher elected to stay home with her new baby, Debra found herself in full-time employment teaching history to junior high students. She had six classes of seventh- and eighth-grade students, and she loved every minute of it. What a marvel for God to give her joy in the midst of sorrow.

A Realtor who attended her church listed Debra's house and within two weeks, she had a legitimate offer. She moved into a two-bedroom apartment complex near her school and traded the expensive SUV for a Honda Accord. An antique dealer offered a generous price for the antiques that remained after she furnished the apartment, and she opened a savings account with the proceeds. In a separate account, she banked the money from the sale of the house until she could get sound advice on how to invest some of it. She placed Chad and Lauren's furniture in storage until they returned. They'd feel much more comfortable in their own beds.

"Finally," Debra said one afternoon after school. She closed her eyes to ease the strain caused by staring at the computer screen.

"Did you finish sending the history assignment?" one of the teachers asked.

"Myra, it took me forever," Debra said. She opened her eyes and clicked the SEND button. "I hope it doesn't take Jamie Walters as long to complete the work as it did for me to enter it."

"Hadn't you used E-mail before?" Myra crossed her arms and peered over Debra's shoulder.

"A few times when parents asked simple questions about their children. All I had to do was hit REPLY and SEND."

Myra laughed. "Tell me you didn't type out the entire lesson on an E-mail."

She glanced up at the woman, her nut-brown face forming a wide smile. Humiliation clouded Debra's mind. "What do you mean? Of course I typed the lesson."

Myra covered her mouth, but a giggle still escaped. "You could have copied it from the existing document and pasted it into your message."

"Huh? Please show me what you mean, so I don't ever have to do this again." Debra fumbled for pencil and paper.

After Myra instructed her on how to cut and paste, the two women chatted for a few minutes.

"How's the investigation going on your kids?" Myra pulled a chair close to Debra.

She shook her head and sighed. "Neither HPD nor the FBI have found a thing. I refuse to give up hope, though. Every phone call becomes the call, and every day I call the police department and the FBI agent assigned to my case."

"I'm so sorry." Myra hugged Debra's shoulders. "Your children are on our church's prayer list."

"Thank you. So many wonderful people have put Chad and Lauren on prayer chains. I'm really grateful."

Debra didn't touch on how the weekends and nights haunted her. She attended Bible studies, tutored students, and volunteered at both church and school to fill up her time. Her counseling sessions with Pastor McDaniel were now once a week on Monday evenings.

She grieved but did not feel ashamed as though she doubted God's provision. At times, she roamed the various malls in a frail hope of seeing Chad or Lauren.

"I'm sure you keep as busy as possible."

If you only knew. "Yes, and I'm involved with a great

Sunday school class, which has helped me tremendously in dealing with it all. It amazes me how God can suddenly bless me with peace when I'm feeling so low that I could crawl under a rock."

"When you get down, call me. I always have a good ear." She wrapped an ample arm around Debra's shoulders.

Debra smiled. She'd made such wonderful, loving friends. Even so, she wondered if her past drinking problem or her inability to please Michael had resulted in Chad and Lauren's abduction. Pastor McDaniel had helped her work through most of those doubts and come to accept God's unfailing love, but sometimes the accusations crept forward.

On Wednesday afternoon before Thanksgiving, Debra found herself waist-deep in depression. The holiday plus the beginning of the Christmas season frightened her. She wanted to escape, run from any reminders of this otherwise joyous time of the year. The excitement from the students and teachers only served to sink her further into a black well.

As soon as she got home from school, she phoned Jill to decline the invitation for Thanksgiving dinner.

"We want you here with us," Jill said. "Come and spend the night. We can have dinner and then head to church together. Don't spend the evening or tomorrow alone."

Although Debra's mood fought any socializing, the idea refused to leave her alone. From her counseling, Debra had learned to let others help her through the tough times. "Okay," she said after a few moments deliberation. "I don't want to do anything but curl up in this silent apartment, but that's not wise."

"I figured as much. You don't need idle time on your hands."

Suddenly Debra blurted out. "Oh, Jill, today my students were so wound up about the holidays, and even the teachers planned shopping sprees for 7:00 a.m. on Friday. For a while I thought I'd throw up."

"Honey, pack your overnight bag and head this way. With both of our families coming for dinner tomorrow, I could use an extra pair of hands."

"Deal. Maybe you can get me out of this horrible mood," Debra said, "and thanks. The next few weeks are going to be tough, and I need to find ways to keep busy."

"Didn't you volunteer for the children's Christmas program at church?"

"Yes, and a basketful of other things, too. I heard on the radio today that Texas Children's Hospital is looking for volunteers in a program to make the holiday season a little brighter for their patients," Debra said. "I'd like to donate my time to the kids."

"Can you handle the stress of working with children, especially under the circumstances?" Jill's voice laced with concern.

"I do it every day with junior-high kids. At least, I'd like to try. If I can't love on—" Her voice broke, and she swallowed the perpetual lump in her throat. "I want to love on children. This is a way for me to fill my time and hopefully make a difference in a child's life."

Silence met her ears until Jill spoke. "You're an inspiration to anyone who has ever experienced the loss of a child. Every time I feel 'poor me' because I haven't conceived, I think how hard it must be for you."

"One day I'll have Chad and Lauren again. In the meantime, I'm still a mother to any child who'll let me hug on them. Jill, I pray God blesses you and Drake with a baby. You two will make wonderful parents."

"Thanks. Now, before you have me crying, I'm going to get the pumpkin and pecan pies baked for Thanksgiving."

"Sure. I'll be there as soon as I call Texas Children's and see if I can get some information about their holiday program."

Later, on the way to Jill and Drake's, Debra made a mental note about Friday. The hospital planned to host an orientation for those interested in volunteering. She'd much rather spend the biggest shopping day of the year thinking about someone other than herself.

Maybe she'd have Chad and Lauren by mid-December. Did she dare look for Christmas gifts?

                                  ॐ   ॐ   ॐ

"Thanksgiving isn't the same without you." Cale's mother's words were burdened with sadness.

"I know; I miss you, too." He cringed at her wistful voice. "And I had my taste buds all ready for a piece of your pumpkin pie."

"I know your absence can't be helped, but it doesn't make me happy."

"I'm really sorry, but this new position has me spinning. Mom, spending the holiday without my family doesn't sit well with me, either. Unfortunately, Christmas doesn't look any better, but I have an idea. Why don't you and Dad come here?"

"Christmas in Houston? What about snow?"

He chuckled. "I haven't even turned off my air-conditioning yet. Seriously, why don't we play it safe with my busy schedule, and you two plan on coming here for Christmas and stay through New Year's?"

"I don't know." She hesitated, and he envisioned her tugging at her ear while she contemplated his request. "I need to discuss it with your dad."

"Put him on."

She sighed. "Robert, your son has a request. Pick up the extension in the kitchen."

Your son, he thought, amused. *I'd be her son if I'd come home for Thanksgiving.*

"Hey, Cale, how's it going?" His dad's booming voice echoed over the lines. "We sure miss you."

"Miss you, too. Everything here is fast-paced and wild, which is why I didn't make it home. I've been thinking, and I'd like for you and Mom to fly here for Christmas. I've plenty of room in my condo."

"What do you say, dear?" Cale heard the optimism in his dad's voice.

Silence.

"Dear?"

"Mom?"

"Will you have a tree?" she asked. "And decorations?"

"Sure. What's Christmas without a tree?" Cale loved the little girl in his mother.

"All right, if you're certain there's no other way," she said.

"I'm certain, and you will love Texas," Cale said. "Folks here are so friendly. You know, the Southern hospitality thing."

"But no snow?" She laughed. "Will we see cowboys and horses?"

Cale grinned. He planned to get theater tickets and take

them to some great restaurants during their visit. The city offered a wealth of entertainment—guaranteed to please even the most stubborn of ladies. "Anything you want, Mom. You tell me, and I'll find a way to get it."

A moment later, he hung up the phone. The anticipation of Christmas masked his disappointment over Thanksgiving. Cafeteria turkey and dressing couldn't be that bad, and they did have great Starbucks coffee. Maybe he'd treat himself to a great meal after work.

chapter 15

After dinner on Thanksgiving afternoon, with the delectable smells of a turkey dinner and all the trimmings wafting through the air, Debra seized the opportunity to talk to Drake before the football game. She had a pressing matter and knew he had the answers.

"Drake, I'm not proficient with computer technology. In fact, all I know about the beast is what's required to enter grades and lesson plans." She paused to gain her composure. She had difficulty thinking about her children without crying, let alone speaking about them. "I've been wondering if the Internet could aid me in finding Chad and Lauren." There she'd said it without breaking down into a puddle of tears.

Drake lifted his gaze. "Aren't you online at school or have E-mail?"

"I have E-mail. We use it for relaying information to the parents, conference appointments, and at times class assignments. But I've never done the Internet thing."

He rubbed his palms together. "Do you still have Michael's laptop?"

"No. He took it with him, but my apartment complex has Internet access."

"I have a PC that I've no use for—recently upgraded to a new one. This weekend I'll set you up with Internet access. The possibilities are endless. I'm surprised the agencies involved in the investigation haven't recommended you look into some sites."

"I never asked, and I never considered it until lately when I overheard other teachers discussing how they searched the Web about various topics." Even her students knew more about computers than she did.

"I tell you what. Let me get you started right now."

"What about your game?" she asked. "I don't want to interfere with your afternoon."

Drake grinned and his eyes sparkled. "Contrary to popular belief, I can exist without my football, but we have plenty of time. The game doesn't start for another forty-five minutes."

Debra followed him into the spare bedroom Jill and Drake used as an office. "Sit here, and I'll walk you through getting connected," he said.

Moments later, he showed her how to use the search engines to locate Web sites about abducted children.

"You look all you want," Drake said. "Let me show you how to print off the material, too."

"Won't this cost a lot of money?" Her fingertips itched with excitement, but she refused to take advantage of her friends.

"No, it doesn't matter how long you stay online."

Anticipation raced through her veins. She had no idea what she'd find, but at least she could do something.

"I need to make sure Jill doesn't need me," she said.

"Stay put," Drake said with a deep chuckle. "Right now she's trapped in a cement wedge between her mother and mine."

For the next three hours, Debra sat captivated as she searched through the many sites designated as having information about abducted children. Evening shadows crept around her, but she still sat fixed to the chair. She carefully read each piece of information and printed out those that captured her attention.

"Are you all right?" Jill asked.

Debra startled. She hadn't noticed her friend standing in the doorway. "I'm fine. Goodness, I apologize for spending all this time in here. Your family must think I'm really rude."

"No, they'd be doing the same thing if they were in your shoes. What all have you found?" Jill pulled a chair next to Debra and flipped on a desk lamp.

"More information than I ever dreamed existed. I could kick myself for not asking about this earlier."

"I hope it helps. Curiosity is killing me, so tell me what you've learned."

Debra picked up a stack of papers. Did she dare reveal her newfound hope?

"I've found out about many organizations that assist parents in finding their children. Many of them have E-mail support groups and utilize chat rooms. I'm not sure what those are, but from what I see, the participants keep a dialogue going about their search. Some sites are merely supportive, while others share information. I saw lots of pictures of missing kids along with stats about them. The FBI's National Center for Missing and Exploited Children has kidnappings and missing persons listed with a short synopsis of each one.

They had Chad and Lauren listed there." She took a deep breath. "It seems I'm not alone at all."

"Of course not." Jill wrapped her arm around Debra's shoulders. "Unfortunately, child abduction is not uncommon."

"One bit of information really shocked me. There are various undergrounds, organized groups of people who hide parents and children, often in violation of the law. Those representing the underground claim they have the children's best interests in mind, but often their fees rule their actions."

Jill's eyes widened. "You mean a person could pay these underground people to hide their children and even the person who abducted them?"

Debra thumbed through the papers for the exact information. "Yes, they falsify new identification for the children and parents in hiding, giving them an opportunity to begin life all over again. It's not foolproof but does reduce the threat of being discovered."

"Sounds like the Underground Railroad during the Civil War," Jill said.

"Exactly the same principle. The FBI is investigating them, but it's difficult to find the proof they need for conviction. Remember, Steven—the FBI agent—said Michael was now living somewhere under a new identity. He probably used an organization like this."

Jill read a printout that Debra handed her. "But these underground people say their work is done in the best interests of the child?"

"That's what they state. Some of them would reveal where the children are for the right price."

"Looks like money talks, not necessarily the welfare of the

child." Jill shook her head.

Debra stretched her tired neck and shoulder muscles. "I'm also wondering if all this information is legit, so I'm going to talk to Alicia and Steven about it. I mean the FBI site is wonderful, but I simply want to do more."

"Good idea. You can put anything you want on your own Web page. Guess it's up to the reader to verify questionable material."

"Do you know if it's hard to make one of these Web sites?" Debra asked. "Or the cost involved?"

"Drake put together one for his company. I don't know about the fees. You'd have to talk to him."

Debra nodded. "Good. I'd like to post Chad and Lauren's pictures, as long as Alicia and Steven don't object." She shrugged. "Sounds more technologically advanced than pasting their pictures on a milk carton."

"How wonderful if someone out there saw their pictures and knew where they were."

Uneasiness crept through Debra's mind. "My thoughts exactly. You know. . .after reading about the underground and realizing Michael could very well be a part of this, I wonder about illegal business practices and other things he might have done."

Jill stared at her. "It's sad, isn't it?"

"As each day goes by, I'm more convinced he is capable of just about anything."

Drake stuck his head inside the door interrupting their conversation. "Telephone call, Debra."

Her heart hammered against her chest. Only Alicia and Steven had this number. "Do you know who it is?"

"Alicia," Drake replied.

chapter 16

Debra trembled as she took the phone from Drake. She wanted to believe only good news would initiate a call from Alicia on Thanksgiving.

"Alicia?"

"Hi, Debra. I have an update."

Debra's heart pounded. She reached for Jill's hand, all the while praying.

"Michael's mother called and admitted she has heard from him. As soon as we can get something concrete, I'll let you know."

"Thank you," Debra said. "God bless you."

"Don't bless me until we find out where Michael has stashed the kids. Talk to you soon, and enjoy the rest of your Thanksgiving."

She hung up the phone and smiled through quivering lips. "Michael has contacted his mother. Nothing else, but to me it's one more sign that God is watching over my babies."

ॐ   ॐ   ॐ

Cale found the day after the Thanksgiving holiday brought high spirits to the entire hospital. With the advent of Christmas, enthusiasm sparkled along with tinsel and lights strung around every imaginable spot, from the visitor's area to the nurses' stations. New items popped up in the gift shop, and a huge tree in the main lobby displayed a thousand twinkling white lights.

He studied the list of activities for the day. A session for those anticipating holiday stress, regular meetings for various departments, and a session with the clergy. Peering up, he saw a minister walk by and head for the elevator. One thing he noticed and appreciated about the hospital was the way people spoke openly about God. Must have something to do with living in the Bible Belt.

Smiling at the receptionist who worked at the visitation center, Cale glanced at his watch and realized he needed to make rounds. Illness and disease didn't take a backseat to holidays.

He'd been studying an intriguing case at Texas Children's. A twelve-year-old girl needed a new heart, or she wouldn't live to see another Thanksgiving. The young girl had been born with congenital heart disease. She'd undergone several surgeries to correct the problem, but a team of physicians determined that the only way to save the girl's life was a transplant. Cale had been asked to assist Dr. Kenton with the surgery. She'd been on a waiting list for months, and hopefully a donor would be found soon.

Shortly after noon, Cale met a few doctor friends in the cafeteria. Hospital food tasted the same in the south as in the north. The only difference lay in a few more Southern dishes. Grits for breakfast had been a new experience. Oddly enough, he liked them smothered in melted butter. Iced tea in winter also surprised him.

Easing into a chair, he greeted the two doctors already deep in conversation.

"You will never guess who participated in the volunteer orientation at Texas Children's this morning," Dr. Derrick Hughes said. "I overheard it at a nurses' station here on the fourth floor."

"Who?" asked Sally Kinslow, a generously proportioned intern.

"Debra Patterson. You know, the lady whose husband abducted her children last summer," Dr. Hughes said. He looked about then wagged a finger at her. "That takes a lot of guts."

Cale drummed a finger onto the table. "I remember the night she lost her children. I heard about it on the news."

"Poor lady has yet to find them." Sally spread a thick layer of butter over a roll then squeezed it together. "I think I'd be ready to kill the guy. What a poor excuse for a man." She shook her head. "I wonder why she wants to volunteer with children during the holidays."

Cale shrugged. "Can you imagine how horrible this season must be for her?"

"No, I can't," Dr. Hughes said before Sally could reply. "If my wife ran off with my kids, I'd probably go nuts. I may work a lot of hours, but every spare minute is with my family."

"I don't have a family to really understand," Sally said. "But I think working with children would be like pouring alcohol in an open wound."

Cale's mind spun. He'd wondered a few times about how the Patterson woman dealt with her loss. "Maybe working with kids eases the pain."

"Or make it unbearable till she loses it," Sally said, sinking her spoon into a mound of mashed potatoes and gravy.

No one commented, and Dr. Hughes veered the conversation in another direction. All the while, Cale thought about Debra Patterson and how distraught she'd looked in the newspaper. What could possibly motivate her to keep going? For him, it would be God, but he didn't know her beliefs. If he had an opportunity, he'd introduce himself and offer his sympathy for her situation.

✦   ✦   ✦

Debra entered her apartment, humming a song from a local Christian radio station. Despite the tragedies of the past few months, God had a way of handing her laughter and joy when she least expected it. Sometimes it happened right in the middle of class—and with moody junior-high students! She knew most teachers steered clear of this age, but she appreciated their spirit.

Immediately her gaze flew to the answering machine. Three messages awaited her. She'd thought of little else today other than the report of Michael contacting his mother.

She took a deep breath and pressed the PLAY button. Ever since the abduction, she'd received calls from "crazies" as she referred to them—people who blamed her for the loss of her children and let her know their opinions in a variety of obscene ways. She'd considered changing to an unlisted number when she moved, but she'd hate to miss a call from someone who might have information about Chad and Lauren.

Jill's voice greeted her on the first message, hoping the volunteer orientation at Texas Children's had gone well. A recorded sales pitch chimed in as the second. The third call came from Steven.

"Hi, Debra. I have news for you, certainly more than what we've had in the past. Authorities have spotted a white male whom they think is Michael in Mexico City, and he did phone his mother from there. That's all I know, and I'll let you know what progresses."

Debra felt chills race through her body. This all could soon be over. The FBI had finally given her hope, or rather God had. She stared at the phone and fought the urge to return Steven's call. She knew he'd planned to spend today with his teenage son, a young man who had given him serious trouble. Her call might interrupt an important conversation.

The clock read three fifteen. Waiting until Monday to find out more information bordered on impossible. She'd call Alicia. Punching in her office number, Debra tapped her foot against the linoleum floor.

After the fourth ring, Alicia answered. "Lieutenant Barnett."

"Hi, Alicia." Debra caught her breath. "I have a message on my machine from Steven. He says the FBI has spotted a white male whom they think may be Michael."

"That's what I heard. Nothing definite. I really don't know any more than you do."

Debra slid into a wooden kitchen chair. "But it does sound good, doesn't it?"

"This is a lead, which is more than what we've had since

this whole thing started."

"So, I can feel optimistic?" Debra asked, wanting desperately for Alicia to kindle a bonfire of hope.

"I think a small dose is in order. I just don't want you to be disappointed if this falls through."

Debra felt her surge of excitement waning. "I understand. Will you call me with any news?"

"Debra, that's Steven's jurisdiction. He'll keep you posted; he's a good man."

"I know," Debra said. "Like you, he puts up with me calling at least five days a week."

"And you keep calling until we get your kids home."

Debra recalled what she'd learned from searching the Internet. "Alicia, is there a reason why neither of you have encouraged me to go online with Chad and Lauren's abduction information?" She felt a twinge of irritation that this avenue had been neglected.

"Frankly, we work through procedures and policy," Alicia said. "But you do whatever you need to. The National Center for Missing and Exploited Children has been very successful and is one of the many tools available."

"What about the FBI and the NCMEC? I saw their parental kidnapping site with pictures of the parents and the children they abducted."

"We're professionals with a job to do, and no doubt you saw your children's pictures. We have an extensive networking system, far superior to anything you could imagine. With all of us working together, surely we will find your children."

Debra sighed. "I believe I want to put their pictures on a Web page. Alicia, I have to do something."

"I completely understand." Sympathy rang through Alicia's words. "If it makes you feel any better, go ahead. But if someone contacts you, then you need to get in touch with us immediately. A word of caution: Whatever you do, don't pay anyone a cent."

"All right. What about the underground? Are there really people who hide children and their abductors for the right price?"

"What do you think?" Alicia asked.

Debra shivered. "He's clever, and he had the money." *Oh, God, must this be so hard? Please let them find Michael and the children in Mexico.*

"My point exactly. If he's taken them out of the country, you're dealing with numerous governmental agencies. But then you would have the terms of the Hague Convention to assist the investigation."

"I read something about that on one of the Web sites," Debra said. "Didn't the conference establish treaties between countries to recover abducted children?"

"Right. Keep in mind some countries cooperate and others do not."

Frustration swelled in Debra's heart. Michael most likely chose a country where he wouldn't face any government involvement in his activities. She resolved to read everything she could get her hands on about the Hague Convention. The information would keep her busy until she spoke with Steven on Monday morning. By then Chad and Lauren could be on their way home. The thought exhilarated her spirit.

As soon as she concluded her call with Alicia, she leafed through the stack of printouts made yesterday at Jill and Drake's until she found the sought-after information—"The Hague Convention of the Civil Aspects of International Child Abduction." The main thrust of the report stated that children under the age of sixteen who had fallen victim to custody disputes should be returned to the country where they resided before the abduction. There, the courts could decide who should be the custodial parent. Each country signing the treaty appointed an agency or authority to carry out the terms.

Debra stopped reading. She didn't like the reports of countries whose courts denied the return of children. Fortunately, Mexico and the United States government were in agreement.

At last, she felt a glimmer of light in all of this. Nearly four months had passed since she'd seen and touched her children. God was good. Surely she'd found the beginning of the end.

chapter 17

Agent Steven Howell yawned and closed his eyes while the plane taxied down the tarmac. Already he craved a cigarette, but he'd have to wait a few hours before he could satisfy the nicotine addiction. Someday he'd quit. He'd really like to sleep, but he needed to review Michael Patterson's file. From the looks of the FBI's findings, he was one cunning man. Then why did he take the chance of calling his mother from Mexico City? Had Patterson gotten too sure of himself? He certainly wasn't a mama's boy—ladies' man, yes, but nothing else. Maybe he needed money. Of course, the Mexican government must suspect something more than a child abduction to call in the FBI. Steven had his suspicions.

He leafed through the file. The Bureau knew Patterson had assumed a different name for him and his children. Now to get that name and figure out where he'd stuck those kids. Steven reached for a stick of gum inside his shirt pocket. The whole situation with Debra perplexed him. What did her estranged husband have against her that he took the kids without so much as an indication of wanting a divorce or separation? Granted Debra called Steven at least five times a week, and that drove him nuts, but her persistence lined up with her need to find those kids. *Bad mothers don't give a rip.*

Since August, she'd gotten rid of that huge house and down-sized her vehicle. She now worked teaching school and volunteered for a ton of worthy causes. Her behavior didn't sound like unfit mother material to him. He'd seen the police reports concerning Patterson's abuse toward his wife. *What a snake.*

Steven hoped he hadn't sold those kids or their trail led to a grave.

Your kids make you do strange things. Steven should know. He'd bailed out his seventeen-year-old son Rod twice from jail. Neither time had his son so much as thanked him. What he did get was a "leave me alone" and "you're so stupid."

Steven blew out a heavy sigh and allowed his eyes to close for only a moment. He wondered if Rod thought his old man got to be an FBI agent by being stupid. Steven was finished making excuses for him. Rod's mother had died in a car accident when the boy started school, but instead of Steven spending every spare moment with his grieving son, he'd wrapped himself up in his work. A glimpse of a dark-haired beauty swept him away into yesteryear, but Steven pushed aside the memories. He admitted his failure as a dad. Actually, Rod's behavior had been okay until he reached sixteen and started driving. Ever since, his friends and habits went hand-in-hand—drinking and smoking pot. Typical scenario. The boy would not have it so easy the next time. A few days in jail might change his mind about his choice of entertainment.

Steven hated leaving him alone with the housekeeper right after his jail release, especially after their argument.

Shoving aside his personal life, Steven made notes on what he needed to find out in Mexico City. He glanced over at his two agents, Ben Frey, an African-American agent who had more energy than a six-year-old on a sugar high, and Julie Simon, a smart gal from the Midwest. Both seemed to be deep in some discussion. Steven would sure like to wind up this case and have the Patterson kids home by Christmas.

✧ ✧ ✧

"Is this a picture of the man who stayed at your hotel two nights ago?" Steven asked the desk clerk in Spanish. The Mexican police had helped him locate the Camino Real Hotel where Patterson had stayed on at least two occasions. So far, they'd been cooperative.

"Sí," the clerk replied. "His name is Alex Wendel." The guy was young—not much more than Rod.

"Was he alone?"

"Sí."

"How many nights?" Steven asked.

The clerk checked his records. "Two."

"Did you see this man talking to anyone?"

"No, sir. You can check in the restaurant, but I'd always seen him alone." The clerk toyed with a pen.

Steven began to feel hopeful. "Did he have any children with him—a boy and a girl?"

"No, sir."

"Has he stayed with you before?"

The clerk again sought the police's permission. At the second nod, he checked the computer. "Twice before."

"What about the other two occasions he was here? Did he have children then?"

"No."

"I'd like to see everything you have on Mr. Wendel."

The clerk glanced at the policeman who again nodded. Steven jotted down all of the information, although he felt certain it was as credible as the name of Alex Wendel. Reluctantly, the clerk divulged to Steven that the rooms Patterson stayed in held one bed.

"I need to see his room," Steven said a few moments later.

"Of course," the clerk replied, "but it's been cleaned. I doubt if you find anything."

If there's a trace of Michael Patterson there, I'll find it.

Turning to Ben and Julie, Steven motioned for them to follow. He whirled around to the clerk. "Before I leave, I want a printout of all phone calls, a list of what he ate, drank, and what kind of car he drove while here—even if he got his shoes shined or his nails done. I'll send one of my agents for it."

Two hours later, Steven left the hotel with Ben and Julie. Not a thing had turned up in the room. Patterson, Wendel— whatever his name—had not eaten or drunk there, nor made a phone call. He'd used other modes of transportation besides leasing a vehicle. Their only leads were to follow up on the taxi companies and run a check on the Visa he'd used to pay for his room.

⸕ ⸕ ⸕

On Christmas Eve afternoon, Texas Children's Hospital organized a special party for the children. Debra volunteered, much against Jill and Drake's protests as well as the auxiliary director at the hospital. No one understood how working with children soothed her grieving spirit. She found making them laugh and urging them to forget the reasons why they were there caused her to forget, too. Those children became her children, their pain her pain. The agony of separation from Chad and Lauren paralleled with the little patients' confusion and sadness in unfamiliar surroundings. She knew somewhere her children were spending their first Christmas away from her. What had Michael told them about their mother? Dare she hope they were happy and healthy?

Debra pushed a young boy in a wheelchair to the crowded area where the rest of the children waited for Santa to appear. All of the eager children who could be out of bed were seated on a parent's lap or around a huge Christmas tree decorated with gingerbread men and candy canes. Each child had a colorfully wrapped package piled beneath the tree, but the gift couldn't be opened until Santa arrived. They'd sung songs and chatted about what they wanted for Christmas, but the children were anxious to see Santa Claus.

Debra held a little girl whose parents had not come for the festivities. She had ugly bruises on one side of her face, and a shoulder-to-wrist cast on her left arm. Debra refused to consider how the child had been injured. "How about a story?" she asked the group.

A chorus of voices rang out with different requests, but the little girl in her lap begged for *The Three Little Pigs*. She looked up with sad, dark eyes, and Debra couldn't resist.

"Okay, it's the story about the three little pigs." She smiled at their happy faces, and for a moment, Chad and Lauren flashed across her mind. But God had given her joy today, and she would not let Him or these children experience her tears. "Once upon a time, there were three little pigs. . . ." The story continued with all eyes on her, and she loved it.

"The first little pig heard a knock at the door—"

"Little pig, little pig let me come in," said a booming voice behind her. Debra glanced up and saw a doctor had decided to join in the story.

"Not by the hair of my chinny, chin chin," Debra said.

The doctor picked up the wolf's part. "Then I'll huff, and I'll puff, and I'll blow your house down."

The two finished the rendition and the eager listeners clapped and shouted for more. As if on cue, Santa exited the elevator and took over his role with the enthusiastic children.

Debra noticed the doctor stayed for the event. He helped distribute cookies and juice to the children and chatted with the parents. The little ones all seemed to know Dr. Cale, as they called him.

When the party ended, wearing out parents and patients, Santa and the nurses helped escort the children back to their rooms. Debra took over cleanup with Dr. Cale's assistance.

"They sure had fun." He laughed. "Most of them weren't a bit afraid of Santa. Oh, by the way, I'm Dr. Cale Thurston." He stuck out his hand.

"I know, I read it on your nametag. It's a pleasure to meet you." She grasped his hand and caught his gaze, kind and caring. "Debra Patterson here, and don't fuss. I can manage this mess." She proceeded to dump paper cups and napkins into a plastic garbage bag.

"No problem, I have a few more minutes before I need to

see my patients." His smile warmed her, and yet he had a mischievous twinkle in his dark blue, nearly black eyes.

"The children adore you." She snatched up an armful of wrapping paper and crumpled it.

He chuckled. "I'm not their doctor; I'm a cardiologist at St. Luke's. Actually, I do have a patient on another floor; she recently received a heart transplant." He glanced down the corridor where a child cried out for his mommy, "But I love kids, and I frequent here every chance I get."

"I see," Debra said. His interest in the children spoke volumes about his character. "Thanks for helping me out with the story."

"Sure. Mrs. Patterson?"

She appreciated his strong, rugged features, but his seriousness caused her to wonder if she'd done something wrong.

"I want to say I have a tremendous amount of respect and admiration for what you are doing here at the hospital in light of. . .your missing children."

She'd heard similar remarks since she started volunteering, but her response always remained the same. "This is a way for me to love on a child when I can't be with my own."

He nodded and wet his lips. "Any news?"

"Not really. The FBI and Houston Police are working hard on the case, but my family seems to have disappeared." She lifted her chin and swallowed hard. No matter how many times someone asked about Chad and Lauren, she had to fight the emotion ready to spill over into tears.

"You have my sympathy." He jammed his hands into his pockets. She noted his high cheekbones, giving him a regal look.

"And I have hope." When he stared at her oddly she added.

"I have hope in Jesus Christ."

A gentle smile spread over his face. "My prayers are with you, Mrs. Patterson. I'm glad to hear you're a Christian."

She gathered up another paper plate and threw it into the garbage bag. "It took this tragedy for me to see how much I needed the Lord, but now I'll never let Him go."

He reached out and took her hand and covered it firmly with his. "May God bless you. May He grant you His perfect peace."

"Thank you," she whispered and turned to tend to the cleanup before he saw the tears pooling her eyes.

✧   ✧   ✧

Cale left the hospital in time to pick up his parents at the airport. He'd made reservations for dinner at a popular steak house, sure to please his dad. Later on tonight, they would attend the Christmas Eve candlelight service at his church and then open gifts. Tomorrow he had tickets for a theater production of Dickens's *A Christmas Carol*, a favorite of his mother's.

Between the hospital and patient obligations, he wanted to spend as much time with his parents as possible. He didn't realize how much he missed them until he moved south.

He wondered how Debra Patterson coped with the holiday season. She said her hope was in Jesus Christ, and he had seen her eyes moisten when she turned from him. What a source of inspiration. Not many people in her circumstances could claim such faith. He didn't want to speculate on how he'd react given such a tragedy. His comparison lay with the loss of his sister and nephew.

What kind of man would take his children from their mother? She certainly didn't look like the type who abused them.

Abuse. He hadn't thought about Julie and Daniel or Kevin for weeks. Cale needed to deal with what happened, forgive himself and Kevin, but not today.

chapter 18

Despite her resolve, Debra woke Christmas morning in despair. She'd dreamed about Chad and Lauren, about a beautiful Christmas with a huge tree trimmed in glittering lights and tinsel. She could even smell the pine; Michael would never have permitted a live tree. Her children giggled and opened their gifts in the fervor she remembered. They posed for pictures wearing hot chocolate mustaches laced with marshmallows. She could hear the Christmas carolers outside the door in a resounding chorus of "Deck The Halls." Then Debra woke to a silent apartment—no Christmas decorations, no carols of peace and joy, and no children.

She curled up into a fetal position and stuffed her pillow next to her, crying into the softness as if it were her mother's breast. She'd told herself she'd be strong on Christmas Day. She'd remember her blessings and not dissolve into a river of self-pity. But as her body wracked with grief, severing her heart from any logic, she wondered if she'd ever be able to stop crying.

She wept for Michael's lost love and for the marriage they could have had with God guiding them. She cried and prayed for him at the same time as fear gripped her about the welfare of Chad and Lauren. An inkling of terror crept in like a prowling cat. Would he have done them harm? Had he, in fact, been deranged and hurt her precious children?

Oh, God, take care of my babies. Shelter them in the palm of Your hand. Let them not fear anyone or have anyone desire to hurt them. Just as You assured me of Your love, have someone shower my children with unconditional love.

The phone rang, but she couldn't bring herself to answer it. She knew the caller was Jill or Drake. If either of them sensed the depth of her depression this celebration morning of Christ's birth, they'd be at her apartment beating down the door. If she didn't answer the phone, they might think she'd left for the day.

A shower. She should shower and perhaps she'd feel better. Once she stopped crying, she'd return the phone call. Whoever it might be. She lay for several more minutes sobbing, unable to stop the agony devouring her. Finally, she crawled from the bed to the bathroom. In days gone by, she'd have reached for the bottle. The thought of escaping from one nightmare to another sickened her. She'd come too far with God to slip back.

The hot water hit her back like tiny needles torturing her flesh. She adjusted the temperature letting the spray wash away the saltiness of her own tears.

This is Christmas, she told herself. *Jesus' birth—a time for rejoicing.* Mary had a baby, but Debra didn't have her babies. She wanted to feel their tender skin and hear their musical laughter—not the haunting sounds that exploded in her nighttime traumas.

"Make a joyful noise unto the Lord," she said aloud. Between the sobs and the heaviness in her chest, she sang.

"Joy to the world, the Lord is come. Let earth receive her king. Let every heart prepare Him room."

She couldn't go any further without wanting to scream, but she must. Somehow, she must. Taking a deep breath, she braved forward.

"And heaven and nature sing. And heaven and nature sing."

Once finished, she soaped her body rubbing vigorously to keep the tears at bay. Taking a deep breath, she began again.

"Hark, the herald angels sing. Glory to the newborn king."

Debra sang until the water ran so cold she shivered. But she recognized a miracle, a God-given marvel; the sorrow ended.

Emotionally exhausted, she emerged from the shower and dressed. With trembling hands, she selected a bright blue pants outfit suitable to celebrate the birthday of her Savior. She would drive to the hospital and volunteer in the pediatrics ward. Some child there may need a substitute mother.

In the kitchen, she checked her messages. Jill had called, concerned about her welfare. Shakily, Debra picked up the phone and pressed the numbers to her friends' phone. Jill answered on the second ring.

"Merry Christmas!" Debra did her best to sound cheery. "I see you called."

"Yes, we were worried about you. I know you didn't want to come here for Christmas, but we wish you'd change your mind."

"I'm going to the hospital." Debra hoped the smile in her spirit transferred over the phone.

"Honey, why torture yourself?"

She remembered the little girl, Jasmine, who had sat in her lap yesterday. One of the nurses had said the child's mother had abandoned her.

"Debra?"

"Excuse me, I was thinking about a child at the hospital who is probably spending the day alone. Anyway, thank you for the invitation, but I want to go where I can be of use."

"All right. Why don't you stop over when you're done?"

"I'll—I'll try."

She replaced the phone and moved about her apartment to gather up her keys and purse. The doorbell buzzed. Startled, she stared at the door. The sound of the second buzz echoed about the apartment. A sharp knock followed.

Slowly she moved to the door until she could peer through the security hole. There stood Michael's mother.

Dread washed over her, debilitating what little strength she had remaining. Pain hammered at her temples. *Father, why? Hasn't this day been hard enough?*

Smoothing her shoulder-length hair, a habit developed a long time ago when Mrs. Patterson's first words were always directed toward Debra's appearance, she took a deep breath and opened the door.

"Mrs. Patterson." She peered into the pale, lined face of the older woman. Anguish etched the corners of her eyes, touching Debra with the reality of Michael's mother not knowing the Lord or able to seek comfort in His embrace. The woman thrust an open cardboard box into Debra's arms.

Debra glanced down to see framed pictures of Chad and Lauren, ones given as gifts, the same the police confiscated when the children were first abducted. She'd been able to scan a few of them, but the quality had been lost.

Gratitude swelled in her for this gift and for the woman who must have had a difficult time parting with the photographs.

Backing up into her apartment, Debra set the box on the floor and bent to her knees to pick up the top photograph. Both children were posed on the branches of an oak tree. Their angelic smiles wrapped comfort around Debra's heart. She held it to her chest while tears of joy and sadness mingled together.

"Thank you, Father," she murmured.

"What?" Mrs. Patterson asked with a huff.

Brushing her fingertips across the picture, she smiled into one of the many truths of Christmas—the wonder of a child's smile. "I was thanking God for your wonderful Christmas gift."

"I brought this box on my on accord." The woman's harsh tone shook Debra, but she didn't experience the old, familiar trembling or the inability to think clearly. "Sounds like you have another crutch. So have you gone from alcohol to God?"

"I have found Him," she said. "The Lord makes each day easier while the children are away." Debra inhaled Mrs. Patterson's familiar cologne, strong and overpowering. "I no longer use alcohol."

"How quaint. Don't hold your breath. Michael is smart; he knows what he's doing. The police and FBI can look all they want, but he has a foolproof plan."

Debra rose to her feet, still clutching the photograph to her body. "I'm not trusting in the police or the FBI or any other investigative agency. My trust is in God." She couldn't believe her courage. The testimony of her faith had flowed without a hint of hesitation. "Please, won't you come in and have some coffee?"

The woman tapped her foot and checked her watch.

"I appreciate your driving here on Christmas Day to bring

me these pictures, and I'd love to sit down and visit for a few minutes."

"I suppose I could for just a bit."

Ignoring the scowl on Mrs. Patterson's face, Debra laid the picture back into the box and scooted it away from the door. She may be the only image of Jesus that Michael's mother saw today. "I have some cinnamon rolls that one of my students gave me for Christmas. Would you care for one?"

"I suppose I have time." The woman stepped inside the apartment and studied the surroundings.

"The furniture looks different here." Debra scrambled for words. She wondered how Mrs. Patterson had found her.

"Why did you leave the house?"

"I couldn't afford to stay." She motioned toward the cream, designer sofa. "Would you like to sit down while I brew some fresh coffee?"

Mrs. Patterson eased down onto the sofa. "Your old neighbor, Jill something or other gave me your address. Anyway, so you're teaching school?"

"Yes, ma'am. History to seventh and eighth graders." Debra reached inside the refrigerator freezer and pulled out the coffee. "I enjoy it."

"The school system must be in desperate need of teachers."

Debra pasted a smile, biting back the caustic words she'd like to toss the woman's way. "I'm sure the school board would be glad to discuss my qualifications with you."

An awkward silence followed while Debra went through the motions of making coffee and warming the cinnamon rolls.

"He's called me twice," Mrs. Patterson said, with no emotion. She looked immaculate, as usual. Her perfectly coifed silver hair, manicured nails, and ultra-expensive green silk suit. "He's quite clever, you know."

Debra's stomach curdled and her fingers shook. "I knew he'd phoned you once. How. . .how are Chad and Lauren?"

"Fine." Mrs. Patterson let out a deep sigh. "The day doesn't seem like Christmas without Michael and the children."

Debra's heart pounded hard against her chest. "No, it doesn't."

"I still believe this whole business is all your fault. If you had been the wife and mother Michael and the children deserved, none of this would have happened."

Help me, Father. "I'm sorry you feel it's my fault, and I apologize for the times I've disappointed you. The truth is, Mrs. Patterson, we're both hurting and grieving our loss. Casting blame won't bring them to us today." Debra lifted her gaze to the woman's clouded eyes. For a brief moment, the hardened façade softened.

"I can't stay." Mrs. Patterson fumbled through her purse. "This was a bad idea, and I really have things to do."

Debra sensed the woman's loneliness, but she attempted to mask it with an indifferent attitude. "I'm sorry. Are you sure you don't have time?"

"No." She positioned her small ultra-expensive shoulder bag. "The day's nearly half over, and I don't have a thing accomplished." She made her way to the door.

"Merry Christmas," Debra said. "I'll be praying for you."

Mrs. Patterson whirled around. "You've changed, Debra."

Right. I'm not afraid of you anymore. "God's changed me. Without Him, I couldn't make it through a single day without my children."

Once Mrs. Patterson left, Debra eased the door shut. Today she'd seen a miserable woman who had no understanding of God or why her son had done such a despicable thing. God could fill the void in Mrs. Patterson's life, if she'd only let Him.

chapter 19

C hristmas night, Cale drove his parents through the River Oaks area to view the panoramic exhibit of the city's most prestigious homes dressed for the festive season. Iron fences and forbidden entrances guarded the mansions of the elite and sharpened the contrast between deterring burglars and "peace on earth goodwill toward men."

Since neither Cale nor his parents had ever spent Christmas in Houston, the idea of running the air conditioner in the pickup struck them as funny, especially with displays of snow-drifts and bundled-up characters dotting the scenery. They teased his mother about her white hair being more authentic than the fake snow among the holiday decorations, and his dad lowered the window stating he needed to get into the mood.

"How is your practice, son?" Dad asked.

Cale glanced at his father, his bald head lit up from the street and holiday lights like an ethereal figure from a medieval painting.

"Remember the little girl who received the heart transplant?"

Dad nodded, offering one of his "I'm so proud of you" smiles.

"She did great and went home today to spend Christmas with her family." Cale hesitated. "I felt real humble being used by God to help her."

"Humility is the mark of true obedience," Dad said. "It's something no one can take away from us."

"Do you still search out the children?" Mom asked.

Cale chuckled. "Of course. Texas Children's is connected to St. Luke's by a hallway from my office and then there is a tunnel down by the cafeteria on level B-1. I'm still pushing wheelchairs up and down the corridors, bringing out my magic tricks, and playing games."

"Any young ladies in the picture?" Her voice edged with hopefulness.

"Nope. I have a love relationship with my job. Don't see anything else in the future."

"What about church? Aren't you involved there?"

She never gives up. "Yes, I'm active, but I haven't met anyone."

Cale turned down a street that held a breathtaking display of white lights outlining the dancer and tin soldiers from the *Nutcracker.*

"Brings out the kid in us," Dad said as the pickup inched past the massive home.

"Julie loved decorating at Christmas," Mom said after they passed a particularly lovely home illuminated by a myriad of lights around a Bethlehem scene. "Remember the year when she chose a penguin theme for her entire house?"

"I do." Dad laughed. "I'm the one who had to help her string all the lights."

"I miss her and Daniel." Mom sighed. "But I know they're

in a better place celebrating Christmas with Jesus."

Dad reached back from the front seat and grasped her hand. "That's my girl," he said barely above a whisper.

Cale swallowed the lump in his throat. He'd had such a good time with his parents, and he wanted it to continue. He knew they needed to voice their feelings about Julie, but too often, it ended in tears.

"Son, is it easier for you not to see Kevin?" Dad asked.

Cale turned a corner onto Inwood Drive. "Yes, much easier."

"It took me a long time before I could forgive him," Mom said, as easily as discussing the weather.

"You mean you did?" Cale's words sounded sharper than he intended. He felt betrayed, but instantly, he heard the conviction in his soul. How could they put the past behind them so easily? He knew what the Lord commanded, but the memories plagued him constantly. Julie would have been thirty, Daniel seven. The animal who had driven them all to such extremes lived on. It was unfair.

"Yes, last Christmas," she said. "Your dad and I called Kevin on Christmas Eve and told him we forgave him for any wrong doing toward Julie and Daniel. The bitterness was eating us alive, and we couldn't go on hating—not when we profess to love the Lord."

Her words yanked at the festering in his soul. "That's good, Mom," he said. "I'm glad for you." *But I can't do it. Not right now.*

"What about you?" Dad asked, turning his attention to Cale. "When are you going to put the past behind you? God will be Kevin's judge, not us."

"I know." He sensed frustration in his words and wished

he could hide his emotions. "It's not as easy as it sounds."

"Holding on to hatred promotes an infection of the soul. It will only grow worse, unless you forgive and mend your relationship with God." Dad's words sounded gentle, just like when Cale used to get into trouble as a kid and Dad talked to him about it.

Silence followed, and Cale lost all interest in the lights and decorations. Always before him were images of Julie and Daniel. In his nightmares, he could see Julie's smiling face and hear Daniel's infectious giggle.

"Talk to us, Cale," Dad said. "How long are you going to blame Kevin and yourself for the plane crash?"

Cale tapped the steering wheel. How could he forget?

"How long are you going to blame yourself?" Dad added.

"I put Julie and Daniel on that plane."

"But you had no way of knowing the outcome." Mom slipped her hand from her husband's grasp to Cale's shoulder. "Are you angry with God, too?"

He shook his head. "I don't believe so. . .maybe."

"Then give it all to Him. You have your whole life ahead of you, and to live it for God's glory means He needs to have full control."

"I'll try." Cale noted his dry mouth. "I'm smart enough to know my hatred doesn't hurt Kevin, only myself."

"And the Lord. None of us know how Kevin has suffered," Dad said. "I can only imagine the guilt of chasing away my wife and son, then having them killed. I doubt if he's had very many peaceful nights."

"Hadn't looked at it quite that way." Conviction hammered at Cale's heart. "I've been too busy playing with the what-ifs."

"Then stop," Dad said. "God is as anxious to hear your repentance as He is to hear Kevin's."

"I've been praying about it, and I'll continue." Cale's shoulders rose and fell. "I know it's time."

chapter 20

With the holidays behind her, Debra dug into her teaching and church work. She decided to continue the volunteer work at the hospital. Although she did not know why, God wanted her among those ill children, and she had no desire to leave them.

After she'd built up her hopes of finding Chad and Lauren in Mexico, she faced another disappointment. The FBI had not found Michael or any traces of him and the children. She'd even allowed herself to consider sleeping arrangements in her two-bedroom apartment and enrolling Chad and Lauren in school.

Sometimes pulling information out of Steven Howell proved next to impossible. Debra wondered if the Bureau actually told her everything. Did he have a file labeled "not to tell Debra" positioned on his desk? Anger at the thought of Steven deceiving her distracted her at home and school. Frustration seeped through the pores of her skin. She had a right to know about her children.

"I have to know the truth," Debra said during a phone call to Alicia. "Are you or Steven keeping anything from me?"

"Absolutely not," Alicia replied. "I don't work that way. Whatever I learn, I tell you."

"What's the FBI's policy?"

"Debra," the woman said. "I'm your friend, so is Steven. We aren't keeping secrets from you. We want to see your children returned and Michael brought to justice. If they need to keep something undisclosed, then that's what they have to do in order to find them."

Immediately Debra felt remorse. "I'm sorry. Mrs. Patterson's words at Christmas shook me—mostly because they're true. Michael had to have a clever plan to fool HPD and the FBI. And look how much time has elapsed."

"It's not over yet. Where is the faith you always tell me about?"

Debra covered her mouth in an effort to stop the tears. "I am praying, but I'm still human. Every day without my children is like being buried alive. Some days I'm afraid I'll run out of air and other times I want to suffocate."

"You can't give up," Alicia said, her gentle tone resounding over the phone. "Keep praying."

"I know," Debra took a deep breath. "Hope is all I have left."

◈   ◈   ◈

Debra watched a boy slide an envelope from his desk to a girl's desk beside him. She slipped it under a Texas history textbook then drew it out slightly to slip her finger beneath the sealed flap. The girl offered the young man a generous smile, obviously forgetting the teacher might be watching. Junior high students didn't celebrate Valentine's Day with chocolate cupcakes and punch, but they still sent valentines. She had a few on her desk to prove it.

She stood and moved to the front of her desk and leaned against it. "Class, I know this is Valentine's Day and most of you believe you are the last of the red-hot lovers." The kids laughed, and she grinned. "But if I see any of you passing those little treasures, you will have to read them to the rest of us."

The two involved with the exchange sheepishly nodded in agreement.

"So, how many of you are ready for next month's Texas history presentation?"

Before she had an opportunity to comment, the vice principal entered her room and pulled her aside.

"You have visitors." She patted Debra's arm. "They're waiting in my office. I'll take over your class until you return."

"Who is it?" Debra asked. A twinge of apprehension slithered up her spine.

"I'll let them explain the nature of their visit. The woman said it was important."

Debra handed her a stack of quizzes to be returned and information regarding the discussion topic. She hurried down the hall to the office, the heels of her sensible shoes tapping against the hard floor. Had Alicia stopped to see her? Had the authorities located Chad and Lauren? How wonderful for her friend to deliver the news personally. Who else could be with her? Steven? Yes, he'd surely want to accompany Alicia with the good news.

She passed a display case on her left featuring the school's basketball team and last year's district trophy. On her right, she noted smudge prints on the glass wall of the library.

Inhaling deeply, Debra stopped outside the vice principal's door in an effort to calm her jagged nerves. With her hand on the doorknob, she hesitated. Did she really want to know what awaited her on the other side?

Lord, if this is about Michael and the children, please don't let me lose sight of You, no matter what the outcome. I've given this search to You, and I know You want the best for me.

She eased open the door. Alicia and Steven sat stiffly in two chairs facing the vice principal's desk. The pair looked strangely out of place among the cutesy valentine decorations, heart-shaped cookies, and pictures of students. A half-cup of coffee rested on the desk, the only thing remotely relevant to Alicia and FBI Agent Howell's world.

"What's going on?" Debra sunk into the armchair in front of the desk.

"We have news." Alicia's forehead crinkled.

Debra's heart hammered against her chest. She'd experienced the aching sensation for several months and considered seeing a doctor but believed it all to be stress related. "And you had to deliver it here personally?"

Steven cleared his throat. "The FBI located Michael in Mexico City. We've had our people working there since the other sighting."

She glanced from Steven to Alicia. Uneasiness wrapped around her quivering emotions. Why weren't they smiling? This should be wonderful news. "What's wrong? Shouldn't we be glad about this?"

"Not really," he continued, with a grim look. "Michael is dead."

♂♀   ♂♀   ♂♀

Cale yawned. He opened his parents' valentine card and laughed aloud at the 1900 black-and-white photograph of an elderly farm couple exchanging paper hearts on a porch swing. "Your mom and dad in the old days," the card read. They'd probably sent one via E-mail, too—complete with music and animation.

Setting aside the bills and advertisements until he responded to his growling stomach, Cale opened the freezer and pulled out a small, frozen lasagna dinner. He calculated the microwave thawing time and peeled back the cellophane wrapping and set the timer. Grabbing a bottle of water from the fridge, he thumbed through the ads and tossed a stack in the trash. As was his habit, he flipped on the TV to catch the even-ing news.

"Debra Patterson, the Houston woman whose husband abducted her children last August, has once again faced tragedy."

Cale whirled around and grabbed the remote to increase the volume. Every muscle stiffened in response to the reporter.

"Today Michael Patterson's body was found in Mexico City. He'd been shot several times, but the cause of the murder is not known. The children have not been located, although Mexican authorities and the FBI are hopeful."

Cale leaned across the counter as the male news reporter talked about the extensive work of the FBI on this case. "Debra Patterson was not available for comment."

No kidding. Why would she want to face anyone from the media? They draw out every conceivable emotion. Poor woman.

He remembered meeting Debra at Christmas. She'd impressed him with her patience and calm demeanor in the midst of the children's party. Oh, he'd seen the tears well up in her eyes, but still she came across as a strong woman. Since then he'd passed her a few times when he'd visited Texas Children's, and they'd greeted each other. Sometimes he asked her about the investigation and other times he elected not to. The sorrow in her face told him the truth.

Lord, I hope Michael Patterson made his peace with You before he died. I wouldn't want to be in his shoes on Judgment Day.

Cale opened the microwave door just as the beep sounded.

What about you? Are you ready to meet Me?

A shiver raced up his spine. He'd been pegged, but good. The nagging thought had been there since Christmas when his parents questioned him about forgiving Kevin. He knew he needed to follow through with mending his relationship with God, but he simply couldn't bring himself to pick up the phone and call Kevin.

✐   ✐   ✐

Debra reached over to the passenger side of her car and took Jill's hand. Her friend's warm touch promised strength for the ordeal ahead.

"No one should go through this alone," Jill said. "I'm glad I'm here."

Debra gazed up at Crestview Funeral Home. The thought of making arrangements for Michael's body to be shipped from Mexico City to Houston set free a whirlwind of emotions. Yesterday's news had devastated her, and today promised no relief. Her head pounded like a jackhammer. She didn't know what to expect, only to get the ordeal over and done.

"The funeral director's name is David Curry, and he's expecting us," Jill said. "I talked to him yesterday about the situation."

She swallowed hard and nodded. "Thank you. I have no idea what I'm supposed to do, the cost, or preparations." Every muscle in her body ached. "But I want to take care of this. I went through all my married life with Michael and his mother handling my life. No more."

"These people can guide you."

Debra released Jill's hand and pulled her keys from the ignition. Dropping them into her purse, she took a deep breath and opened the car door. Every move took courage and stamina that she didn't have. A brisk chill whipped around her, and the sun slipped behind gray clouds. The day fit the occasion.

She remembered the times she wished Michael was dead, and how she'd hated him for what he'd done with the children. Truthfully, she could be a suspect in his murder. Sometimes late at night, her thoughts played back to the night before he left. All the sweet words and gentleness had been part of his game. He hadn't meant a single word. How could Michael have lain there beside her and whispered his love when his treacherous actions were already set in motion?

Moving around to the side of the car, Debra joined Jill, and the two made their way inside the funeral home. The building was a colonial style, with a wide parking lot and manicured grounds. In fact, it reminded her of her own home.

"I don't expect this to be simple—or easy," Debra said, shifting her purse to her shoulder. "I only want to make the arrangements and push this nightmare out of my head."

Inside a cream and tan tiled floor paved the way to a small

desk where a white-haired woman greeted them with a sweet smile.

"I phoned yesterday," Jill said, introducing herself. "This is Debra Patterson, and we have an appointment with David Curry."

"I'll get him for you," the receptionist said. Her quiet voice barely rose above the stringed music in the background.

While they waited, Debra glanced about. A delicate tapestry of Jesus talking to two men caught her eye. Below the framed art was an upholstered chair in rich green, gold, and brick. To her right, a wide hallway displayed the work of Larry Dyke, featuring two of his pastoral paintings. She stepped closer and viewed a shepherd searching for a lost sheep along a rocky, thorn-laden mountain path while the ninety-nine grazed in a green valley. *Like God sought me out.* In another painting, the shepherd tended his sheep beside a quiet stream. The themes depicted the peace she desperately craved. She expected the scent of flowers, but the receptionist's area was devoid of any smells, only cleanliness and warmth met her.

An elderly gentleman with silver hair introduced himself as David Curry. He smiled, and she saw the compassion in his eyes. The director at the funeral home in Kansas City when her mother died had not displayed this kind demeanor. Mr. Curry looked as though he understood her dilemma—a mixture of grief and anger. With a broad gesture, he ushered them into his office.

A photo of three children posed on a bale of hay sat on one corner of his desk, and a small painted rock, obviously decorated by a child, sat beside it. The desk was cleared of any sign of clutter.

"Mrs. Patterson. I understand your husband has been found in Mexico, and you desire to bring his body home for a proper burial." Mr. Curry folded his massive hands on his desk.

"Yes, sir. I have no idea of the process or what you need from me."

"I understand. I'll explain the procedure, and if you have any questions, feel free to voice your concerns."

Jill hugged Debra's shoulders. "Do we need to take notes?"

"If you like, that's up to you," Mr. Curry's quiet voice soothed Debra, comforting her in a way she appreciated.

Jill pulled a notepad and pen from her purse. "I'm ready, sir."

Mr. Curry gazed straight into Debra's eyes. "I am sorry for this unfortunate situation, but we can help you make this transition as smooth as possible. First of all, I need to contact a funeral home in Mexico City to have them prepare the body for burial. I'm bilingual, so this will not be difficult."

"What will the funeral home in Mexico charge?"

He glanced at Jill as she wrote then back to Debra. "I can safely say the charges will be between two and three thousand dollars. They will need the money before they agree to embalm the body."

It sounded gruesome, to barter over a man's body. The thought suddenly hit her that she must pay for all the costs surrounding Michael's burial. She'd have to use some of the money from the sale of their antiques. Even in death, Michael had triumphed over her.

"Will a check do?" she asked. "I can make a transfer today."

"I'm sorry. These people deal in cash. I suggest a cashier's check. I'll call Mexico City when we finish, then let you know later on today about the exact amount."

"What happens after the arrangements are made there?"

"Mr. Patterson will be placed in a plain casket and taken to the airport where the U.S. consulate will examine the body."

"Why is that?" Debra asked.

"To make sure no drugs are being smuggled out of the country."

She nodded. "Go on. I'm sorry for interrupting."

He smiled. "No problem. You stop me with all of your questions. Once the consulate's examination is complete, he will tie a ribbon around the casket, which signifies the casket has been inspected and can be flown to Houston."

"Do you take care of transportation once the flight arrives?" Why did all of this sound so callous, unfeeling? She despised what Michael had done, but she'd once loved him, bore his children.

"Yes. We'll bring the body here and prepare it for your viewing."

She swallowed hard. "I've thought about this, and I do need to see Michael one last time, to make sure it is really him. But I want a closed casket service."

"That is a wise decision. The funeral home in Mexico City will not do a very good job, and it may take as long as two weeks to get your husband here."

Debra shivered and massaged her arms. "Are you saying the body may have an odor?

"Yes, ma'am, and the body may not look its best. That's why I'd like the opportunity to make your husband a little more presentable before you see him. Most likely we'll put a glass shield over the body."

Debra wished away the image of her deceased husband.

"Will he be buried in a casket from Mexico?"

Mr. Curry paused. "Mrs. Patterson, the casket will be of very poor quality. I don't recommend it. I suggest you select one today." He opened a drawer and handed her a brochure. "These are what's available and the prices. Also, in the next few days bring whatever you'd like for your husband to wear."

"All right." She'd have to purchase something since he managed to take everything when he left with the children.

"I'll help you," Jill said. "Don't worry about it."

"I'd like to make a decision about the casket this morning." She sighed. "I want to be done with this."

"Of course. And you have a pastor to perform the service?"

She hadn't phoned Pastor McDaniel, but she felt certain he would do the funeral. "Yes, I do." Her chest started the familiar ache. Someday she planned to see a doctor about the symptoms. At times, she felt she deserved the physical discomfort.

Debra opened the brochure. With an inward gasp, she realized the prices were much more than she anticipated. Premier hardwood caskets ranged from thirteen hundred to seven thousand dollars, and the metal ones were priced from six hundred to seven thousand dollars. Acid rose in her throat, and she willed her nerves to settle. *Help me, Father.* She turned to Jill, who looked as though she read the anguish.

"Do you need some help here?" Jill asked.

Nodding, Debra pointed to the caskets.

"Would you like to view some of them?" Mr. Curry asked.

"I believe so," Debra said. "I'm on a budget."

An hour later, she'd made her decision: a stainless steel casket lined in velvet, moderately priced. "Michael's mother will most likely have problems with the selection," Debra said to Jill.

"What you've chosen is fine—and I'm not so sure I would be so generous in your shoes."

❧   ❧   ❧

Two-and-a-half weeks later, Jill accompanied Debra to the funeral home.

"I haven't seen Michael in six months, and viewing his body will probably be the hardest thing I've ever done," she said.

"You don't have to do this," Jill said. "The authorities have identified Michael."

Debra fought the churning in her stomach. "No, I need to do this."

They met Mr. Curry in the foyer of the funeral room, and he led them to a small viewing room. Debra held her breath, not knowing what to expect, willing her senses to numb. The body beneath the glass barely resembled Michael, but it was him. Her gaze trailed down to his left hand and focused on his wedding ring.

"That's not Michael's ring," she said, staring at the plain gold band.

"What do you mean?" Jill asked.

"It's the one he wore when he arrived from Mexico," Mr. Curry said.

Jill held her breath and fought to maintain her composure. Michael had deceived her even in death. Emotionless, lifeless. Had he married someone else? Why else would he replace his wedding ring? Question after question poured through her mind—none of which had answers.

One last time, she looked into his face. Even when he'd hurt her, he still had a vitality for living. All of his atrocities did not deserve the bullets pumped into his body. How had he gotten himself involved with those who would rather see him dead? Debra sobbed for another thirty minutes before she could venture out of the room.

"All I wanted was my children returned," she said. "I hated what he'd done, but murder?"

Jill placed her arm around Debra's shoulders. How comforting to know God moved among treasured people in her life for dreadful trials like this.

"You were married to him for a lot of years," her friend said. "I would expect no less from you."

Two days later, Debra faced the burial. She chose to forego visitation, which angered Michael's mother. At the funeral home, Mrs. Patterson ranted about Debra's request for a closed casket and even more about the choice. Yet, Debra's wishes were upheld. The woman made a terrible scene in front of Pastor McDaniel, complaining about her rights as a mother and cursing him for attempting to calm her down. Debra pitied the distraught woman; she grieved her murdered son in the only way she knew how—anger and bitterness. Mrs. Patterson worshiped the very image of her son. In her eyes, everything he did and said were flawless. Without Michael, she had nothing to live for. How utterly miserable she must be; her world had been destroyed. Debra understood exactly how Mrs. Patterson felt.

At the graveside, Debra prayed to make it through this last service. The scent of the many rose arrangements assaulted her, all placed by Michael's mother. She sat motionless while the media haunted her. Everywhere she turned, someone stuck a microphone to her face or flashed a camera. She refused to comment. *Let them feed off another carcass.*

Once the massive vault lowered into the earth, the ordeal would be over. Michael had gotten the best of her. He'd gone to his grave with the knowledge of their children's whereabouts.

Pastor McDaniel took his position beneath the tent. He had promised a short service at the funeral home and a brief one at the grave. But for Debra, it couldn't be quick enough. One nightmare after another had plagued her life since last August. Would it ever end?

Mrs. Patterson spat one stinging remark after another. She gave the reporters her version of Michael's disappearance with the children, including Debra's less than desirable qualities as a mother.

The authorities had combed Mexico City and not found a shred of evidence leading to Chad and Lauren. The hotel did not remember any children. The maids claimed no other occupants were in the room, plus Michael reserved only one bed. Mexican police confirmed the hotel's statement by declaring Michael had been in the city alone. What had he done with their children?

She trembled and could not stop. The pain in her chest worsened. Jill wanted her to see a doctor, but Debra had refused. Maybe once she put aside the past few days, she'd make an appointment. Jill squeezed her right hand as though sensing Debra's discomfort. The strength of her dear friend helped more than Debra could ever form into words. Drake, seated beside his wife, had been a powerhouse of strength, as usual. He'd taken time from his job to be with her and Jill at the funeral home and today. Alicia sat on her left with Mrs. Patterson on the other side of Debra. *Oh, dear God, will the nightmares ever end?*

Debra prayed for someone to reach out to her children in love. *Oh, Lord, charge Your angels to guard my babies. Feed them, clothe them, give them shelter, and the love of someone. I know You understand a parent's love. In Jesus' name, amen.*

She would never give up her search. Never. No matter how long it took to find them.

After the graveside service, depression claimed Debra a victim. To her amazement, she grieved Michael's death despite the cruel things he'd done.

"I don't understand my own feelings," she said to Jill. "I thought I hated him, but all day I've been remembering when things were good between us, before he traded our relationship for prestige and power." She shrugged. "At least, that's what I believe pushed him to take the children."

"You can't ignore the love you once had for Michael," Jill replied. "He's the father of your children."

Debra nibbled at her lip. "But I feel like I'm betraying myself. Look what he's done."

"Sounds like you haven't been able to forgive him."

Debra wanted to say she had, but she knew resentment swelled in her heart like a cancer. "Not really. It would be easy to say, 'I forgive Michael,' but I can't forget he took my children away from me." She reached for a tissue. "Following through with the Lord's commands is so hard. I want to be obedient, really I do. Pastor McDaniel and I have talked about it in our sessions, but I can't seem to follow through."

Jill hugged Debra's shoulders. "You can't do it without God's help. It's impossible."

Debra swallowed the old familiar tears. More than ever, she felt determined to be the woman God intended, but she couldn't do it alone. "I'll keep praying."

She'd cried when they lowered Michael's casket into the ground. She recognized the anguish, but God have mercy, the weeping also stemmed from losing a link to Chad and Lauren. How could she ever forgive him?

Sorrow gnawed at her as it had for months. Where were her precious babies? They had to be alive; she dared not think of anything less.

Sometimes she thought if she dwelled on memories of Chad and Lauren for very long, she'd surely lose her mind. During those moments, she clung to Jesus and reached out to Jill and Drake or Alicia or Myra, her dear friend from school. She hated her weakness, but she had not forgotten her crutches from the past. How easily she could slip back into those destructive paths.

God had forgiven her; she possessed Jesus and eternal life. To turn away from His commands meant she didn't trust Jesus. Often her heart cradled Psalm 62:8, a simple verse she had grown to call her own.

Trust in him at all times, O people; pour out your hearts to him, for God is our refuge.

That evening after Jill, Drake, and other good friends paid their final condolences, she pondered over Michael and their years together. Alone in her bed, she weighed the issue of forgiving him. Finally, she realized that harboring resentment only hurt her relationship with God. She had no choice.

She threw back the sheet covering her and worked her way into the living room. Staring out at the apartment's playground with its silvery cast from a slice of the moon, she knelt on the floor. "Heavenly Father, never has anything been so difficult than what You have asked of me. I must forgive Michael, but in my heart I want to go on despising him. Help me, Father. My relationship with You is what really matters."

She paused and reflected on Michael for a moment. Perhaps he had made his peace with God before he died. For his sake, she hoped so. A tear slipped from her eye then another.

"Father, I forgive him for all the terrible things he did to me and the children, and I choose to not hold bitter feelings against him. Help me when Chad and Lauren come home to never say anything derogative about their father." Her thoughts trickled to his mother. "I also forgive Mrs. Patterson in the manner You desire of me. She desperately needs You. In Jesus' name, amen."

chapter 21

Steven stepped off the plane in Mexico City with Ben. Julie had been dispatched there earlier to check out a few leads before the two men arrived. Again, Steven had been sent to find out more about Michael Patterson. This time the FBI investigated the man's murder—along with trying to locate his kids.

Normally Steven didn't get involved in his cases. Oh, he'd be sympathetic when protocol called for it, but he kept his distance emotionally. The Patterson case went against everything he believed appropriate for a good agent. His reaction frustrated him, and he'd spent too many hours deliberating the matter.

Michael Patterson had everything going for him: a beautiful wife, two great kids, a monstrosity of a house, and a respectable law firm. Then he got greedy. But why? When Steven found out the reason, he'd put the pieces together. Until then, the matter drove him nuts.

Then there was Debra. Steven had watched her grow from a terrified, rather wimpy woman to one of strength and courage. He expected the opposite. In the course of a few days' time, she'd lost her husband, children, and mother. Most women would have had a complete breakdown. Instead, she fought the obstacles like an angry she-bear. He'd heard that adversity bred strength, but he hadn't seen it until now. Debra kept busy around the clock with volunteer and church work. She attributed her attitude to God—then Alicia caught the same disease. Well, not actually a disease, but the same faith. If their beliefs made them stronger, why hadn't God answered Debra's prayers for her children's safe return?

Steven still didn't have any answers, but the whole situation had caused him to rethink his life, especially his relationship with his son.

Last night while Rod watched TV, Steven told the kid he'd be leaving for Mexico City and couldn't give him a definite date when he'd be back,

"Whatever," Rod had said.

Steven hated the indifference that added concrete to the wall between them. Usually he slapped the same old response back to Rod, the "it pays for the roof over your head." In the next breath, the two would snarl at each other like two hungry wolves. This time Steven wanted Rod to understand the case and the impact it had made on his life.

"Son," Steven said, "I know I've been a lousy father."

"I'll second that."

You haven't been the model son either. "But if you'll give me a second chance, I'd like to start over."

Rod snorted. "Little late, don't ya think? I'm nearly outta here."

Steven felt anger spring up like weeds in spring. He swallowed the urge to tell him what a good-for-nothing kid he really was. "You're right. Our relationship can't get much worse."

"What's the change of heart, Daddy?"

Steven ignored the sarcasm. "This case I'm working on."

"It's too late. Little League season has been over for years, and I've outgrown my summers with Grandma and Grandpa." Rod picked up the remote and powered on the TV. "I'm not interested."

"I'd like to—"

The kid increased the TV's volume. "Leave me alone."

"Look, son."

"I'm not your son—I'm what you were saddled with when Mom died."

"That's not true, and you know it. You mean everything to me."

"Oh, please." Rod stood from the sofa and headed to his room. "Take your guilt trip somewhere else."

Steven forgot what he wanted to say. With a shrug, he powered off the TV and retreated to pack his suitcase.

"Steven," Ben said, interrupting the remembrances from last night. The two men headed toward baggage claim. "Julie's meeting us at the hotel?"

"Yeah. I had her check out the taxi services to see if anyone identified Michael and to flash his and the kids' pictures around the places where he'd been seen before."

"Do the police have an idea who murdered him?"

"If they do, they're not talking. We're meeting with the authorities as soon as we arrive."

"What about the kids?" Ben asked. "Do we have leads on them?"

"Nope." Steven released a pent-up sigh. "We're back to

square one with this case. Except now we have a murder."

Steven, Ben, and Julie followed up with the Mexican police's normal investigation reports. Ben did a workup on the type of gun used to kill Michael. His research linked the weapon to a drug lord in a mountain village called San Luis, about two-and-a-half hours south of Mexico City.

Julie put miles on her walking shoes flashing pictures and digging up information. She learned Michael had traveled twice to the mountain location, once in the company of the drug lord. The following morning, the three agents were on their way to San Luis.

Steven drove the leased car on the narrow, winding mountain road while Julie navigated and Ben studied the previous day's findings.

"San Luis is a typical mountain village." Ben's towering frame hunched in the backseat. "Not much going on, just poor people trying to get by. Our friend, Patterson, made at least two trips here, one with Juan Hernandez. Says here, our drug lord also dabbles in other ventures; one of them is beekeeping."

"I think we can rest assured that Patterson wasn't interested in bees," Julie said

"Probably not," Steven said. "Although let's not discard it. What other businesses does Hernandez own?"

"Guns, drugs, prostitution, farming, and a cheese factory."

"Interesting," Steven said. "Julie, I'd like for you to look into all of those."

Julie glanced up from the map and her notes. "Does he like kids?"

Ben chuckled. "Nothing here says he doesn't. I see he has grandchildren and gives to the poor."

Steven swerved to keep from hitting a mangy dog. "All drug lords give to the poor. They're his customers. We'll pay Hernandez a little visit. We already know he had Patterson killed, if he didn't do it himself, but I'd like to find those kids—alive."

The road wound around to one small village after another. Always they saw the same sights. Barefoot, dirty-faced children chased their car begging for money. Women washed clothes in the streams. Houses made of rocks or concrete blocks painted in bright colors dotted the scenery. Pigs roamed the streets, and skinny dogs slept on rooftops. Cantinas sprang up everywhere, usually painted white with weathered red signs. Against the off-set of poverty were the giant palms, eucalyptus trees, and dark pink bougainvilleas that bloomed everywhere.

Once in San Luis, Steven approached a few men in the local cantina and told them he wanted to speak with Hernandez. Steven and Ben waited inside while Julia mingled among the villagers with pictures of Chad and Lauren.

Two hours later, a jeep with four heavily armed men approached Steven and Ben.

"You want to speak with Señor Hernandez?" one of them asked in broken English.

Steven nodded.

"We take only you."

✿   ✿   ✿

Steven glanced about Juan Hernandez's estate. Tucked away in the hills, the pale yellow stucco home displayed the drug lord's wealth and fetish for flashy and gaudy furnishings. Steven waited in an elaborate room, the kind he'd expect to see in a magazine not experience for himself.

A bronze statue of Mary holding the crucified Jesus rested on a glass and gold table. He wondered what Debra and Alicia would have thought about a drug lord owning a religious statue. Classical guitar music strummed a soothing melody in the background. A blond, bikini-clad young woman passed by him. She stopped and eyed him from head to toe then waved with her fingers before disappearing outside. His gaze swept to floor-to-ceiling windows that shone through to a swimming pool framed in exotic plants. The sound of children's laughter caught Steven's attention, but he didn't see them.

"So to what do I owe the honor of your visit?" Hernandez entered the room and eased down into a plush, bright red leather chair.

Steven noted the man's impeccable dress in comparison to the filthy children and poor villagers of San Luis.

"In a word, Michael Patterson."

Hernandez raised a brow. "I don't know such a man."

So it's a game, huh? "How about Alex Wendel?"

The man nodded. "Ah, yes, how unfortunate."

"He was killed by the same type of gun your men use."

Hernandez shrugged. "Maybe so. I can't keep track of every gun I own."

"He made a couple of trips here."

"I liked Wendel. He was interested in my bees. I'm sorry about his unfortunate accident, but I cannot help you." Hernandez smiled and reached for a gold-trimmed box containing cigarettes. He offered Steven one.

"No thanks. We're also looking for his children. I don't

suppose you know where they are?"

"Wendel never spoke of children."

"He abducted them from their mother last August in Houston."

"Weren't they his kids, too?"

"Depends on how you look at it." Steven studied the man before him. He almost believed him about the kids. Almost.

Hernandez stood from the leather chair and walked toward the door. "I have many ventures, as you well know, but kidnapping children is not one of them."

Steven reached out to grasp his hand. "Thank you for your time, Mr. Hernandez. My people will be searching the area in an attempt to settle Patterson's death—and find his kids."

"You're wasting your time, Howell, but suit yourself. Perhaps you and your colleagues would like to stay here?"

"Thanks for the offer. I'll be in touch."

Back in San Luis, Ben and Julie had found nothing. No one had seen any American children, but they had seen Patterson. Two days later, the three agents headed back to Mexico City and then on back to Houston. No motive for the murder. No trace of the children.

chapter 22

On Monday, April 15, Chad's ninth birthday brought an onslaught of depression. Debra couldn't sleep or eat, and her concentration level hit near zero. Twice she picked up the phone to call in sick to school, but a nudging of her spirit told her lying was not a cure.

Debra remembered the joy of discovering her pregnancy, the morning sickness that lasted over four months, and the first time she saw her precious baby boy.

"My son is the best tax return ever filed," Michael had said. "And he has the best mom in the world."

The remembrances continued like a movie reel. She wanted to view all the videos made of Chad and Lauren, except Michael had confiscated those living memories. The photo albums were gone along with the discs made from their digital camera. She relived events and conversations, impressing them in her mind until she could reach out to her children again.

No one at school knew the anguish raging through her very soul, and she chose not to discuss it. The only comments made during the day centered on whether or not everyone had filed their tax returns.

Debra wondered if Chad's birthday brought on more chest discomfort, but she noticed the little unexpected stabs more frequently. Ignoring them did not chase them away or lessen her anxiety of the source. A part of her said she deserved a health problem. Her previous lifestyle did not honor God.

"Debra, you need to see a doctor, most likely a cardiologist," Jill said that evening. "I know today has been horrible for you, but chest pains are nothing to fool around with."

"I'm just tired," Debra said. "They'll go away when the children are returned."

"So you want to be worn out and sick when they come home?" Jill tossed her ponytail over her shoulder, and for a moment, Debra thought her friend might shake her.

Debra hesitated. "You're right. I have to take care of myself. Chad and Lauren will need my best."

"God needs your best, too."

She shook her head in silent agreement. "I met a cardiologist at the children's Christmas party at the hospital, Dr. Cale Thurston. He has an excellent reputation, and he's a believer." She patted Jill's arm. "Okay, sis, I'll make an appointment today."

A few days later, as she sat in the waiting room of Dr. Thurston's office, Debra wished she'd ignored the ache in her chest. The whole idea seemed foolish. No one in her family had heart problems, so why would she? Debra completed the necessary, new-patient forms, but she really wanted to cancel the late afternoon appointment. Denial was easier to handle than the truth. Looking about, she saw a Bible on a lamp table. Its silent message brought comfort.

"Debra Patterson," a smiling, young nurse called from the doorway. "The doctor will see you now."

She stood and offered a quick prayer. As always, fragile life rested in God's care.

Shortly thereafter, Cale Thurston entered the examining room and shook her hand. His familiar face helped soothe her apprehension. "Good to see you again, Mrs. Patterson." He sat on a stool and studied her forms then offered her his complete attention. "I understand you're having some chest discomfort. Why don't you describe what you're feeling?"

"There's no particular time or activity to set them off. Little twinges on the left side when I least expect it. In fact, I feel a little silly taking up your time when there are sick people who need your attention."

"I understand. But while you're here, let's run a few tests and check everything out."

Panic sent chills to her fingertips. "What kind of tests?"

"An echocardiogram, a stress test, and I'd like to do a complete blood workup."

"Where do I have these done?"

"We'll handle it all here in the office. It's easy and painless. Even the girl who draws blood seldom receives any complaints." His gaze held a smile.

She relaxed slightly and offered a faint smile of her own. "Guess I sound a bit silly."

"Not at all. Some of my patients are afraid of the procedure. The stress test is done on a treadmill. When you're tired we quit, simple as that."

"When do I get the results?"

"Today, except for the blood work. I'll have those results

tomorrow afternoon. Any more questions?"

"No, I'm ready." She noted his little-boy grin and the sparkle in his deep blue eyes. A handsome man. The moment she thought those words, an alarm sounded in her mind. Michael had been so good looking, and if God ever put a man in her life again—and she hoped He didn't—he'd better be as homely as a fencepost.

An hour later, Debra leafed through a recent woman's magazine and attempted to find interest in spring flowers, momentarily forgetting she now lived in an apartment. A few potted plants graced her patio, none of which were pictured in the magazine.

With one eye on the patient's room door, she waited for test results in the same room where she'd done the treadmill test. The door opened, and Dr. Thurston stepped inside. She sat straighter and closed the magazine.

"So what's the verdict?" Envisions of quadruple bypasses darted across her mind.

"The jury's in." He took a chair across from her then pulled a pair of glasses from his lab coat pocket and opened her file. "And the sentence is light."

"Good." Her entire body relaxed.

He finished reading his notes and slipped his glasses back into his jacket pocket. "Mrs. Patterson, your tests show everything with your heart is fine. Obviously you are under a lot of stress, and that is causing your discomfort."

His gentle voice again eased her apprehensions, and she inhaled a deep cleansing breath.

"What I want to do is prescribe a mild sedative to help you sleep at night. Also, I'd like to see you gain about five to eight pounds and begin an exercise program."

Gain weight? How ironic. She could never be thin enough for Michael. She glanced down at her bony arms. Her watch no longer fit, neither did many of her bracelets. Admittedly, she had difficulty eating since it all happened.

"I used to run every day," she said, "before Michael abducted the children. Guess I shouldn't have stopped."

"Exercise is the best stress releaser," Dr. Thurston said. "You'll feel so much better, and your appetite should return with the increased activity."

"I'll try," Debra said. "Seems like my head is constantly spinning with thoughts of Chad and Lauren. Exercise is not the problem; it's forcing myself to eat."

"I'm assuming you keep busy with your teaching position and volunteering at the hospital."

"And church work," she added.

"Are you in counseling?"

"Yes, with my pastor."

He nodded. "Excellent. You're on the right track. I'll call you as soon as the results from the blood work are here. Do you have any questions?"

Debra paused. "Not really. I do want to thank you for seeing me today."

He grinned, and she thought how much he reminded her of a mischievous little boy. "I'd like to see you in four weeks to review your progress." He handed her a prescription for the sedative. "Meanwhile, if the condition becomes worse, contact us immediately."

She thanked him. Already her chest discomfort had lessened.

"I do want to caution you about the seriousness of stress.

It does lead to heart problems, but I feel in your instance that developing healthy habits will take care of the situation." He leaned forward. "Can we have a word of prayer?"

Never had she seen such compassion in a doctor. "Yes." She hoped he didn't see her display of emotion.

He took her hand into his. "Normally, I pray for my patients in privacy, but I know your faith, and I've seen how you care for the children at the hospital." He bowed his head. "Heavenly Father, I come before You asking for Mrs. Patterson's healing. She's under a mountain of stress, and it's affecting her health. Touch her with Your healing power and give her peace about her children and all of the other things in her life. Help those in search of her little boy and girl to find them and return them to her. Keep them under the shadow of Your mighty arms. In Jesus' name, amen."

"Thank you." Tears dampened her cheeks. "God bless you."

Long after Debra left Cale's office, he reflected on her appointment. Respect and admiration edged his thoughts, and he had no doubt she would follow through with his advice. Such a beautiful woman, inside and out. He prayed her children were found soon.

She stirred something inside him; perhaps it stemmed from her courage in view of her personal tragedy. He raked his fingers through his hair. His thoughts went against ethics—a doctor didn't get involved with a patient. He could admire her beauty and strength, but not pursue it. He could appreciate her wide smile, but not indulge in pulling another one from her. Her eyes could remind him of hot chocolate on a cold night, but he'd better forget the warmth.

Besides, even if Debra Patterson wasn't his patient, she surely had enough going on in her life without any more complications. She'd just buried a husband! As contemptible as Cale viewed the man, he'd still been a vital part of Debra's life. He wondered if she'd been able to forgive him.

The missing children. Michael Patterson had died without revealing where they were hidden. Only God could help Debra now.

Thoughts of Kevin paralleled his mind. Cale had been furious the first time he saw his brother-in-law with another woman after Julie's death. Although the circumstances were reversed in the Patterson case, it bothered him nevertheless.

No matter how he looked at it, thinking about Debra invited problems. He would pray for her, but not let her tug at his heart.

                 *   *   *

"You look great!" Jill called with a wave.

"Thanks," Debra said. "I can't believe how much better I feel." She grabbed her Bible for ladies' Bible study and activated the alarm on her little car. She and Jill had agreed to meet early to catch up on each other's lives.

"Isn't it amazing what eating properly and regular exercise can do for the body and mind?" Jill asked, with a glint in her eyes.

"I shouldn't have given it up," Debra said. "And sleep has probably done more good than anything else. I'm taking some good vitamins, and even my nails are stronger. Best of all, the chest pains have left the building."

"So your checkup went well?"

Debra nodded. "I don't need to see Dr. Thurston unless there's a problem. He's a great doctor. All the good reports I'd heard were true. He made me feel so secure when he prayed with me."

The two strolled toward the church entrance. "How's everything else?"

"The same." She glanced up at the sky. "No one knows where my children are but God." She stopped near the door and managed a quivering smile.

Jill tilted her head. "We can't give up."

Debra glanced away toward the parking lot. "Lauren's birthday is June second. She'll be six." Debra shook her head in an effort to push the despairing thoughts to the most remote part of her head and heart. "I've never been apart from them on their birthdays."

"Seems like the FBI could find something." Jill clenched her jaw. "They've had plenty of time, and they're supposed to be the best."

"Sometimes—"

"Sometimes what?"

Debra tried to speak, repeatedly swallowing her darkest nightmare. "What if they are gone?"

"I don't think we should consider that," Jill said, "and neither should you."

An image of Michael's body viewed through the glass at the funeral home crept across her mind. She shivered. "I keep telling myself those thoughts are not of God—and faith and trust are the answer."

"So many of us are praying, and we know God hears us."

The evening sunlight picked up streaks of gold in Jill's ash blond hair, momentarily diverting Debra's attention. The effect reminded her of God touching one's life with highlights of His Son. Finally she could speak.

"Thank you for being my sister-in-Christ."

"And thank you for allowing me to be a part of your life." Jill opened the church door and held it for Debra to enter.

Puzzled, she moistened her lips. "I don't understand. I'm the high-maintenance one."

"Debra, you don't know your own strength, your influence on others. God has just begun, and I believe He has an incredible plan for your life."

"I pray His plan includes my children." *Oh Lord, wherever they are, keep them safe.*

chapter 23

With a headache pressing against her temples, Debra slipped into bed early. If Debra had thought Chad's birthday dragged her through the mire, dreaming about Lauren's that Saturday night proved even worse. Debra saw pink frosted cupcakes and a dozen silky-haired little girls giggling over Barbie dolls and birthday cake. They turned up their noses at boys and delighted in a game of Candy Land. Birthday balloons floated about, and Lauren grabbed a pink one. It lifted her up into the air, out of Debra's grasp, and eventually out of sight. That's when she woke in a shivering sea of perspiration.

By the time morning arrived, her headache had reduced to a dull pounding, but nothing stopped the hammering of where and why her children were absent from her arms.

Pastor McDaniel delivered a sermon that helped, a message about God's hand in the middle of strife. A few of the ladies in her singles' Sunday school class knew what the date meant and loved on her as though she were a child. Afterward, she accompanied Jill and Drake for lunch, although the thought of food had no appeal.

"I'm fine," Debra said after lunch. "Really. In fact, I'm heading down to the hospital to work for a few hours." She attempted to sound strong, but inside she wanted to crumble.

Finally, evening came and she crawled into bed with the fear of nightmares on her heels. Instead, Debra tossed fitfully all night. The next morning at school, she ached for sleep, and as usual when she'd spent a sleepless night, her stomach churned.

"Not hungry?" Myra glanced at Debra's full plate at lunch.

She wet her lips and pushed aside the macaroni and cheese. Why hide her depression? "I had a bad weekend—Sunday was Lauren's birthday."

Myra's charcoal-colored eyes softened. "Oh, Debra, I'm so sorry. Anything I can do?"

She feigned a smile. "Things are crashing in around me, and I really want to be strong. Pray for me, will you?"

"How about right now? We're alone."

Debra closed her eyes as her dear friend prayed. Myra's Jamaican accent sounded rich and soothing as she asked the Holy Father to comfort Debra, give her strength, and bring her children home.

By three o'clock, she felt much better. *Thank You, sweet Jesus. I know this peace comes only from You. Some days I don't think I can go on, but You always see me through.*

Cale gazed across the sea of lunchtime faces in the hospital cafeteria of St. Luke's hoping for a glimpse of Debra Patterson. A myriad of smells teased his senses and caused his stomach to growl. Ignoring the rumblings, he remembered his mission of hopefully finding her, knowing she often volunteered on Saturdays. He'd told himself it was to check on her, make sure she'd had no reoccurring chest pains. Truthfully, he wanted to establish a friendship of sorts, possibly offer support and encouragement until HPD or the FBI located her children.

Normally, she shared her meals with other workers and volunteers, but today she sat in a far corner alone and reading. Drowning in the cacophony of clattering trays and the buzz of voices, Cale maneuvered his tray of chicken soup, salad, pecan pie, and iced tea toward her table. Odd, his taste buds had quickly latched onto the Southern specialties of pecan pie and sweetened tea. He'd even found a liking for grits, greens, and corn bread.

With a sigh, Cale noted the way Debra's thick, reddish-brown hair fell in soft curves on her shoulders. It looked natural, like her, no pretense and no malice.

"Debra?" Suddenly he felt self-conscious. His words sounded more like a raspy whisper than a man confident of his purpose.

She glanced up, her gaze troubled and her shoulders slumped. A faint smile greeted him. "Dr. Thurston. Good to see you."

"May I sit down? I'd like to talk to you."

A look of apprehension swept over her face then quickly faded. "Certainly, although I'm not good company today."

"I'm sorry. Are you not feeling well?"

"Physically, I'm wonderful. Just. . ." She hesitated and tilted her head. "I learned some rather discouraging information about my children. Please sit down. A diversion from my dismal thoughts may be exactly what I need." She looked at him rather curiously. "What are you doing here on a Saturday?"

"Oh, I rather enjoy the children at Texas Children's." He slid the tray onto the table and unloaded his food before sitting down. "Would a listening ear help?"

She smiled. "I'm sure you hear everyone else's woes. I don't want to burden you with mine."

"Try me." He met her dark brown gaze and noticed she hadn't touched her food. Of course, the burden she carried would zap any appetite. "Why don't I ask the blessing, then we both can eat?"

"Sounds like a great idea." She lowered her head.

"Heavenly Father, thank You for Your rich blessings and the food You provide. May it nourish our bodies to Your glory. In Jesus' name, amen." He lifted his head. "Short and sweet is my motto." He tore across a package of buttermilk dressing and trickled it over his salad.

"Are you sure you want to hear this?" She waded her spoon through a bowl of vegetable soup.

"Absolutely. I'm a heart doctor, which includes the physical and emotional." He chuckled. "Some days I even preach a little."

She relaxed slightly. "Well, the FBI agent who is working my case informed me yesterday that they have proof Michael used the underground in Florida to get him and the children out of the country. Shows you what money can do."

"I'm not familiar with the underground."

"Similar principle as during the Civil War. In essence, he paid an illegal group to provide new identities and paperwork for him and the children to leave the country. Now he's dead, and the children have literally disappeared."

"And no clues anywhere?" Cale leaned forward.

She shook her head. "The FBI found Michael's body in Mexico." She shifted. "Excuse me, I didn't mean to ruin your meal by referring to a dead body."

He waved her comment aside. "I saw the news. Go on."

"They haven't a trace of the children. At least, they aren't relaying information to me about it. Michael used the name of Alex Wendel while in Mexico, but his reason for being there hasn't been disclosed, although it looks like drugs."

"But they aren't giving up?"

"Oh, no. Their work goes on. I guess this all narrows things for them, but for me it's frustrating and terribly depressing. There are so many places in the world where they could be, and it's overwhelming. Plus. . ."

Cale peered into her troubled face. "Plus what?"

"Next week marks a year they've been gone."

I hadn't even thought about the date. "I'm sorry. What a long, hard year. Don't you teach school?"

Debra toyed with her glass of water. "The summer's been difficult, but I taught summer school along with my volunteer work to keep busy."

"You can't occupy every moment of your life." *How well I know.*

"True." She paused.

"Have the investigators indicated the children are out of the country?"

"They're leaning that way. Even if Chad and Lauren were located, then the question arises if the country abides by the 'Hague Convention of International Child Abduction,' and if whoever has them is posing as a parent or guardian."

He lifted a questioning brow.

"It's a treaty between nations aimed at protecting abducted children. The desire is to return these children to their custodial parent."

"Sounds like you have it memorized."

"I do." She pointed to the paper beside her tray. "It's all right here."

"No wonder you're down. You said at my office that you had a good support group within your church."

"Yes, I do, but they can't baby-sit me. Neither would I want them to."

"I understand." He pointed to her bowl. "You haven't eaten a bite, Debra. I know you're not under my care anymore, but if you don't eat properly, you will be."

She wrinkled her nose and folded the papers with a neat crease before placing them inside her purse. "Point well taken, Doctor. And I believe you wanted to talk to me before I unloaded my troubles."

He stabbed his fork into his salad and motioned for her to begin eating, too. "Your circumstances have been on my mind for a long time. In fact, I first heard about the abduction the day it happened while watching the news. Anyway, I never thought I'd meet you, much less be asking you this."

"I don't understand."

"I'd like to be your friend."

"But you are."

"I mean someone you can talk to when things get you down—like today—or have lunch together."

She paled. "Dr. Thurston."

"Cale."

Debra shook her head. "Dr. Thurston. I appreciate your

offer, but I'm not interested. My life is complicated enough without—"

Cale cringed at what must be going through her mind. "Debra, I know exactly what you're thinking, and you've got the wrong idea about me."

"Do I?"

Impassive best described Debra. How could he make her see she had nothing to fear from him? Cale pushed his tray aside, frustrated at his own lack of tact. *What have I done?* "I don't have anything inappropriate in mind, only friendship."

She lifted her chin. "I don't think so." Debra picked up her purse and hurried from the cafeteria.

✦   ✦   ✦

Debra found it nearly impossible to concentrate on her afternoon duties at the hospital. Normally, she loved working with the children: reading to them, playing games, listening to their chatter, and holding them. She relished their sweet smell and smooth skin, but not today. Anger about Dr. Thurston's request took over her best intentions.

Did he think she was so lonely that she'd tumble into his arms because he paid her a little attention? Did she have "naïve" written across her forehead? Debra may have lost her children and allowed her husband to deceive her, but she hadn't drowned in a well of stupidity. The Bible spoke of widows and lonely women being led astray. Well, she wasn't one of them. She'd been given another chance, and she wasn't about to play the fool again. All the games ended when she learned the truth about Michael.

Dr. Thurston is a good man.

Debra shivered. *Where did that come from?*
He prayed with you when you were ill.

She swallowed hard. Until today, his behavior was impeccable and his reputation flawless—as a doctor, a morally upstanding man, and a Christian. Debra remembered their first meeting at the Christmas party. He allowed a little girl to spread chocolate on his white jacket, and then he crawled around on the floor with the other kids. How many other doctors volunteered their spare time to work with children?

Suddenly guilt pelted her for the way she'd responded to his request. She could have declined his offer graciously, thanked him in a manner befitting a Christian woman. Running from the cafeteria like an immature teenager caused her to seep with humiliation.

Debra realized she feared any involvement with a man, whether he offered friendship or wanted more. All she could see were visions of Michael and all the things he'd done to her. In the next breath, she understood the unfairness of comparing every man to Michael.

But what about how she'd treated Dr. Thurston? Should she apologize? Forget about it? That seemed like a cowardly way to handle her mistake.

I have too much to think about—too much to do. My single-most thought is to grow closer to God.

Debra whirled around and saw Dr. Thurston standing before her.

Cale saw the startled look on Debra's face and wondered if she would give him a healthy dose of her mind. He'd thought about that very thing all the way up the elevator, but he had to take a chance.

Yes, he was attracted to Debra Patterson, but not necessarily in the way a man felt the stirrings of a woman. He sincerely wanted to help her in the way friends reach out to each other.

Instead of Debra escaping down the hall, she walked toward him. Her cheeks were inflamed, and he could only imagine what she was about to say.

"I'm sorry," she said, taking a deep breath. "I had no reason to behave that way."

Shock registered to his toes. "Yes, you did. I was out of line, and I apologize. My offer of friendship still holds, but I shouldn't have made it sound like I meant more."

"Hey." She half smiled. "It's all right. I'm really defensive when it comes to relationships, and I have problems trusting anyone, especially. . ."

"A man?"

She nodded. "So shall we try again?"

"Sure."

Debra dampened her lips. "We can't have enough good friends in this world, but anything else is out of the question."

"I understand." Relief flowed through Cale. "Honestly, all I intended was friendship; it just came out wrong." *Lord, she is not the only one who is scared of a relationship.*

Debra stuck out her hand. "So let's just keep it here at the hospital, like we have been."

For now, that would have to be enough. He grasped her hand, and they both laughed. Cale didn't know if God intended for them to be friends. . .or to help her through the road ahead until she found her children. . .or more. . . .

"I—" she began.

Cale's pager sounded, interrupting Debra's words.

"Oh, well." She shrugged. "It can wait." With that, she left him alone in the hall to follow up on his page.

chapter 24

Steven read through Ben and Julie's report, dated August 5, regarding the Patterson case. He'd concluded some time ago that Chad and Lauren Patterson had never been in Mexico, but their father had been sighted all over Europe and South America conducting business dealings with the most unscrupulous characters, and any one of them could have killed him. At least Michael seemed to have steered away from terrorists.

What had Patterson done to enrage Juan Hernandez? Drugs seemed a probable answer, but a hunch told him there was more to it. Were his kids involved? If he'd involved him-self with the other scum of the earth, then would he resort to exploiting those kids to child pornography or prostitution? *Best keep that thought away from Debra. Why torture her?* Even the strongest had a limit.

Patterson used the name of Alex Wendel in South America. He brokered an online international import/export business dealing with imported foods and fresh fruit baskets. On the European front, he'd used the name of Jonathon

Miller, and this identity had an online import/export business dealing in exclusive wines. Both names had American social security numbers and credit information utilizing addresses in the Channel Islands—and a common bank account number.

His pager buzzed, reminding him of Rod's football scrimmage in one hour—a preseason game before the official season. As a high-school senior, his son would start as a tight end. Steven found it difficult to attend the games last year, but that was before he took on the Patterson case and realized what a lousy dad he'd been.

Rod still treated him like a reject from trash day. What else was new?

Steven scanned through the report again. Alex Wendel had made a few trips to Columbia—drugs again. Normally the FBI remained stateside unless a country requested their presence or the case warranted more investigation. *Sounds like I need to make a trip to South America. First, I need to call Debra. She deserves to know some of what this report covers.*

⁂

During an in-service session before lunch, Debra found a message in her mail slot at school to phone Steven. He must have new information, or he'd have called her at home.

Needing privacy, she snatched up her cell phone—glad she'd been able to continue its coverage—and told the secretary she planned to be in her car for the next few minutes.

He answered on the third ring. "Hi, Debra. Thanks for returning my call."

"What's up?" Her attempt to sound light failed.

"A new development in the case, and I wanted to let you know as soon as possible."

"You've located the children?" Her heart pounded until it ached.

"No, I'm sorry. This is about Michael. We've learned he owned an online import/export business, which is why he was seen twice in Mexico. The authorities there have arrested a man linked to Michael's venture. Michael owed him money, and he didn't take kindly to it. Also, the suspect stated he didn't know your husband had children."

Where are they? "Steven, I appreciate your calling me. Do you know where Michael based his business?"

"The address is in the Channel Islands, but we're not sure where he actually lived. Additional information is not to be revealed at this time."

Debra sensed the irritation rising and bit back a retort. "When can you tell me?"

"When I have proof."

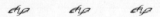

Chad's birthday had devastated Debra. Lauren's sent her to bed with the threat of nightmares. Tonight, the anniversary eve of her children's abduction, she wrestled with her very faith. At one time, the date loomed in the future like an evil omen, but now the day hovered over her with the strength of a dozen demons.

August eighth. The day you lost your children because you were a horrible mother and wife. Where are they now, Debra? Where are they now?

She prayed. She cried. She prayed harder.

"You're spending the night with me," Jill said. Her friend had stopped by the apartment soon after Debra arrived home from school. "Get your stuff together for tomorrow. No argument."

"I won't argue with you." Debra did her best to keep the tears at bay. "The memories are haunting me. I know God will see me through this, but I do need your help."

"And you have it."

"At least I have a job to keep me busy. I never thought I'd be grateful for in-service days."

Jill linked her arm with Debra. "Come on. Not one more minute in this apartment. We're grabbing what you need and splitting this place."

"I should return a call to Pastor McDaniel," Debra said. "He left a message on my machine, and so did Alicia."

"You can call them from my place."

I'm not so sure I can even speak.

The morning of August 8 hit Debra like a rock avalanche, pelting her with bitter memories and attacking her resolve not to let the anniversary of Chad and Lauren's abduction destroy her.

The turmoil began as soon as the alarm clicked onto the local Christian radio station. Instead of contemporary music, the disc jockey cited the historical happenings of this day.

"Today in history: August 8, 1974, Richard Nixon resigns from the presidency. Birthdays are Dustin Hoffman, Keith

Carradine, Esther Williams, and Mel Tillis. Today in 1899, the refrigerator was patented. On August 8, 1945, President Truman signed the United Nations Charter."

And one year ago today, Chad and Lauren Patterson were abducted by their father.

"Help me, Lord," she prayed aloud. "I want to be brave today, but without You it won't happen."

Crawling from the bed, Debra felt the weight of the year's struggles in trying to find her children and to forgive those who had snatched them from her.

I have the Lord. Jesus is enough.

She thought of her job and was thankful the day was filled with activity. *I can do this. I'm not alone.*

Debra showered—so grateful that Jill insisted she spend the night with her and Drake. Unfortunately, the guestroom faced the house where she had lived with Michael and the children.

The joy of the Lord is my strength.

Midway through her devotions, Jill knocked.

"How about breakfast?" Her dear friend stuck her head inside the door.

"Oh, Jill, you're not a morning person. What did you do, set your alarm?"

"Yes, I want to be here for you. Now, what about breakfast?"

Debra sighed. *Thank you, Jesus.* "Coffee and a bagel are all I have time for."

"I'm dressed and ready. I thought we could have a short prayer time after we eat." Jill's voice sounded soothing. In heaven, she'd be offered a special crown. "How does the Café Extraordinaire sound?"

Debra swallowed her tears, mixed with gratitude for God's provision and sorrow for the day. She didn't want to eat or be sociable, but she needed to do those very things. "Thanks, Jill. This means a lot to me."

Later at school, she found a dozen roses on her desk and several cards from various teachers who encouraged her to hold on to her faith. Even the non-believers had cheered her strength in God. Odd, she hadn't mentioned the day's significance to anyone.

"I have something for you." Myra handed her a light blue gift bag.

Debra blinked back the tears. "But you've done so much already with the flowers and cards."

Myra wrapped her arm around Debra's waist. "Only because we all love you. Just open the package. It's not much, only an appreciation of how much I value our friendship."

Debra gingerly lifted the white tissue paper from the bag and pulled out a devotional that accompanied a popular book on the value of prayer. "Thank you, Myra."

"Do you already have one of these?" she asked.

Debra shook her head. "No, and I'll begin using it today." She glanced up into her friend's face. "I don't know how you knew about today, but I'm so glad you remembered."

Myra hugged her. "Jill let me know. No one should have to go through something like this without friends."

Thank You, Jesus.

On her way to lunch, Debra checked her mail slot and saw a sweet message from Alicia.

God held Debra in the palm of His hand. He'd given her friends to shoulder the burden. In a few days, she'd experience the anniversary of her mother's death. That date would be easier; her mom lived with Jesus. What more could anyone ask of those they love?

Debra shuddered. Her own thoughts frightened her.

ℒℴ ℒℴ ℒℴ

A month later, Debra found herself knee-deep in a heated discussion with Steven about the lack of progress in finding the children.

"Looks to me like since you've found his murderer, my children have taken less priority." Rarely did she feel like arguing, but today it suited her just fine.

"That's not true," Steven said. "The FBI is working hard on this case. Investigations take time."

"With all of your connections, it sounds strange that you can't tell me where Michael operated his business."

"I told you I'd give you the information as I establish its validity."

Steven's professional tone irked her. Fire seemed to flare from the pores of her skin. "It's not your children who are missing. Why is it you can locate a banking account in the Channel Islands, discover he changed his identity, find him associated with an import/export business, help solve a murder, but not tell me where you think my children are?"

"I understand you're upset—"

"Upset is a mild way to put it. I'm furious."

"Debra, I'll talk to you when you're more rational." Steven ended the call, leaving her more irate than she'd been in a long time.

Debra realized her little show of temper didn't reflect well on her Christianity. Tonight she'd call Steven back and apologize, but at the moment, she was too angry to do anything but vent her frustrations.

Oh, God, I'm sorry. I don't want to end up bitter. Please forgive me for behaving like a selfish child.

chapter 25

A month later, on a warm Saturday morning in October, Cale stepped off the elevator at Texas Children's in hopes of finding Debra while he visited the children. He'd been in and out of several rooms before he spotted her reading to a few children at the end of the hall. Odd, that's how they first met.

God had given a special word about Debra   patience.

He stood back and admired the gentleness and strength of this woman who lived with the agony of her missing children and devoted her spare hours to these little ones. She had a toddler in her lap and two other children snuggled up on each side of her.

With the attention to her health, Debra's cheeks no longer looked hollow, and her skin glowed with a natural peachy tone. A beautiful woman in every respect of the word, but her eyes revealed the sadness—the sorrow he longed to take away if she'd let him be a real friend. Debra glanced up, startled, then offered a half smile.

"I didn't mean to interrupt you." He gestured for her to

continue. "Keep reading, and I'll see what kind of trouble I can get into with the other young patients."

He turned and headed in the opposite direction, not wanting to pose as a threat. If her emotions were as fragile as he surmised, his listening to her read probably bothered her.

While Cale played Battleship with a precocious nine-year-old by the name of Annie, Debra slipped in with a stack of books and watched the two compete in the game.

"It's good to see you." He fought not to give Debra his entire attention. "This little lady is beating me."

"She likes chess, too," Debra said, leaving a couple of books about horses near the bed. "Last Saturday, Annie captured my queen in less than ten moves."

"You were too easy," Annie replied. "He might be tougher."

"Don't bank on it." He gave the girl a wink. "But if you're still here next Saturday, I'll take you on in a game of chess."

Two moves later, Annie had beaten Cale—and he hadn't tried to lose.

As soon as Cale and Annie finished with proper good-byes and a tentative date for next Saturday's chess match, he and Debra ventured into the hallway.

"And how are you?" he asked as openers, all the while hoping she didn't have plans for lunch.

"I'm okay," she said with a tilt of her head and the same half smile as earlier. She clutched the remaining books to her chest.

"Have you eaten yet?"

She shook her head and greeted a nurse hurrying by.

"Would you consider sharing a table with a friend, at my favorite five-star restaurant known as St. Luke's cafeteria?"

She moistened her lips, and he saw concern lines crease her forehead. "I believe that would be fine."

Cale inwardly sighed relief. A short while later, they walked through the tunnel to St. Luke's. He fished for words and finally settled on talking about the patients at Texas Children's.

In the cafeteria, he suggested a table in the thick of everything going on. The buzz of voices equaled the clash of plastic trays slamming against the hard surfaces. He wanted to do and say those things to ensure that Debra was relaxed in his presence.

He unloaded his roasted turkey and cheese sandwich, a plate full of Caesar salad, and a bowl of beef barley soup onto the table while she set a bowl of chicken noodle soup and a thick brownie to the side. Her hands trembled.

Lord, how can I make her relax?

"Hey, Cale," Derrick Hughes called from an adjacent table. "What are you doing here on a Saturday? Working or pestering the kids over at Texas Children's?"

Cale grinned and waved. "Both. But I did need my weekly kid fix."

"He can have mine for a day," another doctor said.

"Send them on." Cale seated himself and turned his attention to Debra. "Do you want me to bless or will you?" he asked.

"You go ahead." She bowed her head.

"Lord, we thank You for the gift of health and for all the blessings You generously give us. Bless this food and nourish it to our bodies that we may nourish Your kingdom, amen."

Midway through a silent meal, Cale found the perfect conversation starter. "Where do you go to church?"

She laid her spoon beside the bowl. "Spring Creek."

"I imagine the members have been a tremendous source of

encouragement." He met her gaze and saw she still looked uneasy. *Patience.*

"Yes, they've been wonderful. I haven't been going there long, but I'm making friends, mostly through my Sunday school class."

"Where did you attend before?" Cale asked, relieved they had found something easy to discuss.

"I didn't." She swallowed. "I became a Christian after the children were abducted."

He expelled a heavy sigh. "Leave it to me to bring up an unpleasant topic."

"Oh, you haven't." She picked up her spoon and appeared to examine it. "I wouldn't want to go back to the life I led without Jesus." Her eyes grew wide, and he wondered if either of her children held her delightful features.

He smiled—his turn to relax.

"Where do you attend?" She pushed her soup aside and reached for the brownie.

"A church in the southeast part of town, Sagemont. It took some looking around when I first moved here from Detroit, but I'm very happy there."

"Me, too. My church is my family. So you're originally from Michigan?"

"Yes, I had a job offer to join the doctors at St. Luke's nearly two years ago, and since nothing held me in Detroit, here I am."

She laughed lightly. "What a culture shock."

"No kidding, but I do love Houston. My parents came at Christmas, and we had a great time. Although, with mild temps and no snow, it felt strange."

Silence permeated the air.

"How's the investigation?" Had he asked the right question?

She lifted her head. Calmness met him. "About the same. A man is in custody in Mexico City for Michael's murder, but there's nothing to report on the children. Sometimes I wonder if the FBI is still working on the case." She shook her head. "I know better than that. Steven, the FBI agent, is working hard, but not fast enough for me."

They continued in silence, Debra munching on her brownie, and he finishing his sandwich.

"How are we doing in the friends department?" Cale figured he might as well jump in with both feet.

"Definite progress, as long as you have patience." She dabbed at her mouth with the paper napkin.

She said that nearly impossible word.

☙ ☙ ☙

"How about I treat your buds to pizza as soon as you shower and change?" Steven's insides reeled. Rod had not responded positively to any of the attempts at establishing a decent relationship between father and son, but he wasn't giving up.

"Sounds good to me," one of Rod's friends said. "A tie game makes me hungrier than usual."

"Count me in," another player said.

Rod scowled at his dad, but his buds had sealed Steven's request.

"What's it like working for the FBI?" a tall, broad-shouldered young man asked while they waited for their pizzas. "Excuse me." He stuck out his hand. "Bud Thompkins."

"Steven Howell—same as Rod."

The other kid did the same. "Paul Farris."

"Good to meet you guys." He leaned back in his chair. "Honestly, most of my cases are boring—not like the TV shows you've seen." Steven noted Rod looked irritated.

"I think it's cool," Paul said. "Wish my dad had a job like yours. Rod says you travel a lot."

"Depends on the case."

"What are you working on now? Heard you've made a couple of trips to Mexico City," Paul continued.

So he does talk about his old man.

"You guys aren't interested in this, are you?" Rod asked, finishing a cola.

"I am," Bud said, crossing his arms across a mammoth chest. "What's going on in Mexico? Can you tell us?"

Steven's stomach churned. Impressing Rod's buds wasn't the problem, just his son's attitude. "I can't. Sorry, guys. Protocol and procedures require me to keep my cases private."

Bud leaned in closer. He seemed more earnest than the other guys. "I remember a man nabbed his two kids from their mother while they were at a mall. He then cleaned out everything from their house and his business then disappeared."

"I remember something about that," Paul said. "Wasn't he found murdered in Mexico City? Is that your case?"

Steven maintained a placid look on his face. This wasn't the first time folks tried to pull information from him.

"Do you think they're alive?" Paul asked.

"Listen guys, I have no—"

"Can't you tell us something?" Paul asked. "I mean who are we going to tell?"

Red-faced, Rod said nothing. He squirmed in his chair. Steven couldn't figure out if the cause of his son's uneasiness was his dad or his buds.

"Hey, let's lay off. Mr. Howell would tell us if he could." Bud wore a gold cross around his neck, reminding him of Debra and Alicia.

"Thanks." Steven reached for his glass of Coke.

"Has there ever been a case that really got to you?" Bud asked.

"Honestly, some have," Steven said. For the first time, Rod appeared to listen. "Lately working for the FBI has made me rethink my role as a father." He braved forward. "There are a lot of things that can be replaced in this world, but your kids aren't one of them. Now that Rod is a senior, I realize I've wasted a lot of years working."

chapter 26

The months drifted into the holidays, and for the second year, Debra faced Thanksgiving and Christmas without her children. Activities at church and school were nearly identical, except this year more friends than ever offered their sympathies. Many asked her to join them for holiday dinners. She chose to imitate exactly what she'd done the year before, and the repetition helped. Again she attempted to reach out to Mrs. Patterson, even paid her a visit.

"I have nothing to say to you," Michael's mother had said.

"I'm sorry you feel that way. We both have lost so much." Debra hoped her words wove through the woman's bitterness.

"Correction. We have lost those we love, but I didn't cause the problem."

Within the same week of talking to Mrs. Patterson, Debra met with Cale at Texas Children's.

"Are you sure you want to volunteer at Texas Children's on Christmas Day?" Cale asked at the nurses' station on one of the floors. "You could always join me at my parents' place in Michigan."

The thought of him including her in holiday plans frightened her a bit. They were friends, nothing more.

"No, thanks. This is where I need to be."

"Have I upset you with my invitation?" he asked.

Be honest, Debra. "You didn't upset me, just scared me a little." She smiled. "I'll get over it."

If Debra admitted her real feelings, she'd have listed Cale as one who held a special spot on her list of friends.

ダ   ダ   ダ

After Easter Debra began to think about an alternative to finding the children other than the local police or the FBI. Frustrated at the empty-ended reports, she decided to talk to Jill about her thoughts. They met at a coffee shop one afternoon after school dismissed.

"Lately I've been thinking about hiring a private investigator."

"Really? Who would you call?" Jill took a sip of her mocha.

"I have no idea, but this waiting is driving me crazy." Debra stretched her neck and shoulder muscles. "I realize some of the PIs are out to make money and nothing more, but if I'm going to do this thing, then I need to find a reliable source."

"But, the cost."

"I know." Debra sighed. "I have some money left from selling the house and the antiques, and I plan to teach both sessions of summer school. I wanted to save it all for expenses when Chad and Lauren come home, except now I think I need the money to find them."

"So who do you think would give you the name of a reputable detective?" Jill asked.

"Certainly not the FBI, and as much as I love Alicia, I don't imagine she has much use for them either. They have their own way of conducting investigations."

"I understand. I'll ask Drake, but I doubt if he can recommend one."

Debra lifted a latte to her lips. "I'm thinking a good law firm could give me a referral. I believe Michael used them on his cases."

"Go for it. What do you have to lose but time on the phone?" Jill asked.

Debra covered her mouth and bit down hard on her lower lip. "Time is not the problem. It's not knowing whether they are alive to come home to me."

Debra's efforts to retain a private investigator quickly proved futile. Law firms gave her referrals, but their exorbitant fees stopped her cold. In no time at all, she would exhaust her savings—with no guarantee of success. A part of her wanted to use the money, but another part suggested she wait and let the FBI continue their work. They were the best, weren't they? She wanted to believe she was doing all she could to get her children back, but inadequacy gnawed at her like a dog chewing on a dry bone.

Debra needed to be doing something. *Lord, how much longer must I wait before You bring my children back to me?*

Cale stood from his recliner and paced the floor of his tenth-story condo. His mother loved the sleek, contemporary styling, much like the design of his condominium in Detroit.

Truthfully, he loved the look of rich wood and warmer colors, but this had been available in an area close to the hospital. Someday he'd toss the chrome and brilliant black and white for a home in the country, including lots of land and a border collie. He could commute to the city. Lots of people did.

This morning's church services had revived his spirit and encouraged him to venture out into new territory. Cale had an idea—one that pestered him day and night and today gave him the fuel to approach Debra at the earliest opportunity.

On more than one occasion, Cale had considered that Debra's children might be dead. If so, God needed to make sure she possessed the strength to endure another tragedy. The more elapsed time, the more the odds stacked against her. Maybe God intended for her to grow closer to him before allowing her to endure something else.

What was Cale doing trying to outthink God? *Who has understood the mind of the Lord, or instructed him as his counselor?*

I just want to help, Lord. But how can I when she mistakes my motives? Thoughts of Julie and Daniel swept across his mind. His sister refused to trust any man but Cale.

Taking a long drink of water, he remembered something Debra had said months ago. She'd been reading about a treaty among various nations to protect children who had been abducted. The idea focused on returning them to their proper guardian, but some nations didn't comply. Just one more thing for Debra to contend with. Cale made a mental note to search online for information about the Hague Convention. If she ever spoke to him again, he wanted to be up-to-date on such matters.

He stared out his balcony window to the busy, oak-lined

street below. A green-leafed canopy shaded the sidewalk against the unseasonably humid temperatures, and a westerly breeze invited him for a stroll. Officially, the calendar read June 1, but this Sunday the temperatures outside soared into the mid-nineties. He didn't mind the heat. In fact, when he went home last Christmas, he froze. Houston had adopted him.

Stepping out onto his balcony, he caught a serenade of birds, but in the middle of their song, a car alarm erupted along with the piercing scream of an ambulance. A moment later, children's laughter captured his attention. As much as Debra loved children, he imagined that at times their sounds upset her. Sometimes when he saw freckle-faced little boys, his heart wrenched for Daniel.

Sighing, Cale realized he needed to clear his head and formulate his plans for the following week. This need to help restore her motherhood often made no sense to him, yet he realized God's will often looked foolish in the world's view.

Strange and yet comforting, Cale felt certain God had appointed him to assist in the search for the Patterson children. Last night, he'd prayed and asked for direction.

The following Saturday, he searched through Texas Children's until he found Debra and invited her to lunch. As always, the cafeteria at St. Luke's resembled more of a zoo than a mixture of nurses and physicians seasoned with visitors.

Lately Debra seemed more receptive and even responsive to Cale, as though she accepted their friendship and no longer fought it. Nice thought, but he still needed to proceed with caution.

She looked pretty today—fresh and captivating—or was it his heart threatening to push him past the line of friendship and on to the brink of something more.

"Anything new developed with the investigation?" he asked, hedging toward the inevitable.

"Not really. Looks like the war on terrorism is keeping the FBI busy, plus some of the agents are reassigned areas of responsibility to comply with the Bureau's new standards."

"Your agent, too?"

She shook her head. "No, he's simply busy with his job. Oh, Cale, that's wrong of me to second-guess the FBI. I don't know what the problem is. Steven tells me they are working on the case, but I want results. In two months it will be two years."

"Debra I've been doing a lot of thinking, and I'd like to help you more in the area of finding your children."

"What do you mean?" She peered up at him curiously.

"In short, I want to help financially. Maybe a private investigator could uncover clues the FBI have overlooked."

Debra gasped, and Cale feared he'd upset her—again.

"I've been praying over the same thing. I've even looked into it and obtained rates, but I couldn't accept money from you. Besides, their fees are horrible."

"Let me judge what I can and can't do."

She shook her head. "It's completely out of the question."

He leaned toward her. "Would you have dinner with me, and we'll discuss it?"

Debra stiffened. "I don't think so."

"Do you believe God has a plan for all of us?"

"Of course I do."

Her granite-type features told him he'd better do some fast praying and talking. "Incredible as it sounds, I believe one of the reasons God placed me in Houston is to help you find your children. The only reason I suggested dinner is to provide a quiet atmosphere where we can talk."

His thoughts filtered back to Julie and Daniel. Helping Debra find her children wouldn't bring back his sister and nephew, but at least he'd have done something.

"I don't trust easily." Not a muscle twitched on her lovely face. "You already know that."

"I understand, and in your shoes I'd feel the same way. If dinner is uncomfortable for you, why not a library or a park?"

She laughed lightly then captured his attention with a serious gaze. "Cale, under no circumstances can I accept money from you. God will provide a way to locate Chad and Lauren."

Debra's reluctance to accept his offer depressed him. At least his patients wanted his help. "Have you considered I might be part of God's divine plan?"

✽   ✽   ✽

Debra took the elevator up to the second floor of Texas Children's. She recalled the many Saturdays she'd shared lunch with Cale.

Why he persisted in this friendship quest amazed her, but she did value his friendship. Their conversations were always polite, surface talk about everyday occurrences and world events—nothing threatening to her situation. And lately she felt irritated with his eggshell approach. He always asked if she had any news about the children, and her response remained the same.

Except today, he had an unusual request. She meant what she'd said. Cale would not pour his money into finding her children. She dare not owe any man.

Straightening her shoulders to dispel the mental torture of not having Chad and Lauren, Debra lifted her head and proceeded to a toddler's room where Social Services had yesterday brought in a battered little boy, an abuse case. The child wretched at her heart. His thin body held bruise upon bruise, and his left leg had been broken in two places. What if? No, she dare not think about it.

Tomorrow, Lauren would be seven; Chad was ten. Last year, she purchased gifts then returned them. This year, she refused to go through the same heartache.

Later that night, she reviewed her notes for tomorrow's Sunday school class. The lesson was on Ruth and focused on the godly woman's life as a poor widow, caregiver for her mother-in-law, a foreigner, and a model for all single women. Debra believed the study would generate good discussion and possibly an opportunity for hurting women to express their pain. Hurting women and pain, she understood.

Debra read further about how God desired to give His children peace and point them toward obtaining biblical answers to the problems plaguing their lives. The goal of her single woman's Sunday school class was for all of them to choose Jesus—to embrace life instead of tragic circumstances.

As Debra reflected on her lesson, it occurred to her how God used Boaz to bless Ruth's life. Through the advice of her mother-in-law, Ruth turned to a stranger for help, a good man who lived for the Lord.

Staggered by the truth, Debra closed her book and clenched shut her eyes. The bits and pieces of her life that coincided with Ruth's shouted an alarming truth. Boaz and

Cale had offered their assistance to women who desperately needed help. Ruth had accepted; Debra had refused.

Cale's words echoed in her mind. *Have you considered I might be part of God's divine plan?*

chapter 27

Debra's heavy heart continued Saturday evening. Was God talking to her? Was she being stiff-necked like the people in the Old Testament? God worked through her life repeatedly. He put people in her life to help her and people she could help. Last week, she received a call from a women's group who wanted her to speak at their retreat. She wanted to refuse, believing she hadn't been a Christian long enough for such an honor, but God had nudged her spirit to accept.

She shook her head and willed the burning in her throat to disappear. God knew her heart, and He knew where Chad and Lauren were—even if her precious children now lived with Him.

Those thoughts crept into her mind more often than she cared to admit, and not knowing the truth held its own comfort. Although her heart held the love of Christ, she feared if her children were lost to her forever, she'd welcome insanity.

On Sunday the matter continued to plague her. During Sunday school a headache erupted, shooting pain up and down both sides of her temples. By the time church started, her eyes felt as though hot pokers had been plunged through them. She fumbled through her purse for a nasal spray but remembered she'd changed purses and neglected to include her migraine medication.

Easing down on a pew beside Jill, she deliberated whether to leave or stay. She loved church, and Pastor McDaniel's sermons always touched her heart. It didn't matter so much that others saw her red eyes and the water streaming from them. She feared becoming violently ill in the middle of the service.

"What's wrong?" Jill studied her face.

"Migraine," Debra replied, gritting her teeth with the debilitating pain. "And I don't have my medicine."

"Do you want me to take you home?"

Debra shook her head and reached for a tissue to dab her dripping eyes. "I'll manage. I'm only a few minutes away."

"You can't drive if you can't see," Jill stated. She linked arms with Debra then turned to whisper something to Drake. He glanced around his wife to give Debra a sympathetic look.

Will I always be a hopeless emotional cripple?

"I'm taking you home," Jill said. "No questions asked."

Debra and Jill slipped from the sanctuary and out of the church. Stepping into the bright sun, Debra winced and shuffled through her purse until she wrapped her fingers around her sunglasses. Positioning them over war-torn eyes, she allowed Jill to lead her across the parking lot.

"Is your car in the normal place?" Jill asked.

"Yes, but what are you going to do about church?" The last thing Debra wanted was for her friend to miss the blessings of praise and worship.

"I'll either wait for Drake to pick me up at your apartment or drive your car back to church and return it later. Right now, your health and safety are what's important."

Debra wanted to hug her, but instead she retrieved her keys and handed them to Jill. "You are the best friend in the world—next to Jesus."

Jill squeezed her arm. "We're sisters-in-Christ, and we're spending eternity together. We'll have lots of fun then, with no headaches."

Once seated in the car and en route home, Debra kept her eyes closed and prayed for relief.

"What do you think brought this on, Lauren's birthday?" Jill asked. The air conditioner kicked in, releasing cool air and relieving the ultra-warm temperatures. "Guess that would push me into a migraine, too."

Debra hated to burden her friend with Saturday's happenings, but Jill, of all people, would understand. "Her birthday is bothering me, but that's only part of what's on my mind. I had a disturbing conversation with Cale."

"And?"

"He approached me at lunch yesterday about wanting to hire a private investigator."

"Did he say why?" A lilt rose in Jill's voice.

Debra took a deep breath. She relayed how Cale felt God wanted him to help her find Chad and Lauren. He assured her no other motive aligned with his offer.

"Debra, how wonderful. What an answer to prayer, especially after you discovered how much an investigator costs."

A surge of pain rippled across the top of her head, and she waited for it to pass before replying. "I turned him down. I hope you understand why. I didn't cause a scene like the last time or react like an emotionally charged teenager." She sighed. "But it has been on my mind."

"Honey, you've come a long way. You don't even look like the same Debra Patterson of nearly two years ago. Life patterns seldom change overnight, but you're growing in leaps and bounds. This is about trust, right?"

Debra nodded. "I'm afraid to trust Cale. I want to, but I can't."

"I have no idea how hard this must be, but I'll pray for you."

"Thanks." She sniffed and reached for a tissue.

"Are you sure you don't want his help?"

Debra shivered at the thought. "No. I can't accept money from him. He. . .he might expect something else in return, and I could never pay back the amount a good PI would charge."

Jill's forehead crinkled. "Has he suggested anything inappropriate? I mean you told me before he had an excellent reputation as a caring, Christian doctor."

Debra shook her head. "Not at all." She paused until another wave of pain eased. "I'm afraid of men, Jill. I only know of two whom I can trust—Drake and Pastor McDaniel. Even Steven drives me to distraction with his professional, businesslike attitude about this whole investigation."

"Have you prayed about Cale? God could have led him to you."

"I'm not so sure I want to hear what God has to say."

Jill gave her a sad smile. "Well, you are truthful, but His ways are best. Did you explain how you feel?"

"In a roundabout way," Debra said. "I think he understands."

❦   ❦   ❦

Tuesday afternoon Debra entered her apartment and shuffled the papers she needed to grade for summer school onto the kitchen table. She pulled Cale's card from her wallet and stared at it, wishing she didn't have his pager number and could use that as an excuse not to call. Taking a deep breath, she punched in his number. One thing for certain, she didn't need to complicate her life with Cale. She needed to thank him for his offer again and let him know she didn't take his words lightly, but nothing more.

"Yes," she said, when his answering service responded. "I'd like to leave a message for Dr. Cale Thurston."

❦   ❦   ❦

In the middle of a consultation appointment, Cale received a page. Excusing himself, he checked on the call and learned Debra had left a message with his answering service.

"She specifically said for you to contact her at your convenience," the woman reported. "No rush whatsoever."

He replaced the phone. Patients were scheduled back-to-back until five o'clock. Debra would have to wait. Smiling into the face of an anxious businessman who had experienced a mild heart attack some weeks prior, Cale returned his attention to the issue at hand and gave the patient his complete attention.

At six o'clock, he plopped into his cozy office chair and deliberated whether to call Debra now or wait until he'd eaten. His stomach growled, reminding him of the partially eaten tuna sandwich he'd devoured on the run between the hospital and his office. Still, her call might be important.

He punched in her number and closed his eyes, not because he felt the strain of the day; rather he needed the Lord to guide the conversation. Her sweet voice met his ears.

"Debra, this is Cale. I received your page earlier, but I've been swamped with patients. My service said your call was not a medical issue or anything urgent."

"Oh, not at all."

He heard the nervousness in her voice, and from what he'd surmised about how she felt about men, this call must be difficult. "Tell me, what can I do for you?"

She first replied in a faint sigh. "Cale, I owe you an apology for Saturday. I don't think I responded properly to your more-than-generous offer."

"Have you reconsidered?" *Why am I so driven with this thing? Why can't I simply take no for an answer?*

When she failed to say more, he assumed he'd disturbed her again. "Why don't you think and pray about the matter for a while? My offer is open, and I have no intentions of changing my mind."

"I understand, but my mind is made up." Her voice sounded forced, rehearsed.

"Are we still friends? I'd hate to have lunch alone on Saturdays."

"Yes, of course."

"Great. I have another patient at Texas Children's, so I might run into you on Sunday afternoon."

"Maybe we can take a walk to the coffee shop down the street."

Wow! What brought on her change of heart? "Great. I'm a sucker for espresso."

The phone clicked. Cale crossed his arms and leaned back in his chair. He must have made a little progress with Debra. He recalled her statement of not being able to trust. She meant men, and since he fell into that territory, he must have moved up a notch.

Cale's thoughts took on a serious note. *God, use me for Your purpose. Cast aside my own selfish desires and help those kids find their way back to Debra.*

❧   ❧   ❧

"What news do you have on the Patterson case?" Steven asked Ben.

"Nothing. Hernandez made a deal with the Mexican police and turned in one of his men. The authorities there are not backing down from calling the killing drug related."

"And the kids?" Steven asked Julie.

"Just like Columbia—zero. I'm going to shift gears and work on the Jonathon Miller alias."

Steven shook his head. "Debra believes we've given up. I hate this not knowing where he stashed those kids. And I hate more the fact that we aren't able to solve the stupid thing." He turned to Ben. "Tear apart Patterson's online import/export businesses. Something tells me he might have slipped up since he used the same address for Wendel and Miller. Refresh my memory on what he sold online."

"Nuts, cheeses, fruit, Italian wines—all gourmet products," Ben said. "He dealt with only the finest."

Steven toyed with the cup of cold coffee in his hand. "A man could make a lot of money having gourmet food manufactured in South America and labeled from someplace else."

"Gotcha," Ben replied. "I'll get on it right away."

"Julie, look into Hernandez's farm and beekeeping ventures, anything and everything he's associated with."

"I've turned Hernandez inside out." Julie jabbed a pencil behind her ear.

"Then do it again!"

chapter 28

I want to thank you for allowing me to tell my story," Debra said to the group of one hundred and fifty women. "No matter what problems torment your lives, God loves you. And I can tell you; He is enough. He wakes me in the morning, and He is the last one I talk to at night. When I cry, He comforts me, and in those moments of joy and laughter, I know He has given them to me as a special gift. I rest in the knowledge that my heavenly Father lost His Son, too, and He knows my pain. It's been almost two years, and it seems the FBI is no closer to finding my children than six months ago. But no matter where Chad and Lauren are—"

Debra stopped to catch her breath. She heard the tremor in her voice and swallowed the lump in her throat. She blinked back the tears and prayed for strength. The ladies' retreat had been difficult to prepare for, often ripping open the wounds she thought had healed. Her notes seemed to bleed with the raw emotions she revealed to the women, but she'd felt God's hand every step of the way. Taking a deep breath, she moved to close her speech.

"Wherever my children are today," she said, "God is watching over them. He loves them more than I could ever comprehend, just like He is pouring out His love to you."

Debra stepped back from the podium and removed her wireless microphone as the women applauded and rose to their feet. She saw their tear-glazed faces and knew without a doubt that God had used her to speak to these dear ladies.

Jill and Myra stood to her right. Myra gave her a thumbs-up while dabbing her eyes, and Jill lifted her hand in a sign of praising God.

When the crowd quieted, Debra felt the need to add to her closing comments. She lifted the mike to her lips. "If any of you need to pray or simply talk, I will be available in the back of the auditorium with the other conference leaders."

She left the stage and made her way to the rear of the outdoor retreat center, nestled in the pines of Sam Houston National Forest. For two days she'd functioned on pure adrenaline, reveling in the stillness of the woods and listening to God pour out His love through those around her, and now she felt a peak of exhilaration. For the first time, she understood the joy of serving the Lord. Someday she planned to tell her children about the blessings of following Him.

Already a line of women waited for her. A surge of emotion echoed the truth. She, Debra Patterson, had little to offer, but God through her could do so much.

"Thank you for this weekend." A woman near her age took Debra's hand. "I never realized how much I cherished my husband and children until I heard your story. May God bless you."

Another woman could only cry, and Debra wept with her.

"Would you speak at my ladies' Bible study?" a grand-mother asked.

"I'm single," yet another woman said, "and so many times I wished I didn't have my two children to raise alone. I'm so sorry for my selfish thoughts. You've helped me see that I am not alone, and I will never allow those thoughts to stand in the way of my relationship with them or God again."

Hours later, Debra drove home. She'd been one of the last to leave; so many women wanted to talk and pray. Exhaustion had finally caught up with her, and if not for the music blaring in her ears, she'd have pulled over for a nap.

A thought crept over her, the same nagging sensation she knew came from above. A month ago, when she studied Ruth, Debra sensed God tugging at her to take action. She'd allowed foolish pride to determine her steps.

Picking up her cell phone, she turned down the volume on the radio and punched in Cale's home phone. His voice greeted her, strong and robust.

"Hi Cale, this is Debra."

"Hey, what a pleasant surprise. How was your retreat?"

"One of those mountaintop experiences." She laughed and heard her own voice tremble. "I'm not so sure I want to climb down. Right now I'm basking in the afterglow."

"I'd liked to have heard you," he said, "but I guess I'd looked funny with all those women. I'm sure you were great."

"I tried. Anyway, I'd like to ask you something, and this is hard so please bear with me." She took a deep breath. "Does the offer still hold to help me find the children?"

"The door's wide open," he said, and she heard the sincerity.

"Would you like to meet me for lunch after church tomorrow?"

"Absolutely."

❦   ❦   ❦

Debra pulled her car into the parking lot of Hannah's Home-style Restaurant. Her stomach rumbled. She'd skipped breakfast to sleep in from the rigorous weekend, and already she could taste the broccoli-cheese soup and corn bread. Peering around for a parking space, she wondered what kind of car Cale drove. He looked like the sporty type, not a Cadillac or Town Car. Swinging in beside a shiny red pickup, she checked the time and realized she'd arrived nearly ten minutes late.

Her heels clicked across the pavement. She'd asked him for lunch, and he probably assumed she'd stood him up. All night, her thoughts had vacillated between the retreat and meeting with Cale, and the excitement proved overwhelming. A quality, private investigator sounded like a dream—another ray of hope.

She heard Cale call her name, and he waved from the front of the restaurant. His confident stance unnerved her a bit, especially when she felt so insecure around him. The way he carried himself seemed to demand attention, and she hoped he didn't notice the effect he had on her.

"You parked right beside my truck." He grinned like a teenager showing off his prized possession.

She caught a pleasant sparkle in his dark blue eyes. Maybe this wouldn't be so difficult after all. "I didn't know it was yours. I expected more of a. . .city look."

He laughed and she saw he carried a rather thick file folder tucked underneath his arm, and she longed to see what it contained.

"I'm starved." Cale patted his stomach. "I skipped breakfast."

"Me, too," she said, "and this food smells great."

After a brief wait, they were seated at a booth and chatted through the meal about her retreat and his Saturday at the hospital. Both ordered peach cobbler and ice cream for dessert and discovered they both loved strawberry-rhubarb pie. Debra lingered over her cobbler, praying for the courage to bring up the subject of a private investigator.

"Are you ready to talk?" he asked, as if reading her thoughts. He pushed aside his empty plate and took a sip of coffee.

She nodded and met his gaze. "I told you once that I have a difficult time trusting," she began. "Getting to know you as a friend has been a real stretch for me, except you have been kind and understanding—much more patient than I ever imagined. At times, I've been embarrassed at how much you tried and how little I gave in return." She dabbed her mouth with the napkin and scooted her plate toward his. "What I want to say is thank you."

His face softened, accenting his chiseled features. "You're welcome. I'm curious as to what brought about the change."

She brushed a few crumbs from the wooden table. "God's been speaking to me through a study of Ruth and in preparation for the retreat. I kept pushing away His urging to trust you until last evening, but now I'm ready to accept your offer."

"Wonderful." He leaned forward. "I'm honored to be called your friend. You're a strong lady, and I have a lot of admiration for you." He reached down on the bench beside him and produced the file. "I brought along some information for us to go over."

Curiously, she looked at the opened file in an attempt to read the upside-down papers. She made out "children" and "lost" before he turned them sideways for her.

"My guess is you've read all the things ever produced on the Internet about child abduction, but last night I printed everything I could find."

She smiled, pleased with his interest as she leafed through each page and quickly scanned the information. "So far I've seen these sites and saved the information." She stopped and read a page about yet another organization offering online meetings to help those dealing with the pain of abducted children. Like so many groups, they held heartbreaking stories about precious children snatched away from the custodial parent. Some children, like hers, were listed on every site imaginable. She replaced the page and leafed through many more.

"Is it all redundant?" Cale's voice edged with regret. "There's information near the bottom about various PIs. I don't know if having a Web site makes them any better than the next one, but last night I took advantage of being online. I found an extensive list, but I did nail it down to these."

"After I called?" she asked, glancing up. When he nodded, she added, "I appreciate this, really I do."

She continued through the papers until she found the various investigators. One name matched a referral from a large law firm that she'd researched. "This PI is supposed to be good. He's done work for Grimes and Huffman Law Firm and also for Michael." She handed the pages to Cale. "Another firm recommended this next man."

Cale took the information. "Looks like we have a start."

Anxiety wrapped around her emotions. "Do you have any idea what these investigators charge?"

He continued to read, "Yes, I do, several hundred dollars a day for a reputable PI."

"Cale, you could be throwing away your money."

"Do you put a price on your children?" he asked without hesitation.

"No, of course not!"

"Then neither do I."

The thought of her children placed on an auction block appalled her. "You're a very generous man, Cale, and I don't understand why God has allowed me to be the recipient of your kindness, but I am sincerely grateful."

His smile warmed her. "You're welcome. We will simply have to be in prayer about this whole thing until your children are found."

She tilted her head. "You believe they are alive somewhere?"

"I believe God has them in the palm of His hand."

His resolute words strengthened her, urging her not to give up. Still a matter plagued her. "It's important for me to know why you are doing this."

A grieved, faraway look settled in his eyes, and she wondered if he had lost children.

"To ease a guilty conscience," he said after several moments.

Her heart pounded with an inkling of fear. "Why?"

"I had a sister—a beautiful, kind, compassionate woman— and a nephew. I loved them very much, but they were killed in a plane crash."

"I'm sorry," she said, "but I don't understand."

"Although I wasn't piloting the plane, I blame myself." He sighed and leaned back against the booth. "Logic tells me to get on with my life, but it's tough."

"I'm still confused."

"Julie had an abusive husband. He's a doctor, and the stress involved with his work pushed him to take it out on her." Cale's words grew bitter. "She asked me to help her and Daniel get away from him. I did, and the plane crashed killing them both."

Debra's heart quickened. "How could such a tragedy be your fault?" she asked, confused by his confession.

"I arranged for the plane, didn't I?" His eyes narrowed. "And her worthless husband wouldn't even attend the funeral."

Debra studied her friend's face. Clearly, he'd spent many a sleepless night over the loss of his sister and nephew. "Didn't forgiveness ease your pain?"

He raised a brow. "As in forgiving myself?"

"Yes, and your brother-in-law."

His jaw stiffened, and Debra knew exactly what had happened.

"Cale, I'm a baby Christian. I don't know all the Bible stories or have tons of verses memorized, but I do know that until I forgave Michael, his mother, and myself, I had only heartache." She took a deep breath. What she felt compelled to say risked all she held dear. "Don't help me find my children in the hope of easing your conscience, because it won't work."

He said nothing. His features hardened, and he glanced away. "I know you're right," he said. "I've held a grudge against

Kevin for over four years. Even my parents have been able to forgive him, but not me."

"Maybe now is the time."

✑   ✑   ✑

Cale drove back to his condo in a sea of emotion, his mind repeating Debra's words. Maybe she was right. Could his reasons for financing an investigator be purely selfish, a way to bargain with God to release him of his anguish? He'd spent a lot of time here and in Detroit working with kids for the same reason. Understandably, his fondness for them was genuine, but his motives could very well be wrong.

Mom and Dad had encouraged him at Christmas, and Cale knew God would not forgive him his sins until he forgave Kevin. The truth sounded simple. Foolishly simple. Then why couldn't he get down on his knees and talk to God about it? Why couldn't he pick up the phone and call Kevin?

Cale remembered being five years old and stealing a chocolate bar from the drugstore. His dad made him break his piggy bank to pay for the candy and march right back to the store with his confession. Sure would be easier if dear old Dad had done the same for him with Kevin. Except this time, his heavenly Father urged him to make amends.

Once at home, Cale paced the floor until the sun cast dancing shadows through his patio window. Unable to live another moment with the guilt, he dropped to his knees, and for the next hour, he poured out his heart to the One who really cared. He shouted about God's unfairness in taking Julie and Daniel from him. He remembered good times with them.

He wept. And he asked God to forgive him for his hard heart.

Rising, Cale reached for the phone and called Henry Ford Hospital. A moment later, he dialed Kevin's pager and waited for his brother-in-law to return the call. In the slowly settling darkness, he waited until the phone rang. Immediately he recognized Kevin's voice.

"This is Cale," he began, noting his carefully formed words had just left him. He needed to rely only on Him.

"What do you want? Is not seeing me at the hospital where you can offer your barbs in person getting to you?"

"No, that's not why I called."

"Then what is it?"

Cale heard the irritation in Kevin's voice. "I called to ask you to forgive me for the way I've treated you the past four years."

Silence met him.

"Is there a catch?" Kevin laughed.

"No. I can't live with myself, blaming you for Julie and Daniel's deaths."

Kevin expelled a heavy sigh. "Well, I blame you for putting them on that plane."

"Sometimes I do, too."

"You should have kept your nose out of it."

Cale fought the words he wanted to spew at Kevin. God had not called him to judge, but forgive. "It was an accident, and I'm sorry for making your life miserable. I have found God can heal the ache in your heart, Kevin."

"Spare me your sentiments. You know what you can do with your religion. I'm my own man, and I don't need any supernatural mumbo-jumbo."

As much as he disliked the man, Cale felt pity. Suddenly

he realized Kevin's guilt and shame were much worse than his own.

"Neither of us can change what happened," Cale said. "I should have insisted the pilot wait for the weather to clear—"

"Right," Kevin said grimly.

"God helped me deal with their deaths, and He can help you," Cale said.

"This conversation is a waste," Kevin said. "I don't have a need for your God or anything else from you. Don't bother me again."

The phone clicked in Cale's ear. He'd heard and felt his brother-in-law's bitterness. Not until this moment had Cale realized Kevin's misery, the misery eating him like a parasite.

Cale knew he could go on and be the man God intended and leave the past where it should be. In all his personal pain, he never thought he'd pledge to pray for Kevin, but obedience to God ruled out any selfish motives. Helping Debra locate her children must not have been the only reason God led him to Houston. Now he could help her with a clear conscience. Tomorrow they'd begin interviewing PIs and take one more step in finding those children.

chapter 29

Debra stared at October's calendar in the teacher's lounge. She wondered if Chad enjoyed fifth grade. How much had he grown? Next year he'd be in junior high, the same age as the students at her school. Did he have an opportunity to play soccer? How many teeth had her baby girl lost? Did she still cuddle her dolls? Debra hoped no one had cut her thick blond curls. She hoped they had not forgotten her.

Her stomach tightened. Some days, like this one, depression welled up inside her like a bomb threatening to explode. She wanted to give in and cry, but not at school. Her students deserved the best.

Her weeping spells had diminished considerably since the abduction a little over two years ago, and she understood the dangers of turning inward and becoming self-absorbed. Tears were healthy—she'd learned that from Pastor McDaniel—and she fully intended to exercise her right as soon as she drove away from the parking lot. Until then, she had to pray for strength to get through each moment.

The verses from Ecclesiastes, chapter three came to mind. She used this passage frequently in her speaking: *a time to weep and a time to laugh, a time to mourn and a time to dance.* But she wasn't ready to claim a time to search and a time to give up. The thought of God asking her to stop looking for Chad and Lauren haunted her. Surely, He would not.

Promptly at three thirty, she stepped out into an invigorating fall day, and in admiration for the trees nodding in the breeze, she momentarily abandoned her depression.

"Debra," Myra said behind her. "Got a minute?"

She whirled around to see her friend rushing from the building with an armful of books and papers. Her round face and charcoal-colored eyes appeared distracted. "Sure, what's going on?"

"Not me, you," Myra replied, slowing her steps as Debra grabbed a teetering stack of papers. As they stood side by side, Myra caught her breath. "I thought you might need to talk. You haven't been yourself the past few days."

Debra forced a smile. "Oh, I'm all right."

Myra gave her an "I know better" look, just like Debra's mom used to do.

She might as well confess. "Actually, I'm down a bit. Some days are like that, and I'm frustrated with the PI."

"Not getting anywhere?" Her friend's voice softened.

Debra shook her head and pressed her lips firmly together. "We retained him with glowing recommendations, but he seems more interested in collecting his fee than getting out of his office and looking for leads. Anyway, we were pleased in the beginning, but he hasn't turned up a thing."

"Oh, man," Myra said in her typical Jamaican manner.

"For what you're paying him, he should have come up with those children a long time ago."

"Correction, what Cale is paying him, and the amount is astronomical. To be honest, I'm ready to toss this guy."

"Then what?"

Debra shrugged. "Oh, we have names and a list of other private investigators. It's all so discouraging."

"Those children are still on my church's prayer list," Myra said, "and they will be until they come home."

Debra couldn't help but smile at her friend. "You sound like Jill."

Myra's brown face beamed. "It's hope, honey. Faith and trust and hope always brighten our lives. Don't you have a speaking engagement tomorrow night?"

"Sure do. The largest group yet—nearly eight hundred women," Debra said as they walked slowly toward Myra's car.

"Whew, girlfriend. I think you should take to the road!"

Debra felt a breeze pick up the tendrils of her hair and tickle her face, as refreshing as Myra's sweet company. "Truthfully, I'm filled up through the rest of the year."

"I want a copy of your speaking schedule. You pack in the ladies, and I have a few friends who could use a dose of God's power. Are you still volunteering at the hospital?"

"Every chance I get. I really need to get my master's to increase my pay scale. When the kids are home, I'm going to need more money." She waved to another teacher heading home. "Goodness knows how long it will take to pay back Cale."

"Honey, he isn't expecting you to pay him a cent." Myra frowned.

By this time, they'd reached Myra's car. "I know, but I don't want to be a charity case."

Her friend unlocked her back door, and they piled Myra's papers and books onto the seat. She turned and eyed Debra strangely. "Are you two seeing each other?"

Debra felt a slow rise of color. Jill had hinted about the same thing. "Not at all. Are people talking?"

Myra shook her head. "Who would be gossiping? Me? Jill or Drake? Seems to me you and Cale are more than friends."

"Nothing else. He has his agenda, and I have mine. The last thing I need is another man."

"Don't compare Cale and Michael," Myra said.

"I know, like night and day." The thought sounded ludicrous. "But the only thing occupying my mind these days is my relationship with the Lord and finding Chad and Lauren. Anything else will have to wait."

"Can't argue with those priorities." Myra slammed her car door. "Well, I'll be grading papers until the wee hours of the morning unless I leave now."

"Sure. See you tomorrow, and thanks for lifting my spirits. I planned to head home and have a crying session, but I think I'll go over tomorrow night's speech instead." Debra reached to hug her. "Sure glad we're friends. Next time, it's your turn to unload on me."

All during the evening, Debra toyed with the idea of dismissing the investigator—a pleasant man, but congeniality didn't find Chad and Lauren. Shortly after nine, she paged Cale. He replied moments later.

"I want to talk to you about our PI." She doodled on a piece of paper by the phone.

"Your expectations went south, too?" he asked.

"Exactly. I'm disappointed he hasn't gotten any farther with the investigation. Something is missing, Cale, something the police, the FBI, and the PI haven't turned up."

"But what? Last night I wondered if we could do a better job ourselves," he said. "I'm irritated about the lack of progress from these so-called professionals. Think about it, Debra. We have a file with all the information given to these guys, including everything about your children from their Social Security numbers to their blood types. We've utilized software to help with the search, contacted public information brokers, and know more about Michael than ever before."

She recalled learning about Michael's less-than-ethical business practices during the trial, which convicted the man who had been arrested in Mexico. The investigation revealed three other persons who had motives to kill him, including a woman with whom he'd had an affair. She indicated Michael had ended their relationship because she bored him.

"I could spend next summer doing more of what we've already done," Debra said. "At least it would provide time to think about all the information I've given the various agencies. I've turned my brain inside out, but it seems useless."

"Did Steven find out about our investigators?"

"Yes, and he wasn't happy. He insisted the FBI did the best job and reminded me they had helped solve Michael's murder. They still don't know where he lived during the period of time before his death. She fought the urge to cry. "Where do we go from here?"

"I think we need more prayer before we start interviewing again." Frustration crusted his words.

"Cale? Is there something you're not telling me?" Numerous fears swarmed her mind: if he knew something about the children or he'd given up on the search.

"Not at all. I was thinking about a billboard I saw off the Sam Houston Tollway last weekend. It advertised finding missing children. I know I've seen the sign before, but this time it caught my attention."

"Did you write down the number?"

He chuckled. "As a matter of fact, I did—the Web site, too. Do you want to call?"

Debra flipped up a clean sheet on her scribble pad. "Why not? What have we got to lose but more of your money?" She glanced at the clock: *nine thirty.* "Think I'll try now."

"Call me back here at home."

Apprehension mixed with a shot of excitement caused Debra to shiver. What could this new person do that hadn't already been done?

She punched in the number, wondering if anyone would answer at this hour.

"Faith Covenant for Missing Children," a male voice said.

The name startled Debra, and she scrambled for words to continue. A religious organization? "Ah, yes. I need some information about your services. A friend of mine saw your billboard and wrote down your number."

"I find missing children," he said. "I don't post their pictures at Wal-Mart and the local grocery. I don't charge expensive fees. I go out and find them."

Debra faltered her words. "How many have you found?"

"Since 1989 I've returned one hundred twenty-five children to their parents or custodial parent."

His stats sounded incredible. No one had given her such success figures. "How do you conduct your search? The police department, FBI, and a private investigator have been working on this case for over two years."

"First of all, I pray for God's guidance before I take on a client. This is a ministry, and I don't take my calling lightly. I require a ten-page questionnaire, and I need photos with every bit of information you can think of."

Debra's heart hammered against her chest, but then she always had the same reaction to new hope. "I would give you my heart if I thought you needed it. Do you have any references from past clients?"

His chair squeaked, and she heard what sounded like a drawer open and shut. "Yes, and I can do better than that. With your address, I'll send you a packet of information, including articles from *World* magazine and the *Houston Chronicle*, which explain my methods of locating children. Would you like my Web address, too?"

"I have it," Debra said. "Can you mail the packet tomorrow?"

"Of course. What's your name and address?"

Debra quickly rattled off her information.

"I remember your situation," he said, as though recalling the particulars. "I've been praying for your children's return."

Chill bumps raced up her arm. He knew about Chad and Lauren? "Thank you. Perhaps you can do even more."

"And it's been two years since they were abducted?"

"Yes, sir, two years in August. Excuse me, but I don't know your name." She held her pen so tightly her fingers cramped.

"Jordon Jackson. You can reach me at this number day or night."

She cleared her throat and willed her nerves to settle. "Mr. Jackson, I don't put a price on my children, but what are your fees?"

"If you don't have any money, then my services are free. If you want to compensate me, then I'm grateful."

At last Debra sensed hope, like a budding flower ready to burst into bloom. She prayed this would not be one more disappointment. "You may be an answer to prayer," she said. "I wish I had your information now."

"Would you like to pick it up tonight?"

"Oh, yes, very much."

"Let me give you directions. I'm on the southwest side of town. Take 59 south to. . ."

As soon as she hung up, Debra grabbed her purse while phoning Cale. "I'm going after the packet of material now," she said. "He might be just another fraud, but his claims may be valid."

"Wait, I want to go with you. Curiosity is driving me crazy. Besides, I don't think it's wise for you to drive this late at night to a stranger's house."

"But, Cale, I can handle this," she said. He'd done so much for her, and for once, she wanted to reciprocate.

"I'm a stubborn man, and I'm on my way to your apartment. We can ask him questions together and see if he's legitimate."

chapter 30

Debra scanned Jordon Jackson's ten-page questionnaire. She wanted to complete it right there and have him start his investigation tomorrow morning. Suddenly doubts flared. Could Jordon be too good to be true? She wondered if she could handle any more failures from professionals who claimed success. Cale, on the other hand, appeared relaxed as he asked Jordon questions and jotted down the answers.

She studied the investigator before her. His well-over-two-hundred-pound frame and muscular physique probably helped when it came to fending for himself in rough circumstances. The more he talked, the more she realized his altruistic qualities.

"How did you get interested in this line of work?" Cale asked.

Jordon inhaled deeply. "When I was eight years old, my mother abducted me from my dad. They'd divorced right after my birth, and he was awarded custody. We moved around a lot, and Mom told me the courts had decided I should live with her. Anyway, when I was thirty-two, I finally found my dad. He'd all but given up on ever seeing me again. We had a great reunion. Dad led me to Jesus. An awesome experience." He paused. "Not long after that, I felt God drawing me into a ministry of helping parents find abducted kids. Let me make it clear here that I pray over every case, because not every parent who seeks my services is the proper parent for the child. I have to walk hand-in-hand with the Lord to discern what He wants me to do."

"Have you ever broken the law?" Cale's face revealed no emotion, as though Jordon were on trial.

"I make every effort to obey the law. The Bible instructs us to do so. But if I feel God is moving me to take a step that is contrary to what the law states, I obey God. I realized a long time ago that I might spend time in jail for helping people."

"Thanks. I appreciate your honesty," Cale said. "As soon as Debra returns the form, then you can get started?"

"Yes, immediately," Jordon said. "I've read enough about your case to know this is a God-sized project. I prayed before you came about taking it on, and I believe the Lord would have me offer my services."

"Excellent." Cale crossed his legs. "Right now, do you see any holes in what the FBI and the past PI have done?"

Debra glanced up from her reading, every nerve tuned to his response.

"Can't tell," Jordon said, "and I'm thinking out loud here. My gut reaction is that Michael's mother doesn't have a clue to the whereabouts of her grandchildren. She'd have managed to visit them by now. I think the answer lies in the three suspected killers. . . . Maybe not them, but through them."

Puzzled, Debra stole a look at Cale then back to Jordon. "I don't understand."

"This is purely speculation," Jordon said, his blue eyes clear as glass. "Michael skimmed money off the top of his law firm and stashed it away. Obviously, he used the funds to start an import/export business. With Michael's greed, I imagine he made other enemies, as well as the ones brought to light in the Mexican investigation. I really don't think an ambitious man like Michael would take on all the facets of abducting his children without a little help."

Cale fought off a yawn and shook his head in obvious need of sleep. "I agree. So what are you suggesting?"

"I'm thinking of snooping with a heavy dose of prayer for direction."

Debra trembled. "A woman," she whispered. "A woman to help with Chad and Lauren—and give him emotional support."

"It's a thought," Jordon said.

Silence reigned across the small office.

"No one has suggested this before," Debra said. "Oh, I imagine the FBI considered it, especially when a woman was questioned in regards to his murder."

"We all need to pray about this," Jordon said.

"What's in this for you?" Cale asked.

"To see families reunited," he replied. "That's why I need proof of the custodial parent, marriage licenses, divorce decrees, and whatever legal documents available. My interest is in the welfare of the children."

Debra took a deep breath. "Why do you feel you're successful when others have failed?"

"Tenacity," Jordon said. "It doesn't do a bit of good to pray about something and not do the work God requires of me. In fact, let's have a word of prayer before you leave."

"Good idea." Cale took Debra's hand into his.

"Heavenly Father-God, we come before You asking for

direction and wisdom in locating Debra's children. Keep them safe under the shadow of angels' wings. May they find food, shelter, and love until they are brought home to their mother. Enlarge our territories, Father. Give us supernatural strength and insight so that, in finding Chad and Lauren, You will be glorified. In Jesus' name, amen."

After midnight, Debra crawled into bed. Her body screamed for sleep, but she doubted if her mind would succumb to it. Her thoughts repeated every portion of tonight's meeting. She'd read the articles about Jordon and listened to his statement of faith on a cassette tape.

In the course of securing missing children, he'd spent a week in a Mexican jail, dodged bullets in Iraq, survived a month in the wilds of South Africa, and pulled a teenage girl from a religious commune in California. He'd been beaten, threatened, and considered a saint. Because of his commitment to children, he had volunteers who assisted him in areas of language barriers and international negotiations. If the reports of his exploits were true, Jordon had earned the title of "Mighty Giant."

She agreed to meet him the next night in order to return the questionnaire and the other requested information. Despite her uncertainties about his rather eccentric and bizarre methods of tracking down children, she wanted to trust him.

In the darkness, Debra opened her eyes and stared at the ceiling. "He may be able to find Chad and Lauren," she said. "Oh, Lord, let it be so."

꿍 꿍 꿍

At 1:00 a.m., Cale powered down his computer and resigned

himself to bed. The evening's events rolled against his brain like water slapping against the side of a boat. He'd learned more about finding lost kids than he'd ever known before. Jordon Jackson knew his stuff, plus he called his work a ministry.

Tonight Jordon initiated prayer—a simple request for God's hand to lead them. A Christian investigator had Cale's vote anytime, especially one who delivered what he claimed. Of course, only God gave guarantees.

The all-too-familiar suspicion entered his mind and slammed the door. What if Debra's kids weren't lost or missing but lying in an unmarked grave? Cale despised himself for allowing such disquieting thoughts. He wanted those children returned unhurt and with a minimum of painful memories. Many times, he envisioned Debra's smiling face with each arm wrapped around a child. Once again Cale remembered only God could handle his request.

All during the next day, Cale considered phoning Jordon. When he finally closed his last patient's chart, the notion flared up again. Tossing aside his usual qualms about not being a member of Debra's family and hesitant to take the initiative about the case, he pulled Jordon's number from his wallet. The man's business cards certainly weren't the best card stock, and his home office looked shabby, smelled musty, too. The furnishings, although clean, resembled rejects from the Salvation Army. Obviously, Jordon could upgrade, if he charged a decent fee, but many of his clients probably didn't have any money, and Cale had seen enough investigators driven by pecuniary motives. Lack of funds shouldn't stop a parent from locating missing children, and Jordon had taken on many of their challenges.

Cale lifted a half-full bottle of water to his lips and took a long drink. *Find your guts, Doctor. Pick up the phone, and make the call.* Shaking his head, he punched in the numbers.

"Jordon, this is Cale Thurston. How's your day going?"

"Business as usual. What can I do for you?"

"I understand Debra is bringing by the papers for you this afternoon. With your track record, both of us are hopeful. I do have a concern, however, and I'd rather not voice it in front of her."

"I wonder if it's the same as mine," Jordon said.

"The likelihood of those two children being alive?" Cale despised his own fears.

A moment passed before Jordon replied. "Yes, but it's a possibility in all of these cases. We have to believe and work toward the opposite end of the spectrum."

"I agree. My request is this: If you discover Debra's children are, in fact, dead, I'd like to be present when you tell her."

"Most definitely so. I can tell you care deeply about Mrs. Patterson, and if our findings reveal a tragedy, she'll need all the support she can get."

Cale jerked to attention. He thought he'd kept his emotions guarded. With the present state of things, Debra didn't need her life complicated with his profession of love. "She's a great lady, and I want the best for her."

"I agree."

He felt as if he needed to say more, to clarify his position in Debra's life. "We're good friends with a common goal—finding her children."

"Then we're all friends together," Jordon said, and Cale silently praised his subtlety.

"One more thing," Cale said. "I intend to pay for your time and reimburse you for all the expenses. If you'd keep track of them for me, I'd appreciate it."

"I don't charge, Dr. Thurston. I'd prefer you make a donation at the close of our dealings."

Cale chuckled. "You don't give me much choice. A donation it is."

&p   &p   &p

Two weeks later, Cale drove to Debra's apartment on Saturday evening. He hoped he wasn't imposing with his unannounced arrival. Debra hadn't been at the hospital today; a speaking engagement had forced her to cancel her volunteer work. He wanted to discuss Jordon, to see how she felt about his progress. Uneasiness settled upon Cale. How low of him to use Jordon as an excuse to see her.

Who am I fooling? The realization hit him with the force of a cannonball. Although they'd never touched each other, except to hold hands in prayer, Cale had fallen in love with Debra.

He couldn't do this. His impetuous act was not fair to her. Taking advantage of a woman in a distress mode listed as pretty low on anyone's scale. Her life lay in turmoil, and she needed friendship to see her through—nothing else implied. He pulled into a gas station and turned his truck around to head back to the medical center.

Calling Debra made more sense. She answered on the third ring, and her sweet voice tugged at his heartstrings.

"Hi, Debra. This is Cale. I won't take up your time since

you're probably exhausted from the retreat."

"Oh, I'm fine. How nice of you to call."

Be glad I'm not at your front door. "The retreat went well?"

"Very nice. There were about one hundred women, and five of them made professions of faith."

He smiled. Her speaking engagements always seemed to usher in God's presence. "Keep going, and someone will want you to write Bible curriculum."

"I don't think so, but thanks for the boost."

He took a breath. "Debra, all of this with Jordon has happened so fast, and I'd like to discuss his progress."

She failed to answer, and he knew from experience that she often took time to think through her response. "I have church in the morning, and Jill and Drake invited me to lunch."

"What about the afternoon?"

"I'm not sure. I do have papers to grade." She hesitated. "But I'd rather get together."

"What about the zoo? Or a museum and dinner?"

"A museum, but there's no need for dinner. You've spent plenty of money on me without adding more."

"We have to eat—doctor's orders."

"All right." She laughed. "We can talk about it tomorrow."

"How about I pick you up around two thirty?"

"Sure."

"Have you heard from Jordon?"

"Yesterday. He has his preliminary work done. And you'll never guess, but he wiggled himself into Michael's mother's house."

He loved the lilt in her voice. "How did he convince her to let him in?"

"He said charm, but I've never known her to be easy prey. Jordon is convinced she hasn't a clue to the children's whereabouts."

"Where from here?" Cale asked.

"Well, he's been to Chad and Lauren's old school, interviewed neighbors, talked to Michael's ex-partner, and secured a list of their past clients, some of whom he's spoken to, and he's flying to Mexico City tonight. He plans to stay in the same hotel where Michael stayed before the murder."

"Our man is busy," Cale said, "and certainly faster than our other investigators."

"I'm pleased—very pleased—with his actions so far," she said. "Enough about me. What have you been doing?"

"Performing surgeries and seeing patients." He palmed his forehead. "I nearly forgot. I'm supposed to look into chartering a boat for a deep-sea fishing tour. A couple of doctors said it would be a great trip, and I got elected to schedule it since I'm the only single guy. Do you want to come?"

"No, thanks. I don't do well on boats. Michael used to deep-sea fish. In fact, quite often."

"Who did he use?"

"A company in Galveston. Hold on a minute while I grab the phone book. The name is right on the tip of my tongue."

While he waited for her to return, he wondered how he'd managed to slip in the invitation when it hadn't occurred to him before.

"Here it is: Gulf Coast Charters," Debra said.

"Let me write down the number." Cale snatched up a pen and paper from the console while she rattled it off. "Thanks. This helps a lot."

"Don't know how I forgot about his fishing weekends," Debra said. "Those were the only times he came home in a good mood."

Cale immediately surmised the man either loved fishing or had a lady friend and used fishing as an excuse. Another thought assaulted him. "You said you forgot about his deep-sea fishing. Does that mean you've never told anyone about it?"

He heard her draw in an unsteady breath. "Oh, Cale, I've never told a soul. I don't even know who he went with on those weekends."

Cale glanced at his watch. "I imagine Jordon's left by now. We'll have to tell him when he gets back."

"Cale," she said, "can we visit Gulf Coast Charters tomorrow instead of doing something else?"

Her request startled him. "Of course. Are you thinking of doing a little PI work on our own?"

"Yes. It may mean nothing, but that's exactly what I want to do."

chapter 31

On Sunday afternoon as Debra and Cale strolled toward Pier 19 and Gulf Coast Charters, the scent of fish tickled her nostrils, and seagulls called out overhead. It all seemed peaceful against the trepidation raging inside her.

She desperately wanted to find out if the owner of the charter service knew anything about Michael's dealings, but she felt a little sneaky. Then again, Michael had been the ultimate deceiver.

"Play the role as my friend. You know what I mean. You're accompanying me while I check on their fishing trips." Cale brushed her shoulder with his. They were dressed in khaki shorts and T-shirts—two people out for a day of sun and fun.

"I never did well as an actress," Debra said. "I'm so shaky." She noted the breeze coming off the gulf, a pleasant change from the summer months. She wished it could calm her ragged nerves. "All along I've wanted to do something to help find Chad and Lauren, and now that I might have the opportunity, I'm afraid I'll do or say something wrong. Then again, this man probably knows nothing."

"Just remember you really are my friend." He offered a quirky smile. "Aren't you keeping me company while I check on the charter tours?"

"Of course." She took a deep breath to convince herself. "We might even prove ourselves as amateur detectives." She met his gaze. "Really, I don't want to build up my hopes."

"I know." He took her hand. His touch comforted her, and once again, she thanked God for blessing her with this godly man's friendship.

Moments later, they stepped into the tiny, dingy office of Gulf Coast Charters. She glanced about the male-occupied domain and noted a half-dozen pictures of saltwater fish, various bathing beauties, and two rod-and-reel calendars. An eerie sensation crept over her. Michael had spent a lot of time here, a place where she'd never been.

"Good afternoon," Cale said to a balding, latte-colored man seated behind a cluttered desk. When the man glanced up, Cale extended his hand. "I'm Dr. Cale Thurston, and this is Debra. I'd like to have some information about your deep-sea fishing tours."

The man stood, looking very much the part of one who made his living by the sea. Dressed in white shorts and a blue-striped pullover, his casual appearance plus a brilliant white smile should have made her feel welcome, but it didn't.

"Pleasure to meet you Dr. Thurston." He nodded to her. "And you, too, Debra. My name is Nicholas Sagliarino; call me Nic. I own this place. Can I offer you folks something to drink? A soda? Bottle of water?"

Cale released Nic's hand and glanced at Debra. "What about you? I'd like a bottle of water."

"So would I." She offered Nic a smile. "The temperature in here is much nicer than outside."

"I agree." Nic retrieved three bottles from a small refrigerator. He continued his pleasantries. "Thanks for stopping by. Do you have a date in mind for your fishing trip?"

Cale pulled a personal digital assistant from his shirt pocket. "The first weekend in November."

He handed Debra and Cale their drinks, and while standing, he leafed through the planner lying open on his desk. "We can accommodate you. How many will be in your party, and how many days?"

"Seven people total, and for one day." Cale's good-natured tone amazed her. "We're all doctors anxious for a little rest and relaxation."

At times, she envied Cale's affable ways. He didn't appear to be the least bit nervous.

Nic jotted down the information then handed Cale a brochure. "This tells what we do and what to expect while we're out at sea. It also includes pricing."

Cale handed the brochure to Debra, and she took a quick glimpse at the colorful cover of happy people catching lots of fish before tucking it into her shoulder bag.

"Do you have any pictures of past cruises?" Cale asked.

Nic grinned broadly. "Sure do. Why don't you two have a seat and take a look?" He pointed to a couple of worn chairs nestled between a door and the wall. On one of them sat a royal blue picture album.

"Thanks," Cale said, and Debra followed him to the chairs.

With trembling legs, she sat beside Cale and together they studied each page. Smiling faces in glossy color prints displayed catches of red snapper and kingfish. Other photos were fishermen raising their arms in a toast or simply posing for a group shot.

"Not everyone cares to look at those." Nic lifted a bottle of water to his lips and took a seat at his desk. "But I keep adding more pictures in hopes folks might be interested."

"These are great," Cale said, not lifting his gaze from the album.

Near the back of the photographs, Debra spotted Michael with Nic and an attractive, blond-haired woman. She stood in the middle, and the men had their arms wrapped around her shoulders. Regret raced through Debra's senses. Michael rarely looked this happy at home. Old poignant accusations about her inadequacy flashed across her mind. She pushed the thoughts away. Michael had made his own choices about his life. A tear fell, and she hastily wiped it away.

"There." She pointed to the photograph.

"Hey, I see an attorney I once knew." Cale's enthusiasm equaled any actor she'd ever seen. He turned the album so Nic could view the page. "Michael Patterson."

He cleared his throat. "Yeah, that's him."

Cale ignored Nic's obvious indifference and continued to stare at the picture. "Is the woman his wife?"

Nic peered out a window. "No, she's my wife, or rather was. We divorced over three-and-a-half years ago."

Cale glanced up. "Sorry to hear that. I knew Patterson had a reputation as a ladies' man, and I thought. . ." He grimaced. "Looks like I put my foot in my mouth."

Nic waved his hand then grabbed his bottle of water. "Don't worry about it. But you're right, Patterson was about as faithful as a stray cat—and he did enjoy my wife's company."

Debra nibbled at the corner of her mouth, unable to lift her gaze to Nic. Suddenly she felt dirty for deceiving this poor man who appeared to grieve the loss of his wife.

Cale closed the album and handed it to Nic. "Thanks. I believe we're all set here as long as you have the day reserved. I'd like to put the deposit on my credit card."

"I can do that."

While Nic processed the card and wrote Cale a receipt, Debra glanced about the office. There, on the far corner of his desk sat a small picture of his ex-wife. *He still loves her.*

Cale gripped the man's hand. "We'll be in touch. Call me if anything comes up."

"Sure." Nic returned the shake. "You and your friends will have a great trip. There's nothing better than deep-sea fishing to help a man relax." He nodded at Debra. "Pleased to meet you."

Outside the office, she felt dizzy, incoherent. Taking a deep breath, she lifted her chin and strolled alongside Cale.

"Are you okay?" he asked, reaching for her hand. "You're shaking."

"I'm fine." Debra watched two boys race by them on skates. They looked to be Chad's age. She swallowed the ache for her children and squeezed his hand. "What do we do now?"

"I think we need to let Jordon know what we learned today. Nic's wife may have been one of many, but it needs to be checked out."

"What about the FBI agent?"

"Yes, but after we talk to Jordon." She felt a twinge of sadness and hopefulness entwined in a strange swirl of emotions. "I have Jordon's cell number at my apartment."

He flashed a wide grin. "I have his number in my truck."

A surge of excitement raced through her veins. "Good. We can call right away."

While they made their way back to the truck, Debra replayed Nic's every word and mannerism. "Do you think this is a possible link to my children?"

He nodded and paused before replying. "I'm wondering if we have stumbled onto something, especially since no one knew about his fishing ventures."

"My negligence." Debra fought the urge to condemn herself for forgetting Michael's Galveston trips. She shook her head to dispel the thoughts. "But it is valuable information, and we have it now, although the FBI probably has known about it since the beginning."

"But they haven't found your children. We have new hope, Debra."

chapter 32

Debra laid Cale's phone on the truck seat. So much to think about, so much she dared to hope and believe. Sometimes when she shut her eyes, she could hear her precious children's voices, not hauntingly as in the past, but calling for her to be patient. Love whispered her name over the barriers of miles and time. Soon they would be with her again. She heard it in the wind, God's reassurance touching her in His ineffable whisper. Sometimes she wondered how God's love could be greater than a mother's, but she knew it to be true. She felt it every minute of the day.

"Are you okay?" Cale asked.

She'd been so engrossed in her own reflections that his voice startled her. "I'm sorry." She glanced at her folded hands, embarrassed by her billowing emotions. "I was thinking and caught up in prayer and worship, all at the same time." She tilted her head, knowing her confession didn't hold true to her reticent personality.

"Oh, Debra, I don't want you to be disappointed," he said.

The timbre of his voice told her what she suspected, but she couldn't confront him with it. Not now. Better Cale believe she knew nothing of his feelings for her, especially when she didn't understand the way her heart lifted at the sound of his voice.

"I'll be all right." She turned her attention his way. "I know many believe Chad and Lauren are gone, but I refuse to bury them until I see their little graves. They are in God's care. . . somewhere."

"Debra, I'm here for you," Cale said. "I am with you for as long as you need me."

"I know." Debra turned away from his gaze, determined, as she had so many times before, to be strong. "I need to tell you what Jordon said."

His concern changed to a faint smile, and for the moment, she could push away what she'd heard in his words and seen in his eyes. "First of all, he hasn't learned much in Mexico City, but he wants to stay two more days. Just like the FBI, he's found nothing to substantiate anyone ever accompanied Michael on his trips to Mexico. Jordon looked into the four nights Michael stayed at the Camino Real in February. A bartender at the hotel said Michael drank heavily, which is so unusual for him. He prided himself on staying in control."

Cale nodded. "I remember you said he wasn't a drinker."

"I'm wondering, or maybe I'm hoping, he had some regrets," Debra said. "Cale, he changed so much over the years. In the beginning, we shared the same dreams and aspirations. None of them bordered on anything illegal. It just troubles me that his priorities changed from family to greed and selfishness." She shrugged. "Guess I'll never know what ruled his mind."

"Did Jordon have anything else to report?"

"I'm sorry, didn't mean to get carried away. The bartender

also said Michael was surly and tried to pick fights with the other patrons. The management asked him to leave each night." Debra stared out the window at the traffic building up on I-45 heading back into Houston. "I don't recall Michael ever being drunk, and he thought too highly of himself to pick a fight—at least one where he might lose."

"Alcohol affects people differently."

"I know, but I'm wondering if his belligerence got him killed." She shook her head. "He could level anyone with his sarcasm."

"What did Jordon have to say about the Sagliarinos?"

Immediately she felt a tingling in her stomach. "He sounded optimistic, and he will get on it as soon as he returns." She tossed Cale a wide grin. "He called us Christian sleuths and asked if we wanted a job."

Cale chuckled. "I can see his brochure: 'Cardiovascular surgeon and junior high history teacher resign from current careers to help parents find missing children.' "

"You're already doing that," Debra said. "And doing a terrific job, I might add."

He reached across the seat for her hand, and she considered pulling it back. But deep inside the abyss of her heart, she'd found a special spot for Cale, and she didn't want to let go.

"You know, don't you," he said, his attention glued to the highway. "I'm having a tough time disguising it."

"My heart has a wall around it," she said. "All I can think about are my children."

"I understand. I'm not asking or expecting anything in return. I simply wanted you to know."

She'd rather he hadn't brought up the topic, but now that

he had, she must be honest. "Cale, your friendship is priceless. You've shown me the traits of a true man of God, something I hadn't seen before except in my friend Jill's husband and in my pastor. If any man could ever reach me again, it would be you."

      ip   *ip*   *ip*

On Wednesday Jordon phoned Debra and announced he'd returned to Houston.

"I'm heading to Galveston in the morning," he said in the same excited tone she'd come to recognize as part of his personality. She and Cale had decided he worked on adrenaline alone. "I should be back sometime tomorrow night or Friday. I want to thoroughly investigate the Sagliarino couple and their connection to Michael."

"Did you learn anything more in Mexico?" she asked.

"No, nothing more than I told you on Sunday. Chased down a few loose ends and rumors, but nothing to lead me to believe your children were ever there. The FBI does a good job, Debra, but I had to check on a few things myself."

Debra groped for words but failed to find a reply that would not give away her disillusionment.

"This trip cleared up any doubts about your children living in Mexico," he went on, as if sensing her mood. "We can now move on to something else."

"I know, and I appreciate what you've done." She realized her words sounded flat and insincere, but she couldn't muster the energy to feign optimism.

"I'll call as soon as I finish in Galveston," Jordon said.

Debra replaced the phone and took a deep cleansing

breath—the kind needed to rid her mind of misgivings about Jordon's ability to find Chad and Lauren.

She needed to talk to Jill; she'd boost her spirits by the mere sound of her voice. The idea of phoning Cale tempted her, but with his confession on Sunday, she decided against it. The last thing she wanted to do was lead him on or abuse their friendship. Debra stood and wrapped her arms around her shoulders. She'd actually begun praying for God's will concerning Cale. Everything, absolutely everything in her life belonged to the Father, and she refused to make any decisions without His leading.

Sinking onto her sofa, she realized talking to Jill made sense. Although they'd been together on Sunday for church and lunch, Debra hadn't told her about Jordon. Her friend would sense the need to help Debra release those lingering emotions threatening to take a bite out of her strength in the Lord. Snatching up the phone, she lightly pressed in Jill's number.

In the minutes that followed, Debra carefully explained to her friend the findings of the past several days.

"The other investigators weren't Christian," Jill said. "We both know the value of prayer, and the new investigator obviously seeks the Lord in what he does."

"I'm very hopeful." Debra curled up on the sofa and tucked her legs under her.

"Maybe a little scared?" Jill asked.

Debra smiled. "A lot scared. I visited with a woman at one of my speaking engagements who said finding her children proved as frightening as not knowing their whereabouts. They'd been living in filth like little animals."

"Talk to me, Debra. You sound like you're carrying a big load here."

"I knew I called you for a reason." Debra twisted the phone cord around her fingers. "I feel Jordon will find them, and deep down I believe they're alive and well. But sometimes when I reach a brick wall, the idea of them being abused or worse is more than I can handle. The not knowing may be easier than finding out the truth." A cold shudder overtook her body. "Does this mean my faith is not strong enough?"

"Not at all," Jill said. "You're human, and you need prayer and support. Who knows? What you and Cale discovered might lead in a positive direction."

"True. Guess I'm having a case of the blues, but talking to you has made me feel better. Thanks, Jill, you've always been there for me—even when I didn't deserve it."

"Hey, it goes both ways. Remember right after the Fourth of July, when I returned from my sister's house with the news of her third pregnancy? I was so jealous and angry at God, but you lifted me right out of a huge depression."

How well Debra remembered. Jill had cried buckets, pleading with God for a child. When neither Drake nor Pastor McDaniel could help, Debra and Jill spent a weekend at a bed-and-breakfast. They rode horses at a nearby stable, and Jill gave her riding lessons. Through tears, prayer, and encouragement, Jill climbed out of the dark hole. "I remember," Debra said. "It's a small thing when you give to a friend."

"My point exactly."

⌘　　⌘　　⌘

Debra rubbed her palms together, tucked her hair behind her ears, then patted her foot against the floorboard of Cale's truck.

"I'm going as fast as I can," Cale said, "without breaking the speed limit."

She smiled. "Shows that much, huh?"

"I'm anxious, too. Jordon said he 'found out some interesting information.' " Cale mimicked the big man's deep voice. "Couldn't he have told you more?"

"I asked," Debra said. "He said he preferred talking to us in person." She glared at a minivan traveling at a snail's pace. "But he sounded excited—as usual. I can only imagine how his hyperactivity drove his parents and teachers nuts."

Cale flipped on his left turn signal and passed the minivan. "I agree. Right now I feel like one of those storm chasers—maybe I need another analogy."

"Yes, me, too," Debra said. "I've been in the middle of a whirlwind for over two years. I did find shelter, though."

He smiled. "I love your way of looking at things, Debra. With all my grandiose education, I'll never have your ability to philosophize a situation."

She laughed, the first time since last Sunday. "I'm a Christian woman. We're supposed to see the world in a different perspective."

Twenty minutes later, Cale knocked on Jordon's office door. Debra's knees weakened. Surely, with the turmoil racing inside her, the news would be good.

"Sit down." Jordon motioned to the same chairs they'd used at their previous meeting. "I won't mince words. Let's get right to business."

"Good. I'm a nervous wreck," Debra said. "Tell me it's good news, Jordon."

"Maybe so." Jordon's tone sounded gentle in contrast to

his huge frame. He pulled a chair from behind his desk and placed it in front of Debra and Cale. "Let me tell you what I found out, and you two be the judge. Michael and Helene Sagliarino were having an affair long before the time of the children's disappearance. In fact, she had obtained a divorce and left the country to go back to her hometown in Germany about six months before Michael abducted the children. She's never returned to the States."

"Why didn't Nic come forward with this information when Debra's children were taken?" Cale asked, irritation rising in his voice. "Or when authorities found Michael's body?"

Jordon shook his head. "My guess is he didn't pay much attention to the abduction, simply because he'd buried himself in his work after Helene left him. As far as offering information after the murder, frankly, I don't imagine he wanted to get involved. Sagliarino is a private person. No one knew about the problems in his marriage until after the divorce. He loved his wife very much—my guess is he still does."

Debra remembered the picture of Helene on Nic's desk. Uneasiness swept over her. "Shouldn't the FBI have discovered this information?"

"Yes, if they haven't already, but remember they didn't have this lead. Nic would have been the only link."

Cale cleared his throat. "Are you going to the FBI with this before or after a trip to Germany?"

Jordon's gaze bore into Cale. "After. Helene is living in Celle. It may be a wild lead, but my guess is either she has those children or knows their whereabouts."

Debra gasped and felt herself grow pale. "I'm going with you. I can't wait here."

chapter 33

"Not yet," Jordon said. He pulled his chair closer to Debra and took her hand into his. "I need you here, to be my prayer support."

Debra swallowed hard. Her lips quivered, and she willed her frenzied nerves to calm. "What could be more important than finding my children? I'm their mother."

"This is a hunch, not a definite," Jordon said. "I don't have any proof Chad and Lauren are in Germany. My only lead is that Helene originally lived in Celle, and her maiden name was Schmidt. She may be in any country for all we know."

"How does Germany view abducted children?" Debra rummaged through her mind for what she'd read about this country's interpretation of international abductions.

"Not in our favor," Jordon said. "They are very loyal to their citizens and believe if an abducted child has a German parent, then the child needs to remain in Germany. In short, governmental agencies would need to step in and prove your parentage."

"But Michael is dead. I'm the only surviving parent."

Debra searched the faces of Jordon then Cale and back again. "How can they keep me from my children?"

Jordon placed his other hand on top of Debra's, like a doctor forced to give a heartbreaking diagnosis. "We don't know anything yet, but bear in mind Michael changed his identity and possibly married Helene. I believe the German government would assist us, but that may take a little while. Let's see what I can find first."

Debra remembered the wedding band on Michael's finger.

"If we find the children, then we'll pray about which avenue to take," Jordon continued. "I'm afraid I might have you all worked up for nothing. Please remember this may all amount to nothing."

She nibbled on her lip. "I. . .I understand. Can I do anything? What about passports?"

Jordon patted her hand. "There's no point in wasting your time and money until we have something substantial."

Debra leaned forward. "It'll give me something to do. Michael took their birth certificates, but I've obtained legal copies and can use those for identification."

Jordon's hesitance showed in the lines on his face. "Okay, just in case we're blessed with success."

"Jordon," Cale said, "I want to go with you."

"I operate better alone. Who knows how long I'll be there? I require little sleep, and I'm always on the go."

"Two can work twice as fast, and I know what it's like to work without sleep."

Jordon continued to deny Cale's offer. "What about your schedule? Don't you have surgeries to perform? Patients to see?"

"I can rearrange things and be gone a few days. It's important to me, and I'm not sure I can give you a reason why, except I'm committed to help in every way possible."

"You two certainly are a stubborn pair." Jordon expelled a frustrated breath. He stood and paced the small room. "Cale, the company does sound good, and you could drive while I make notes and look. If we could share a room, we could also bounce off ideas." He hesitated. "How quickly can you be ready to leave?"

"I'll phone you tomorrow shortly after noon. I have two surgeries in the morning at eight and ten thirty."

Jordon turned to Debra. "How do you feel about this?"

She wanted to cry and plead, but whining fell under the classification of immature. "I guess if Cale can be of more help, then it's best he accompany you. Just call me as soon as you know anything."

"Of course we will," Jordon said. "There's a seven-hour time difference, but I don't imagine you care about when we contact you. By the way, I have a global cellular."

That night Debra's body refused to give in to sleep. Her mind argued with her heart. *Don't get so excited. This could very well be nothing.* She didn't dare think about the horror of another woman claiming to be Chad and Lauren's mother.

She adjusted her pillow, turned on her radio to classical music, drank a glass of milk, and read her Bible. Still, her body refused to relax. Her mind spun with how Chad and Lauren must look by now, and how magnificent their reunion would be. She walked through the darkened shadows of her apartment to the spare bedroom. Both children would have to sleep there until she could afford a bigger place. Maybe she could make half of it look like a boy's room and the other half like a girl's. Better yet, she'd give up her bedroom since it was larger, and she'd move into the smaller room.

What about clothes? She guessed about sizes, but the two would most likely want to pick out their own. Social Security from Michael provided extra income—a college fund for each of them. She had money left from the house and the antiques, but those funds belonged to Cale for all of his expenses.

And counseling. Yes, the three of them needed Pastor McDaniel and his gentle ways of helping people work through tough issues. She must never, absolutely never, speak of Michael in a derogatory manner.

Debra's heart pounded. Oh, the joy of explaining Jesus to them and seeing them come to know the Lord. Imagine, all three of them attending church and Sunday school like a real family—well, almost a real family.

God may have in mind for her to marry again one day. An image of Cale rose, as did a reminder of his tender mannerisms with children. She'd be a liar if she did not admit her attraction to this dear man. She appreciated the way his hair fell unruly across his forehead above those incredibly dark blue eyes.

Debra touched the rough grain of her Bible and praised God for her teaching position. The children could spend the summer with her: swimming lessons, picnics, long walks in the park, the zoo. Chad would be old enough for church camp, and she could go along as a counselor. In her joy, the tears began to flow. Slipping to her knees with only the light from a silver slice of moon gracing the spare bedroom, Debra poured out her heart.

"Oh, dear Lord, let it be true. Help Jordon find my babies. Please give me another chance to be a godly mother. I can't give them the material things they once had with Michael, but I can show them the blessings of following You." She started to rise, but paused. "I'm not making any deals, Lord. I'm begging for my children."

Debra stood as a sense of peace—the same relief she'd known in the past—flowed through her body. Unexplainable, unfathomable love rained on her. No matter the outcome, no matter how painful or penetrating the grief, God was still enough. God would always be enough.

✑   ✑   ✑

Cale sat at his desk and stared at the picture of Julie and Daniel. He no longer felt the guilt of the past, only cherished memories of his dear sister and nephew. The burden of their deaths vanished the night he'd called Kevin. Cale remembered the joy in his parents' voices when he told them about forgiving Kevin and himself. The mere act lifted the burden he'd carried for so long, and it cemented his relationship with the Lord. Why did man insist upon making life miserable when God offered a way out?

Cale spoke to Jordon shortly before noon and told him he could free up his schedule in two days' time and be ready to fly to Germany. His patients would be under the care of a valued friend and cardiologist in his absence. He felt confident his practice would be in capable hands, and even more self-assured that he was doing exactly what God intended. Strange and wonderful how God worked things. Cale could only pray he and Jordon learned the whereabouts of Debra's children, and the two were alive. Odd, he'd begun to think of Chad and Lauren as his own, perhaps a reality in due time. Certainly, his love for Debra and his dream of a family were not unknown to the Father.

On a warm mid-October Saturday, Cale and Jordon flew out of George Bush Intercontinental Airport at four thirty-five in the afternoon via Lufthansa en route to Frankfurt, Germany, where they would connect with another Lufthansa flight to Hanover. There, Cale had arranged to lease a car to transport them on to Celle.

"Do you speak German?" Cale asked once their flight left Houston.

"A little. Enough to get by," Jordon said. He held up a book. "I have fourteen hours to refresh myself—this ten-hour flight and the four-hour layover."

Cale chuckled. "And I have fourteen hours to learn something. Ever been there before?"

"Once to Frankfurt. It's beautiful country. You'll see."

The hours in flight gave Cale plenty of time to think—mostly of Debra and what she'd come to mean in his life. Everywhere he looked, he saw her cocoa brown eyes and wide smile. He'd memorized the way light played off her hair, highlighting the red like waves of fire. Debra had captured his heart with her inward and outward beauty. Michael Patterson had been a fool.

"How did you meet Debra?" Jordon stuck a bookmark into his English/German dictionary book and gave Cale his attention.

Cale closed his own German book, unable to concentrate

with thoughts darting in and out of his mind. "I first heard about what happened to her family on the late-night news. Then nearly two years ago on Christmas Eve, I strayed into Texas Children's Hospital to see what the kiddos were doing, and I met her there."

"Instant friends?" Jordon asked.

"A slow relationship," Cale said. "Debra's husband hurt her badly, and she tends to shy away from men."

Jordon raised a brow. "That's obvious. I really want to find her children. I mean, I always want to help others, but Debra is unique. She's had one adversity after another, and still she keeps right on going. The pitfalls in her life simply make her stronger."

"I admire her strength, too," Cale said.

Jordon chuckled. "You're in love with her. No denying those feelings."

"Guess I am," Cale said, not so sure he liked his secret feelings surfacing to the top of their conversation. "I sure didn't plan it, but first things first. We need to find those children."

"It won't be easy once she does get them home," Jordon said. "I've seen so many cases like these, and the kids always need a lot of love. They are insecure and afraid to let the parent out of their sight."

"I figured Christian counseling would be in order for a long time. Who knows what they've seen or been through during the past two years?"

The plane landed in Hanover just before two Sunday afternoon. Both men had napped on the planes and were anxious to set their feet on solid ground. Cool air whipped about them, causing them to dig through their luggage for a jacket.

After stuffing their bags into the backseat of a dark green Volkswagen Passat, Cale took the driver's seat while Jordon studied the map.

"Where to?" Cale asked, filled with anticipation about what they needed to do.

"We want to take 191 into Celle. Should take us around thirty to forty minutes. We'll check into the Espirit Hotel and map out the next few days. Did you read about the city?"

"Sure did. It's very old, ancient according to American standards. If not for our mission, I'd enjoy doing a bit of sightseeing."

Jordon laughed. "My friend, we will be doing a lot of sightseeing, but unfortunately not the touristy spots."

"What's your plan?" Cale asked, watching the road ahead for signs of 191.

"I'm going to try the easy route first by phoning every Schmidt in the phone book from our room. My guess, there're a million of them. Since Helene grew up here, there's bound to be a relative who'd know how to find her."

"What makes you think one of her relatives would give you any information? She probably has alerted them all to the possibility of Americans trying to find her."

Jordon shrugged. "Umm, maybe not. If Michael and Helene did not eventually end up together, then she has nothing to hide."

"If you don't find out anything from the phone book, then what?"

"I'll check marriage records for the past two years. Michael used the name of Alex Wendel and Jonathon Miller, but he could have used a different one with Helene and the children.

He wore a wedding ring when the police found his body, but I'm not sure that is substantial enough to assume he'd married again. What a scum. I'm using Helene's maiden name to try to locate her. If she has them, her relatives would believe the children were legally hers."

Cale settled into his own reflections and pushed aside a hint of depression. He didn't want to consider this little trip into Germany might prove futile.

The two checked into the hotel, exhausted yet eager to begin their search. Since it was Sunday and all the stores were closed, most of the residents should be at home or arriving in the evening. Glancing through the phone book, Jordon moaned with the number of Schmidts living in Celle.

"I should have known," Jordon said. "There are a ton of them listed."

"Wish I could help, but I'd stumble through my German." Cale had begun to wonder if he could actually be of assistance to his new friend.

"Oh, I'm simply complaining. As if you didn't already know, I'm a little hyper, and I really want to find those children. How about a short walk to ease out the kinks from the flight? You could enjoy a little bit of the scenery you talked about earlier."

As they walked, Cale's insides churned. He believed they needed to do something more with their time other than calm Jordon's hyperactivity. If this trip led them nowhere, his nerves would need an overhaul. He took a deep breath and attempted to enjoy the magnificence around him.

Cale marveled at Celle's centuries-old architecture, a mixture of German and European touches. He was awed by an elaborate, baroque-styled church, which had served the community for hundreds of years. A moment later, he stared at rows of brick and half-timbered buildings with their tall-peaked roofs to deter the winter's heavy snowfall. Down the street, a renaissance-styled gable on an ancient town hall competed with the attraction of bricked streets and unique shops.

When the weariness of jet lag settled on his body, Cale suggested eating before heading back to the hotel. He refused to give in to sleep until the sun went down.

"I want to start phoning," Jordon said. "It'll take awhile to get through the list, and tomorrow those people will be heading to work. All we can do in the daytime is locate a city map and look up the streets where they live and check marriage records." He glanced up at Cale with a grin. "You can pray while I make the calls."

Back in their hotel room, both men sprawled on their beds. Jordon flipped open his cell phone and started down the page of numbers.

"Hello, I'm looking for Helene. I know her maiden name was Schmidt, but I don't remember who she married," Jordon said in German. A moment later, he looked for another number. "He didn't know a Helene Schmidt."

Twenty-eight more calls resulted in discouragement for Cale, but not Jordon. He punched in the twenty-ninth number and repeated his question.

By now, Cale had the German memorized. With his hands behind his head, he prayed again.

"Yes, I'm an old friend from the States. Do you know how I can reach her?" Jordon scribbled down several numbers. "Thank you very much. What's her address? I may just drive by and surprise her." He wrote down the information.

"A winner?" Cale asked, immediately pulling himself to a sitting position.

"Sure hope so. Keep praying while I see where this number takes us."

Cale held his breath, hoping against hope that Jordon had a good lead. Exhaling, he listened to every word.

"Hello. I'd like to speak with Helene." A few moments later, Jordon began again. "Helene, I've been trying to reach you. I'm from the States." Jordon's gaze flew to Cale. "She hung up," he said. "This may be one blessed day." He jumped from the bed. "Let's take a look."

After obtaining a city map from the hotel lobby, Cale drove while Jordon navigated. The homes in this part of the city were situated in a fairly new area, neatly kept brick dwellings with white picket fences. Hopefully, Debra's children lived in a nice neighborhood like this one.

"We're looking for Otto von Boehn Strasse, number three." Jordon traced the map with his fingers. "If she's our gal, I bet she stays inside and doesn't stick her nose out until she feels it's safe."

After the two men located the home, they parked farther down the street and watched Helene Schmidt's house. Just as Jordon figured, no one stirred.

Due to jet lag, Cale slept hard that night and woke refreshed and ready, once again, to track down Helene Schmidt's address—and anything else Jordon deemed necessary. "The children in the area should be emerging from their homes for school. Let's pray Chad and Lauren are among them."

"And if they are?" Cale asked. "What then?"

Jordon held up a pen. "This is actually a digital camera. I intend to snap a few pictures."

Once they reached the street, Jordon asked Cale to park the car. "Wish I had a dog," Jordon said. "Who would suspect a man walking his pet?" He glanced about them. "Wait here while I take a stroll."

Cale glanced in his rearview mirror. "A group of kids are headed this way."

Jordon nodded. "I'll wait until they pass."

From his mirror, Cale watched the children. A boy with reddish-brown hair caught his attention. He gripped the steering wheel, wanting to shout at Jordon but couldn't for fear of capturing the children's attention.

"It's Chad," Cale said barely above a whisper. "I've seen his picture enough to recognize him anywhere."

chapter 34

Debra entered her apartment and dumped a mound of papers on the kitchen table. The students had their first history reports due, and tonight she needed to look over their beginning research notes. With her thoughts foremost on Jordon and Cale's trip to Germany, she realized how difficult it would be to give her students the attention they deserved.

Her stomach growled. She'd skipped lunch to meet with an anxious parent who feared his son might not make it to the ninth grade. Unfortunately, the boy had barely passed seventh grade and had not gotten off to a good start this year. He needed a tutor, and Debra suggested the father secure one as soon as possible. The man did not handle it well. Then there were two meetings after school regarding cafeteria behavior and hallway monitoring. Anxious to get home and sit by the phone did not begin to describe her scattered emotions.

She reached into the refrigerator and pulled out a peach yogurt. Grabbing a spoon from the drawer, she settled back on her sofa to let her body and mind relax. Fat chance of that when the possibility of finding her children consumed every thought.

The phone rang, piercing her silent dream world. She scrambled for it and dropped her yogurt and spoon on the carpet. "Rats." She hurried to the kitchen for a towel while pressing the TALK button. Instantly she recognized Cale's voice.

"I wanted to make sure you were home from school," he said. Did she detect a tone of excitement, or was it wishful thinking?

"You have news?" Her mouth felt like chalk. She placed the towel over the peach and white mess on the floor and slumped onto the sofa.

"Yes, we have," he said. "Debra, are you sitting down?"

Immediately heat flooded her face and her pulse quickened. A lump grew in her throat. "Tell me, please," she said. "Now."

"We've found Chad and Lauren. They're living here in Celle with Helene. I saw them, Debra, both of them, and they look good. Jordon took pictures, and he's downloading them now to his laptop." She heard the investigator's voice in the background. "In fact, he just e-mailed them to you."

Debra couldn't speak for the joy filling her heart. Tears spilled from her eyes, and she wanted to shout from her balcony for the whole world to hear. "I. . .I don't know what to say. Praise God. Oh, praise God. Thank you, sweet Jesus." She attempted to calm herself between the weeping and the elation.

"How did you find them?" She raced across the living room to her computer in the spare bedroom. She powered it on and listened while Cale repeated his story.

". . .Then right behind the boys walked a pair of little girls, hand-in-hand. Jordon started snapping pictures with this tiny digital camera, and we hurried back to the hotel."

"I don't know how to thank both of you," Debra said. "Cale, I'm overwhelmed with all of this. When Jordon came into the picture, you could have easily bowed out, but you became even more involved. How will I ever repay you?"

"I didn't do a thing for payment. You know the story about my sister and nephew. I can't bring them back, but I can help you find your children." He paused. "We don't have them home yet. We'll celebrate when we hit American soil. And keep praying."

"I will. I'd better take a half day off tomorrow to get their birth certificates and passports."

"Sounds like a great idea to me." She heard the smile in his voice. "Jordon wants to speak with you."

She took a deep breath while she waited for him to take the phone. "Debra, is this not great news?" Jordon's enthusiasm reached over the telephone wires. "Isn't our God good?"

She sniffed. "Oh, yes. I'm so grateful."

"I know you are. Listen, I know we talked about this, but get your children's passports and put a rush on them. Also, keep this information to yourself. In the wrong hands, it could blow what we need to do."

Debra shortly tried to figure out the harm of telling everyone about locating the children, but Jordon did know best. Of course, if Helene had connections in the States, she could be alerted.

"We're sticking around to make sure the children walk the same path to the school bus each day and to further investigate the situation here," Jordon said. "I want to check if Michael and Helene were married and possibly what names the children are using. In the meantime, keep those prayers going, and we'll keep in touch. Oh, and don't forget to put a rush on those passports. Talk to you soon."

"When can we get them?"

"I want to come home first and wait a full two weeks. If Helene suspects anything at all, she might bolt."

Debra laid the phone aside. Trembling, she clicked on the SEND/RECEIVE button and waited for her E-mail to download. It seemed to take an eternity. Instantly, she spotted the message from Jordon and waited again while the attachment of her precious children's pictures unfolded on the screen before her.

As a tousle of cinnamon-colored hair filled the top of the screen, then a round face smiled at her, uncontrollable sobs escaped her lips. Chad had grown so tall. He no longer had a chubby little body but looked leaner and older. He had friends she didn't know and a language she couldn't speak.

A moment later she stared into the face of her little girl. Debra wiped the tears blurring her vision. Lauren's blond hair reached midway down her back, and it had been styled with little butterfly clips. She laughed with her little friend, and Debra could almost hear her giggle.

Debra viewed two other pictures of her children. Each one looked more beautiful than the next. She laughed and cried at the same time while her lips praised God. Soon she'd draw them into her arms and once more feel the joy of holding her children next to her heart.

❦   ❦   ❦

The two weeks following Jordon and Cale's return home flew by in a flurry. Betrayal swept over her again when she learned

Michael and Helene had lived together as husband and wife under the name of Jonathon Miller. According to German law, Helene Miller was the mother of Spencer and Christine Miller. Her poor babies. Whatever had Michael told them about their mother?

The passports were easy to obtain. In fact, so easy that it alarmed her, and fortunately she already had one when Michael took her to Spain a few years ago.

She arranged for a substitute to take over her class while she took the time off for personal reasons. Her principal needed more of an explanation, or she wouldn't have a job when she returned, but Jordon had forbidden it. When it came to her children, she didn't have a choice.

Her skin tingled each time she thought about assuming her role as a mother. It all sounded too wonderful to be true—but the aspect of Christian motherhood frightened her. She didn't want to make any mistakes.

Sometimes she wondered how she'd ever repay Cale for all the money he'd spent on her behalf, but she must for her own peace of mind. For the past several months, they'd grown so close, and she found it nearly impossible to imagine life without him. This, too, rested in God's hands. The Father had taken care of her children, and she refused selfishly to consider any additional blessings.

Her stomach remained in a flutter to the point she found it difficult to eat.

"Debra, you aren't going to do Chad and Lauren a bit of good if you don't stay healthy," Jill said to her one evening. Debra had told her dear friend and Drake all that had happened and cautioned them to keep her secret. They were family and had given far more than she ever deserved. It took all of her strength not to phone Pastor McDaniel, Myra, Alicia from the police department, or Steven, except she dare not risk it. She even considered contacting Michael's mother, although the woman remained bitter and had aged significantly over the past two years.

"Okay, I'll fix a peanut-butter-and-honey sandwich." Debra realized Jill made sense.

"You fix it while I'm on the line," Jill said. "Then talk to me with your mouth full. Is the peanut butter creamy or crunchy?"

"Crunchy." Debra feigned annoyance as she reached in her cupboard for the jar. "Do you want to know the brand?"

"Umm, not necessarily. Pour yourself a glass of milk and grab a piece of fruit, too."

"Sure, sis," Debra teased, grateful for two soft slices of bread and a speckled banana.

"Debra, can you really believe what is happening? This time next week, you'll be fixing P-B&J's for Chad and Lauren." Jill fairly squealed.

"Pinch me over the phone," Debra said. "I still can't believe it." She considered the trip to Germany. "I know I should be more concerned about losing my job, but I'm not. The principal knows I love those kids in my class, and he knows I also honor my commitments, but my own children come first. He was not happy that I refused to tell him why I needed the time off."

"Maybe he will be later once he learns the truth."

"I hope so. Anyway, my mind is spinning with intercepting Chad and Lauren on their way to school. What if they don't want to come? Or what if they don't remember me?"

"Honey, it's been a little over two years. They will know you. Trust me. . .trust God."

Debra dipped a knife into the peanut butter. "Would you do me a favor?"

"Name it."

"I'd like for you and Drake to be at the airport when we come back. I want you to share in the blessing."

"Consider it done. I wouldn't miss it."

"I'll call you once we're in flight."

"Perfect. Now, let me hear you crunch on those peanuts."

Saturday afternoon, Debra, Cale, and Jordon boarded a Lufthansa flight to Frankfurt. She felt shaky all over, like a child at Christmas. More than Christmas, but like many Christmases and birthdays mixed into one with Jesus hosting the dinner—as close to heaven as she'd ever come to know in this world.

Once the plane left the ground, she attempted to study Cale's German book, but her mind whirled, and she couldn't concentrate. The mere thought of hearing Chad and Lauren say "Mom" again brought her to tears.

"You should try to sleep," Cale said once the hour grew late.

She flashed him a nervous smile. "I don't think I can."

In the shadows, his voice revealed the telltale signs of love. "Do you know how happy it makes me to be a part of this?"

"I can see it," she said. "You are a saint, Cale. You've given me more than I could ever return to you, not just the money but the friendship and trust."

"I would do it all again and more." He reached for her hand.

She shivered. "I'm frightened about all of this: seeing my

children again after so long, being a good mother, and wondering what God has in store for my little family. . .and for you and me."

His mouth curved into a smile. "We'll have to take each day as it comes. I do care about you—very much."

Gazing into his face, the man she'd come to trust and love, her feelings surfaced stronger than ever before. "I care about you, Cale, and—"

He touched his fingers to her lips. "No need to say more. God will guide us through whatever lies ahead. Right now, we have a job to do, and the last thing I want is to pressure you about a relationship."

She settled back into her seat and allowed him to continue holding her hand. She felt more peaceful than she could ever remember.

When they arrived in Hanover the next afternoon, Jordon rented a Volvo—big enough to hold all of them with the children. He'd already determined it best for him to be in charge of the car and take a later flight the next day back to the States after they obtained Chad and Lauren. They would be in a tight squeeze on Monday morning securing the children at 8:00 a.m. then heading back to Hanover to catch a 10:45 flight.

In Celle, they stayed again at the Espirit Hotel. Debra felt the enchantment of the quaint city, but her emotions were wound too tightly to enjoy the scenery and tourist attractions. A part of her wanted to take in the sights. After all, this had been her children's home. Cale reported Chad and Lauren looked well and happy. Helene must have cared for them, and Debra shivered with a twinge of jealousy.

I'm sorry, Lord. I asked You to take care of my children, and You did. Help me to forgive this woman.

Sadness for Helene replaced the bitterness. The woman had lost Michael and would soon lose Chad and Lauren. She must love the children, or she'd have returned them to Debra when Michael died.

Debra knew the agony of losing those she loved.

Once registered at the hotel, Jordon and Cale placed their luggage in their room and met Debra in the lobby.

"Stay here and try to rest," Jordon said. She marveled at how such a big man who looked more like a linebacker than a private investigator could be so considerate.

"Where are you going?" she asked.

"We're going to drive by Helene's house."

Her eyes widened. "I'm going, too."

Jordon pressed his lips firmly together. "We can't risk it. Debra, if Chad sees you and tells Helene that he just saw a woman who looked like his mother, what do you think she'll do? Especially after I phoned her a few weeks ago."

Debra swallowed the perpetual lump in her throat. She shook her head and turned from him.

"We might never find them again," Jordon said in a calmness he seldom exhibited. "You don't want to be this close, then let them slip through our fingers, do you?"

"No," she said through a ragged breath. She slowly turned to face Cale and Jordon. "You're right. I'll stay here."

The men were gone for nearly three hours. Debra attempted to pray, then sleep, but memories of her children took precedence.

Jordon and Cale reported they saw nothing. Where were

Chad and Lauren? Had Helene found out what they planned? Had she taken them somewhere else?

After an endless Sunday of rehearsing the plan for Monday, Debra slept fitfully until she rose at five and made ready to leave Germany with her children. Her stomach churned; she wanted to cry. Every breath became a prayer.

At seven thirty Jordon drove the Volvo to the point where they'd seen Chad and Lauren walk to the school bus. Once parked, he prayed aloud for God's hand to be on their mission.

At seven fifty, a group of children headed toward them, their lively shouts and calls echoing against the cool morning. Debra's heart pounded so hard she feared Cale and Jordon could hear. But it didn't matter.

"Debra, are you ready?" Jordon asked.

She nodded. How many times had they rehearsed this?

A group of children sauntered their way. "Just like the other time, the boys are ahead of the girls," Cale said.

"How can you two sound so composed?" Her teeth chattered.

"Take a deep breath," Cale said, "and pray for strength."

The children grew closer, and for the first time in over two years, she saw a tousle of auburn hair and a familiar wide smile.

"Now," Jordon said. "Do exactly as we rehearsed."

Debra's hands shook so badly she could barely open the door. *Lord, help me. I can't do this alone.* Somehow, it opened, and she stepped near the boys.

Her attention focused on her son. "Chad," she said in a weak voice.

He stared at her and stopped, his sights fixed on hers. His face grew pale.

He knows me! Thank You, Jesus. "Chad. It's Mom. I've come to take you home." She bit her tongue to keep from dissolving into a mass of emotion.

He sucked in his breath, hesitated, and flew into her arms. "Mom, oh, Mom. I knew you weren't dead."

As much as she wanted to stand and hold her son, she remembered Jordon's instructions. "Chad, into the car, quickly now, son."

Chad whirled around. "Come on, Christine. . .Lauren," he said. "It's our mom. She's alive, and she's gonna take us home."

The little girl froze. Shock registered on her tiny face in a pasty shade of white. Debra stepped toward her, but Lauren slumped back and shook her head. *Oh, no. My baby is afraid.*

Chad spoke to Lauren in German, but she wrapped her arms around her tiny shoulders. She looked even more like Michael.

"Mama," she screamed in German and backed away from the small group. "Mama," she screamed louder, and Debra knew she meant Helene.

"We have to go," Jordon said. "Helene may hear Lauren calling her. Someone could be watching us."

"Lauren, please. It's Mommy." Debra could not decide whether to venture farther or continue to plead.

Lauren turned and ran down the sidewalk. All the while, she screamed in German for her mother. Debra left Chad with Cale and hurried after her.

Help me, Lord. Help me.

At that moment, Debra recognized Helene racing toward Lauren. The woman opened her arms and caught the little girl. Breathless, Debra dare not stop. She heard Lauren cry and saw Helene hold her close. They resembled each other, even the blond color of their hair. The sight wrenched at Debra's heart.

"Lauren," she shouted. "Please, baby, this is Mommy."

Helene stared, her face a mask of disbelief and horror. She clutched Lauren's hand and ran, shouting something in German. Debra's legs and lungs burned in protest, but she couldn't stop the pursuit. Only when Helene and Lauren rushed up a set of steps to a brick home did she recognize defeat.

"Lauren, I'm at the Espirit Hotel. Call me, baby. Please, Helene. She's my little girl."

The door of Helene's home slammed shut, but Debra climbed the steps. She banged on the door begging Helene to talk to her.

Sweetheart, let me hold you. Let me touch your soft cheeks and your baby-silk hair.

chapter 35

D ebra, get in the car." Never had Cale's words demanded such attention.

She whirled around to see Jordon had driven
after her, and Cale had exited the car.

"My baby," Debra said. "Helene has my baby."

In a moment, Cale was beside her. He grabbed her arm
and pulled her toward the car. "This will not work," he said.
How could he sound so calm? "Helene can have us arrested.
Let's go somewhere and think this through."

"But I can't." Debra trembled in rage and fear.

"You must. Do you want to lose Chad, too?"

Cale's reminder shocked her to her senses, and she allowed
him to escort her to the car. In the next moment, Jordon sped
away. Numb, Debra could only wrap her arms around her son
and hold him as she'd dreamed all these months.

Snuggled next to Chad, she heard him sob. She couldn't
halt her own weeping; a mixture of gratitude and defeat
etched her emotions. Finally he ceased crying and lifted his
gaze to her. He gently wiped the dampness from her cheek.

"Dad said you died, Mom. What happened?" Chad's English was flawless. He clung to her, as though a toddler again.

"He made a mistake," she said, without hesitation.

"Is Dad alive, too?"

She moistened her lips. "No, honey."

"Our other mama said he had an accident." His dark brown eyes stared earnestly into hers.

"She was right." The reference of Helene as mama ripped through her, but she held her composure. *I have to be strong.*

"I love you, Chad." She touched his forehead with a kiss. "I've always loved you and Lauren."

He blinked back another tear. "I have so many questions."

"I know, sweetheart, so do I, but we have a long time to catch up on those things."

A thought suddenly stuck Debra, and she gasped with the reality of what she'd done. "Jordon, Cale, I've done something stupid. I told Lauren and Helene we were staying at the Espirit."

Cale revealed no emotion.

"We'll check you into another hotel," Jordon said, "and I'll find another one for me. Sure glad we already have our bags."

"How will Christine, I mean Lauren, find us?" Chad paused. "Our other mom probably won't let her anyway." His face turned serious. "That mom believes you're dead, too."

"I'm not sure what we will do," Debra said. "But God will work it out."

⁂ ⁂ ⁂

Cale instructed Debra and Chad to stay outside the hotel while he checked into the Caroline Mathilde Hotel under the name of Mr. and Mrs. Douglas Sanderson. Cale detested the deceit, but he knew the importance of keeping their location a secret. He feared in no time at all the police and media would have Chad's picture flashing for everyone to see.

Debra reclined on the bed with her son. The boy nestled within her embrace, and her face radiated with joy. When Cale caught her attention, a cloud passed over her placid features. She undoubtedly reflected on Lauren and the present situation.

"What now?" she asked. "I'm grateful to have Chad, but I want my little girl, too."

Cale shook his head. "We simply wait. Jordon will be here shortly, unless he senses someone following him."

"Who would follow Mr. Jordon?" Chad asked. "Do you think my other mom is so upset that she'd try to get me back?"

Debra moistened her lips. "I'm sure she's sad."

"Like I've been kidnapped?" Chad asked.

Debra's heart seemed to skip a beat, but she needed to downplay his question. "Possibly."

"Maybe I should call her," he continued. "If I explained you're not dead, I bet she'd understand."

"Not yet, Chad," Cale said. "Your mother, Mr. Jordon, and I need to think this through. We'll get your sister."

The boy sat silent as though pondering everything. "My sister should be here. Our other mom—I don't know what to call her since you're alive—is nice and she loves us a lot. When she found out that Dad died, she told us she'd always love and take care of us. But I want you. Guess I'm a little confused."

"Of course you are." Cale took a seat beside him. "For now, let the adults figure out the best thing to do. How does that sound?"

Chad shrugged.

He looks so much like his mother.

"Okay. Can I still ask questions when I don't understand?"

"You bet." Cale turned to Debra. "What do you say, Mom? Are questions fine?"

Debra smiled, a shaky one at best, but a smile. "We'll do our best."

Cale stood and gazed out the hotel window in hopes of seeing Jordon. *This could have been so easy. According to plan, Lauren and Chad should be on their way to the airport with Debra. Why, God? How can this be a part of Your divine plan? Must it be so hard? Help us, Father, because I don't know what to do.*

I lift up my eyes to the hills—where does my help come from? My help comes from the Lord, the Maker of heaven and earth.

Cale felt the flesh on the back of his neck tingle. A sense of peace settled over his restlessness. How he treasured the unexplainable workings of the Father. He desperately wanted Lauren returned to Debra. Surely God wanted the same thing.

"Cale."

He gazed into the face of the woman he treasured. The sight of her with Chad, renewing the bond they had once shared as mother and son moved his spirit to praise God for His blessings.

"Jesus is enough." Debra straightened her shoulders and lifted her chin. "Jesus will always be enough."

chapter 36

Debra watched her son; she couldn't take her eyes from him. How he'd grown, and now she could see an image of the man he'd one day be. He resembled her father with the beginnings of broad shoulders and a narrow waist.

Helene had provided well. Chad's clothes were of the finest quality, and he was in excellent health. She had no doubt about Helene's love for him and Lauren—surely a blessing. Debra felt more than one pang of jealousy, but God had answered her prayers. Could He also be saying no to Lauren? Debra shivered. Should she settle for half of her heart's desire? Was it enough to know her little girl had the love of a woman who cherished her?

I can't give up, Lord. I'm trusting You for both of my children.

Cale's cell phone rang startling her. A moment later, he handed it to her. "Jordon wants to talk to you."

"Debra," Jordon said. "As I told Cale, I'm checked into a hotel under an assumed name, and I'd rather not give that to you. No point in getting you into any more trouble than we're currently in. Call me on my cell if you need me."

"Are we all right at the present?"

"I doubt it—and I'm being honest. While I was settling up my bill at the Espirit, Helene phoned for you. I heard the desk clerk state Mrs. Patterson no longer stayed at their facilities. I took the call."

"And?" Debra caught her breath.

"She wants to talk to you—left me a number. If you'll grab pencil and paper, I'll give it to you."

She scrambled for her purse, fully aware of Chad watching her every move. She turned so he wouldn't see, momentarily forgetting Chad could have given her Helene's number. "Got it," she said.

"Use Cale's phone—possibly away from the room."

"Sure."

"Be careful, Debra. This could be a trap."

"Or the hand of God answering our prayers." Debra held on to Cale's cell. "Do you mind if I use your phone in the hall?"

"Go ahead. Maybe Chad will give me a few German lessons."

She slipped from the room and punched in the number. Helene answered on the first ring.

"This is Debra Patterson."

"This. . .is quite a shock to me." Helene had a heavy accent.

Debra took a deep breath. "I understand."

"My husband said you were dead."

Dare she say a word about Michael being married to her when he took on another wife? "He was mistaken."

"I think of Spencer and Christine as my children."

"I understand, but they are legally mine." Debra felt her anger rising. "I am their mother."

"Can we talk?"

"Yes, of course. I have lots of questions for you." Debra hoped her words conveyed confidence.

"Shall we meet in the lobby of the Espirit in an hour?"

"An hour and a half would be better." *I need time to pray.*

"Certainly."

Debra felt her heart pound. She had to meet with Helene. Perhaps the whole mess could be sorted out by tonight—and she'd have Lauren.

✤   ✤   ✤

Despite Jordon and Cale's objections, Debra took a taxi within two blocks of the Espirit and walked into the hotel fifteen minutes ahead of the prearranged time. She had Cale's cell phone in case something went wrong, but what could he do if Helene decided to keep her baby girl?

Standing in the lobby, Debra played out several scenarios with Helene then she scolded herself for not relying on God to work out the problems. *How easy this all would be if Helene did not care for Chad and Lauren.* Was the woman a willing party to the kidnapping? Had she married Michael without knowledge of his wife? Had she been lied to? Question after question poured through Debra's mind, and not an answer to any of them.

In the middle of a prayer, Helene walked into the hotel. She was dressed smartly in a black pantsuit. When Debra looked into Helene's face, she saw the telltale signs of tears.

"Debra," the woman said, moving her way.

"I thought you might bring Lauren."

"Christine is with my mother. She's a very upset little girl. She doesn't remember you; neither does she understand why her brother is gone."

Debra nodded, not sure how to venture into dangerous territory. "I believe once she talks to me, she will remember everything."

Helene stiffened. "I don't intend to give up either of my children."

"How can you say that? I can prove they are mine." Debra knew her voice laced with desperation. "Once the authorities receive the truth, they will turn them over to me."

Helene's cell rang, and Debra waited while the woman briefly conducted a conversation in German. Once she concluded the call, Debra sought to appeal to the woman's sense of reason.

"Helene, be reasonable. Michael abducted the children, obtained new identities for them, married you without a divorce, and told them I was dead. Now, how do you think you can gain custody of my children?"

Debra's attention was diverted to the hotel's door. Four policemen stepped inside, guns drawn.

Helene stood. "Do you think I'm stupid? You are under arrest for kidnapping my son."

✋   ✋   ✋

Cale paced the floor of the hotel room. There was so much he wanted to say to Jordon but couldn't because of Chad. Alarm had long since taken over his mind. Debra had been gone over an hour, and she had promised to call. At first annoyance dominated his countenance, but not anymore. Something had gone wrong.

"I'm calling her," he said.

"Go ahead," Jordon said. "We've waited long enough. She's had thirty minutes to talk about things."

Chad stood from the bed where he'd been reading a book about soccer that Debra had picked up for him. "I'm not a child anymore. I've been thinking my father took Lauren and me from my mother, gave us new names, brought us to Germany, and did a whole bunch of other things I don't understand. Now my real mom has found us, and she suddenly disappears. You two are worried, just like I am. I know Mom went to talk to her. I know she's trying to get Lauren. What are you not telling me?"

Cale studied the boy. He'd seen too much of life at such a young age. "You're right, Chad. We're concerned about your mother."

Jordon handed Cale his cell and punched in the numbers. The phone rang until voice mail picked up. *What has happened? Why isn't Debra answering?*

"Try the hotel." Jordon handed him a card with the Espirit number. "One of the front desk employees speaks English."

Cale nodded and made the call. "Yes, I'm looking for a woman who may be waiting in your lobby. She's an American, with shoulder length, auburn hair and attractive."

"The police have just arrested a woman fitting your description. Who are you?"

ঔ   ঔ   ঔ

Debra swallowed hard and studied her jail cell from the single bed. Her quarters were neat, clean—much nicer than she'd have ever imagined. Perhaps much nicer than she deserved. A radio positioned on a small table linked her with the outside world, but in a language she didn't understand. What did it matter? She'd lost Chad and Lauren, probably for good. She'd willingly broken German law to try to get them, and now she sat in jail waiting. . .waiting to hear she may never see her children again. Steven had warned her against taking matters into her own hands, and Alicia had told her to allow the proper authorities to handle the case.

Once more, she was apart from her children. She struggled to keep from blaming Helene and God for her arrest. Each time anger and bitterness rose to the surface, she attempted to shrug it aside. *There is a reason. There is a purpose. Forgive Helene. Allow God to work.* Those words repeated in her mind, simple phrases that gave her hope and strength.

For the past two years, Debra's every breath had been to find Chad and Lauren. She'd refused to give up. Her life had seeped with sin, but when God revealed His love, she turned her life over to Him. The Holy Father never deserted her, and she'd lived for Him trusting His ways and not her own.

Jesus is enough.

How many times had she used that truth in her speaking engagements and personal testimony? She wanted to grasp those words now and not let go, but she couldn't. The pain in her heart refused to subside.

The past several months had taken her from hell to the portals of heaven. God had not brought her this far only to desert her in this dark hour. He didn't work to harm those He loved. Did He?

Jesus is enough.

Stop it, Lord. You don't know how I feel. All of this for nothing.

Neither Jordon nor Cale had been to see her, but she imagined there were warrants for their arrest, too. Debra imagined they would visit the American embassy to plead her case. Even if they secured her release, what good would it do? She'd rather stay in jail than live without her children. With kidnapping charges pressed against her, the German government would not be interested in her rights as Chad and Lauren's legal mother. Her actions simply proved Michael's accusations against her.

The solitude brought back a flood of memories, from those nightmarish days after the children's disappearance to the events leading to the Lord.

Sweet thoughts of Jill planted gratitude for the dear woman who had served as the best friend anyone could ever want. Debra trembled and bit back the urge to dissolve into a pool of grief. She couldn't be strong on her own, but she could through the Lord. How she wished she'd spent all of her past years serving Him rather than herself. Maybe now, she'd have more memorized scripture and stronger faith.

Jesus is enough. Give thanks in all things.

Lord, how can I be thankful when I will never see my children again. How can Jesus be enough?

Whom do you serve, My child?

Shame washed over her. She held her breath as realization pierced her heart. All this time, she'd claimed to serve the Lord with her whole heart, when in truth she'd used her actions to gain His favor.

I'll do this for God, and then He will return my children.

Heaven forgive her, she'd attempted to barter with God. She'd put her children above God and lost.

Debra clenched her fists, determined to hold on to her faith. But she was more frightened than she'd been in a long time.

She slipped to her knees and wept. *Heavenly Father, forgive my sins. I am guilty of putting my children above my relationship with You. Oh, God, You are the beginning and the end of all things. You are the one true God. You are my strength and my salvation. You sent Your Son Jesus to die for me. Yes, Jesus is enough. Jesus will always be enough.*

chapter 37

Helene wrapped her arms around the little girl in her lap and continued to rock. This was a habit begun over two years ago when Michael first brought her the children. He'd said his wife had severe mental problems, and he feared for their safety.

"The police will not believe me," he'd said. "I'm afraid Debra will hurt them, and I know the courts will not grant me custody. She has so many friends who would testify on her behalf."

"But, Michael, you're an attorney. You know the law. You can protect your children," Helene said.

He shook his head and huge tears rolled over his cheeks. "Not even my mother believes my stories about Debra. That's why I have to get them out of the country." Michael gathered up her hands and brought them to his lips. "I love you, Helene. I want to spend the rest of my life with you. I want you to be the mother of my children."

Helene believed Michael. She loved him with every ounce of her being. After months of planning, he arrived in Germany with Spencer and Christine, the children's new names. Michael became Jonathon Miller, and their new lives began.

Within a month, he reported his wife had committed suicide. Shortly afterward, the two married. The children had a difficult time adjusting to new names, faces, and a foreign language, but they were resilient. Helene loved them fiercely. She'd always wanted children but had been unable to conceive. Life looked perfect. Michael doted on her and the children. Never had she been so incredibly happy.

Then Michael's behavior began to change. He appeared preoccupied with something, and his anger erupted when she least expected it. One moment he loved her, and the next he compared her to Debra. Many nights she wakened to find him sitting alone in the dark with no explanation. Confused, Helene decided she must find a way for him to talk to her, but before she could, he was the victim of a horrible murder. She learned about his death from Nic. He wanted her to come back to him, but she refused. She never mentioned the children.

While searching the *Houston Chronicle* online right after Michael's death for information regarding his murder, Helene discovered Debra Patterson still searched for her children. Why had he told her Debra was dead?

"She is an alcoholic and abuses the children," Michael had said over two years ago when he abducted the children.

In order to protect Spencer and Christine, Helene hid their identity. She must keep Michael's children and raise them as her own. He had risked everything for them, and she could do no less.

As days passed into weeks, suspicion filled Helene's mind about other things she'd ignored in their married life. Michael had refused to discuss his business dealings, which provided an exorbitant income.

"Isn't it enough to know I love you and provide you with everything you could ever want?" he'd asked. "Don't concern yourself with my business trips and the time away from home. I want only the best for you and our children."

She loved Spencer and Christine too much to ever let them go back to a woman who had abused them. They were her cherished children, and no one would ever learn the truth.

More online reading of the *Chronicle* created more doubts. With the realization that Michael had hidden the truth about his business dealings and Debra's suicide, had he also lied about his wife's mental condition?

"Mama."

Helene kissed Christine's cheek. "Yes, sweetheart." No one could love this little girl and her brother more. Debra sat in jail. The police searched for the others who had assisted her, and soon she'd have Spencer back, too.

"I've been remembering. That woman is my real mama."

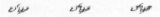

Early the following morning found Debra deep in prayer. Repeatedly, she had whispered the words, "Jesus is enough," until she fell asleep only to waken in the darkness with the same truth on her lips. She'd never spent a night in jail, and the sounds plus her rambling thoughts had kept her awake. Prayer swept through her mind until she perspired in its intensity.

God had not deserted her. Their relationship had been restored. He had answered her prayers for Chad and Lauren.

They did have someone to love them. They were well cared for. She had found them. If her Lord deemed fit for the children to stay with Helene, then she must accept it. But to her dying day, she'd never stop praying for Chad and Lauren's return.

The sound of footsteps caught her attention. She glanced up to see a guard approach her cell. Once he opened the door, he escorted her to another area where Helene sat opposite a metal barrier. Debra trembled. What did this mean? Hadn't the woman done enough damage?

"I'd like to talk," Helene said through a quivering smile. She sniffed and dabbed her nose with a tissue.

"All right." Debra slid into a chair. "First tell me about Lauren. Is she okay?"

Helene eyes pooled with tears. "Yes. She misses her mommy."

Debra's heart plummeted. Must this woman continually rub her relationship with Lauren in Debra's face?

"Debra," Helene glanced down at her hands folded around a tissue. "I'm afraid I've made a terrible mistake."

$$\wp \qquad \wp \qquad \wp$$

Steven pulled a stick of gum from his shirt pocket. He quickly unwrapped it and popped it into his mouth. With the help of Ben and Julie, the three had finally put together the pieces about Michael Patterson—his life, death, and possibly his children.

The key had been in a phone call from the owner of Gulf Coast Charters. Nic Sagliarino said Michael Patterson had been involved in an extra-marital affair with his wife.

"I know I should have called with this information before,

but frankly Patterson got what was coming to him. He snatched my wife right from me."

"Where is your ex-wife now?" Steven had asked.

"She's living in Celle, Germany." The wheels began to turn.

Snatching up his bifocals, Steven read through the roughly sketched report. Michael had gotten in over his head when he skimmed too much off the top of his law firm's profits. He knew he was about to get caught and left the country with his kids and obtained new identities. He changed his name to Alex Wendel for business purposes, but to his new family, he was Jonathon Miller, and his children were Spencer and Christine. With new names and a new life, Michael settled in Germany where he married Helen Sagliarino, a woman he'd met while deep-sea fishing in Galveston. She'd divorced her husband for Michael and went home to Celle, Germany, to await his arrival. There, he started an import/export business with gourmet foods, which he basically operated online. He still had a penchant for money and decided to manufacture some of his products in other countries where the costs were cheaper. That's where he met up with Hernandez, who agreed to provide him with cheese through one of his companies. Michael slapped on a made-in-Germany sticker and sold the cheese at a substantial profit.

What Michael didn't know was Hernandez used him to smuggle cocaine into Germany. He had an insider handle the warehouse unloading of the cheese and distribution of the drugs. That worked well until Michael stumbled onto what was really happening. He made contact with Hernandez and flew to Mexico. Michael confronted Hernandez and refused to have anything to do with drugs. Michael also announced that cheese could be obtained elsewhere. Hernandez had him killed. When caught, the killer revealed information about Hernandez in exchange for a new life.

The Patterson kids had to be in Celle, Germany, with Helene. The government would cooperate with the FBI once they proved the children were not legally Helene's.

Steven stuck the report back into the file. Debra couldn't learn about any of this until the children were located and negotiations made with the German government.

He leaned back in his chair. Finally, things were coming together with the Patterson case, and life with Rod had gotten a whole lot better. They talked more. In fact, father and son planned a weekend of deep-sea fishing via Gulf Coast Charters.

chapter 38

I sec now I was lied to, like you," Helene concluded. "After hearing your story, I believe you never threatened the children." She paused and shook her head as though in disbelief. "I wonder if Michael ever told me the truth about anything. I'm so sorry. I should have gone to the authorities. I should and shouldn't have done a lot of things."

Debra's heart softened with Helene's confession. She felt pity for this woman who, like Debra, had not only lost her husband but now her children.

"You and I have suffered," Debra said. "We are both guilty of loving a man who deceived us, but we both have been blessed with his children."

Helene nodded. Her tissue now lay in shreds. "I'll make the arrangements to have the charges lifted. I am the one who needs to be behind those bars now."

Debra allowed Helene's words settle in her mind and heart. A part of her wanted to see the woman punished, but the tender side of her could not put the woman through any more torment. "No, Helene. I forgive your part in this. All I've ever wanted is my children. My prayers have always been for God to provide someone to love and care for them, and He did. How can I fault you for that?" Debra hesitated before speaking again. "I'm not saying this is easy for me. I'm human, and when I think of the heartache during the past two years, I want to scream with the unfairness."

Shock registered on Helene's face. "I don't understand. I've committed a horrible crime."

"Yes, you have, but I refuse to allow this to continue. Let me have my children and go home."

Debra waited in the lobby of the police department with a representative of the American embassy. She wanted no problems or questions asked when she took custody of Lauren. Jordon stood with her, but Cale and Chad remained at the hotel.

She felt hot and cold at the same time while every inch of her trembled. The thought of something going wrong assailed her thoughts no matter how hard she tried to push them away. For over two years, she'd anticipated the moment when her baby girl would once more be in her arms. Not a night had slipped by without the heart-wrenching longing that only a mother could feel. She knew God held Chad and Lauren in His embrace, but she never knew if He would return them to her in this lifetime. All Debra had was hope, and that hope helped her climb out of bed each day and dream about the moment when her relationship with her children was restored. God had given her back Chad, and their reunion gave her chills and filled her eyes with joyful tears. She'd been weak with prayers of thanksgiving. Now—now, the time approached to touch the face and shower kisses on her precious Lauren.

A police car stopped in Debra's full view. An officer opened the back door, and Helene climbed out. She held the hand of the most beautiful little girl God ever created.

Debra gasped, and tears flowed unchecked down her cheeks. She swallowed repeatedly. Lauren deserved to see a smiling mommy.

"Praise God," Jordon said.

Debra could only nod; her gaze fixed on Lauren. She wanted to run through the doors and wrap her arms around the child, but she had been asked to wait until Lauren stepped into the police station.

Thank You, Lord. Thank You for all You've done.

The door opened. "Mama!" Lauren called and flew to Debra's arms. "My mommy, my real mommy." The little girl's gray-green eyes radiated the love that Debra had feared was gone.

"I remembered you. I didn't really forget."

Debra no longer cared about the tears. With Lauren in her arms, nothing else mattered. Her baby smelled so sweet and pure, just as Debra remembered.

"I love you, Lauren. Mommy loves you so much." Debra glanced up at Helene's grief-stricken face. "Thank you for caring for and loving my children."

Helene said nothing but turned and walked from the police station.

At the airport, Debra stood with Cale and her children ready to board the plane taking them from Frankfurt to Houston. *Home. What a pleasant thought.* The small group sat in their own row with Debra between her children and Cale on the other side of Lauren. The children slept in a sporadic pattern, but neither let go of Debra's hand. She knew they were confused. Lauren had instantly warmed to Cale, just like Chad, and at one point, she chatted away to him in German.

Chad took a deep breath. "She will be sad that we're gone. Can I write her a letter when we get home?"

She knew her son didn't know how to refer to Helene, and, as of yet, Debra didn't know how to help him. "Of course. She loves you very much."

"But she's not you, my real mom."

While the children slept, sheltered beneath Debra's arms, she vowed to do whatever she could for the rest of her life to make sure they were secure, safe, and understood God's provision—and, more importantly, that Jesus is enough.

"Cale," she said.

He glanced up from a book he was reading.

"Have I thanked you properly for all you've done? I would have been lost without your support and encouragement."

"Only about a hundred times." The sound of his voice eased all the trepidation threatening to shake her newfound joy. He was a godsend, a true blessing.

"I'm going to miss all those hours we shared together."

"Me, too, but you will have lots to do," he said.

"Maybe you could join us sometime?"

His smile warmed her. "I'll join you anytime."

The plane landed in Houston on schedule. Debra sensed the exhaustion in her children as well as herself. Cale, too, looked as if he could sleep for three days. She wished Jordon could be with them, but he'd arrive later.

As they stepped off the plane and down the corridor, she breathed a sigh of relief. Debra took Chad and Lauren's hand into hers and, with Cale, they moved ahead. She'd never take any of God's blessings for granted again.

"We're home." Cale smiled through a splattering of tears.

Liquid emotion flowed down her cheeks. Finally she could speak. "This is a new beginning, isn't it?"

"I believe so."

Thank You, Lord, for all You've done for my children and me. Thank You for the wonderful man before me. I will treasure him for as long as there is life within me.

Once they finished with immigration and customs and exited to the terminal lobby, Debra spotted Jill and Drake, and the couple waved wildly. Debra gasped. Not only were her dear friends waiting, but also Pastor McDaniel, Myra, Alicia, Steven, and even Mrs. Patterson. No doubt, their relationship would always be strained, but the children needed a loving grandmother. Behind them, a group of people she recognized from church and her school cheered.

Myra and Alicia held up a huge banner that read WELCOME HOME, CHAD, LAUREN, AND DEBRA. WE LOVE YOU.

epilogue

October—one year later

Dear Helene,

Thank you so much for the birthday money and the book about Celle. I'm glad it's written in German and English so I won't forget the language. I'm playing soccer for the junior high team at my school.

I'm making good grades in school, and so is Lauren. We go to a private Christian school where we talk about God. It's like Sunday school but with all the regular school stuff. Our teachers made a big fuss about Lauren and me speaking German, and Mom has a tutor teaching us more.

Mom and Cale were married last Saturday, and I was the best man, and Lauren was dressed just like Mom. They gave each of us a promise ring. It means my new dad promises to love us and show us how to live like Jesus wants. He cried when he told us that in the ceremony. I hope someday you find a husband like my mom did, but he has to be Christian.

I've been praying for you, and Lauren is, too. We love you and thank you for taking such good care of us until our real mom found us.

Love,
Chad Patterson Thurston

DiAnn Mills wrote from the time she could hold a pencil. In 1995 her husband suggested she fulfill her lifelong dream to write a book. With God's direction, her first novel, *Rehoboth,* was published in 1998. That launched her career and has kept her creating ever since.

DiAnn believes her readers should "Expect an Adventure" when they read her books. Her desire is to show characters solving real problems of today from a Christian perspective. She is the author of nine novels, one nonfiction book, nine novellas, as well as numerous short stories, articles, devotions, and the contributor to several nonfiction compilations.

DiAnn lives in sunny Houston, Texas, the home of heat, humidity, and Harleys. In fact she'd own one, but her legs are too short. DiAnn and her husband have four adult sons and one grandson and are active members of their church.

Visit DiAnn at www.diannmills.com.

Ekaterina

Heirs of Anton, Book 1

*by Susan Downs
and Susan May Warren*

Upon receiving an unusual package in the mail, Ekaterina "Kat" Moore boards a plane to Russia, her ancestral home, to seek some answers. What she finds leads her on a perilous journey through time as Kat must flee the Russian underground. To further complicate matters, she finds herself falling in love with FSB Captain Vadeem Spasonov, a man trying to forget the nightmares of his own past. When Kat's secrets lead to the answers Vadeem needs, the treasures they find unleash an avalanche of God's design.

288 pages / 1-59310-161-9

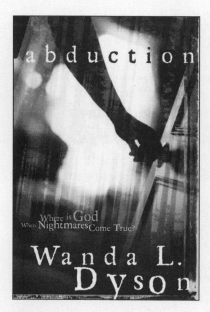

Abduction
by Wanda L. Dyson

"Where's Jessie?" Even as she breathes out the words, Karen Matthews knows that her worst nightmare has become a reality. Her seven-month-old baby is gone, stolen during the night. When the police call a famous psychic, Zoe Shefford, to use her mysterious "powers" to locate the child, Karen hesitates. When her husband suddenly disappears as well, Karen becomes the prime suspect. Apparently, God has forgotten about poor Karen Matthews, left to mourn the loss of her baby, her husband, and even her faith—or has He? That's what Karen—and Zoe—must find out before it's too late.

368 pages / 1-58660-812-6

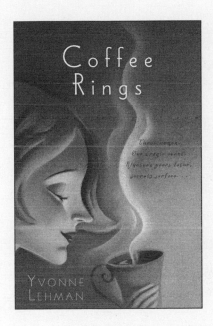